HOUSE OF
WOLVES

James Patterson is one of the best-known and biggest-selling writers of all time. Among his creations are some of the world's most popular series, including Alex Cross, the Women's Murder Club, Michael Bennett and the Private novels. He has written many other number one bestsellers including collaborations with President Bill Clinton and Dolly Parton, stand-alone thrillers and non-fiction. James has donated millions in grants to independent bookshops and has been the most borrowed adult author in UK libraries for the past fourteen years in a row. He lives in Florida with his family.

Mike Lupica is a veteran sports columnist – spending most of his career with the *New York Daily News* – who is now a member of the National Sports Media Association Hall of Fame. For three decades, he was a panellist on ESPN's *The Sports Reporters*. As a novelist, he has written sixteen *New York Times* bestsellers.

A list of titles by James Patterson appears
at the back of this book

HOUSE OF WOLVES

JAMES PATTERSON
& MIKE LUPICA

PENGUIN BOOKS

PENGUIN BOOKS

UK | USA | Canada | Ireland | Australia
India | New Zealand | South Africa

Penguin Books is part of the Penguin Random House group of companies
whose addresses can be found at global.penguinrandomhouse.com

First published in the UK by Century in 2023
Published in Penguin Books 2023
001

Printed and bound in Great Britain by Clays Ltd, Elcograf S.p.A.

The authorised representative in the EEA is Penguin Random House Ireland,
Morrison Chambers, 32 Nassau Street, Dublin D02 YH68

A CIP catalogue record for this book is available from the British Library

ISBN: 978–1–529–15972–1

www.greenpenguin.co.uk

Penguin Random House is committed to a
sustainable future for our business, our readers
and our planet. This book is made from Forest
Stewardship Council® certified paper.

HOUSE OF
WOLVES

ONE

ALONE ON HIS BOAT and half drunk, the Golden Gate Bridge off to his left and Alcatraz dead ahead, Joe Wolf started to sing about having left his heart in San Francisco.

Then he suddenly threw back his head and laughed, remembering the last time he'd belted out the song, with his second wife out here on *The Sea Wolf,* both of them knowing the marriage was over.

"*What* heart?" she'd said.

Oh, he had heart, all right, and brains and balls to go with it. How did she think he ended up with his own football team and his own newspaper—by winning the goddamn lottery? He apologized to nobody, not even for the deals he'd had to cut to get what he wanted, especially when he felt, as he did tonight, as if he owned the whole city.

Did he have secrets? Who the hell didn't have secrets? And regrets. He never talked about his biggest secret, but his biggest regret was his family. It was the way his three sons had turned out, the way they'd disappointed him. His fault? Or theirs?

Then there was his only daughter.

She was the best of them, the rising star of the family. Only she'd turned her back on him. And in that way became the biggest disappointment of all.

"I'm not like the rest of you!" she'd said the last time they fought.

Was that fight earlier this year or last year? There were so many he'd lost track. But that was when she told him she was walking away for good, and she meant it this time.

No, he thought. *You were supposed to be better.*

He drank Grey Goose out of the bottle. The good stuff. But worth it because he was.

Hardly any wind tonight, though. No other boats anywhere in sight, just the smell of the water and the occasional screech of California gulls, the night shining with starlight—bright enough, Joe Wolf thought, to light Wolves Stadium.

His stadium, even if it was too old now, the way they said he was.

He raised the bottle to his lips, realized it was empty, was about to go below and open another one when he heard a noise behind him.

Turned and saw who was standing there.

Shit.

Had to have been hiding below when Joe boarded.

"You?" Joe Wolf said.

"Me."

"What the hell do you want?"

"To ask you a question."

"So ask."

"Simple question, really."

"From you or him?"

"It doesn't really matter."

"Then get to it already," Joe Wolf said. "I'm not getting any younger."

4

"Did you think we'd wait forever for you to give up?"

"That's it? You came all the way out here to ask me a question you should already know the answer to?"

"Pretty much."

The boat had been at rest, rocking gently, the night suddenly still except for the lap of the water against the hull, the gulls having gone silent.

Joe Wolf turned toward the wheel now, ready to start the diesel back up and head back, his evening shot just like that.

"I'll give up when I'm dead."

Suddenly the voice was right behind him.

"Fine with me."

TWO

MY STAR QUARTERBACK ROLLED to his right and faked a pass, faked the closest linebacker out of his shoes and nearly his pants, then ran twenty yards untouched to the end zone. If he'd decided to keep going, he could have run untouched all the way to Sausalito.

I blew my whistle and walked toward Carlos Quintera, the linebacker who'd just blown the play. By now the varsity team at Hunters Point High, in the section of town between Hunters Point and Bayview, knew that they weren't playing on one of those teams that ended the season with participation trophies.

I felt a smile forming on my lips. Undergrad at Cal. Stanford Law. And about to read an eighteen-year-old kid the riot act because he'd messed up at a high school football practice.

If I didn't love football as much as I did, I would have asked myself what in the world I was doing here.

"Carlos, we're going to need to get back to basics after that effort. Would that be all right with you?"

"Sure, Coach Jenny."

Still smiling, I held up the ball.

"This," I said to him, "is a football."

"You need to stop right there, Coach," Chris Tinelli, quarterback and captain of the team, said. "Pretty sure you're going too fast for him."

They all laughed. Even Carlos joined in, at least until I told him that we were going to hit the Pause button on today's practice while he ran five laps around the field.

By now all my players had long since put their teenage male egos, and their jockness, in check enough to allow them to be coached by a woman. And they had been made completely aware, really from our first practice together, that I didn't let shit go.

Inherited trait.

"Five laps, for real?" Carlos said.

"Or ten if we're still having this conversation ten seconds from now."

When practice had started in August for the Hunters Point Bears, they'd treated me like some sort of substitute teacher, thinking they really *could* get away with things, maybe because I was a woman. But it hadn't taken long for me, the political science teacher at Hunters Point, to show them differently.

After today's practice, Carlos walked over to me, helmet in hand, and said, "You know you sound like Bill Belichick when you keep telling us to do our job, right?"

I grinned at him.

"That candy-ass?"

I was the last one on the field, as always, starting to make the long walk toward the back entrance of the school, when I saw what looked like my whole team running at me, the guys still in their pads.

Chris Tinelli was the one who got to me first, out of breath, face red. Eyes red. He had his phone in his right hand.

I never brought my phone with me to practice. Once I got to the field it was all football for me, same as for my players.

"Coach Jenny," he said. "I'm so sorry."

"Chris, what's wrong?"

"Your dad died. It's all over social media."

He looked like he might cry. Maybe I would later. Just not now. Not in front of the players. I was the coach. A tough guy.

Another inherited trait.

"How?" I said.

"They say he drowned."

THREE

DANNY WOLF STARED DOWN at the field from the floor-to-ceiling window behind his desk, watching the Wolves practice.

His general manager, Mike Sawchuck, was standing next to him. This was going to be Mike's last year with the Wolves, even if the poor bastard didn't know it yet. Another guy Danny's father had hired who thought he had more tenure than a Supreme Court justice.

"Your dad loved the view from up here when this was still his office," Sawchuck said.

Here we go, Danny thought.

Now he contemplated throwing himself out the window.

"It's not his office anymore," Danny said, "as often as you seem to forget that fact."

"C'mon, Danny Boy. I know who's calling the shots around here now."

Danny Wolf turned to glare at him.

"How many times do I have to tell you not to call me that?"

"Hey, your dad does."

"I rest my case."

"I didn't come up here looking for a fight," Sawchuck said. "We're a team, you and me."

I should fire his ass now.

"Not fighting, Mike," Danny said. "Just explaining. And not to put too fine a point on things, you and I aren't a team. We were *never* a team. You're an employee."

They both watched now as the team's aging quarterback, Ted Skyler, wildly overthrew the team's number one draft choice, DeLavarious Harmon.

Harmon had been wide open behind the defense twenty yards down the field. Skyler threw it thirty, at least. Ted Skyler had stayed around too long; the general manager had stayed around far too long. So had Joe Wolf. Sometimes this place felt like the NFL version of an assisted-living facility.

Sometimes when Mike Sawchuck started to get weepy about the good old days, Danny wanted to throw *him* out the window in front of them.

"Lot of new guys this season," Sawchuck said, desperate to change the subject back to football. "But even if we get off to a slow start, in our division we're still gonna have a shot. I don't see anybody running away with the thing."

"Really. Even with Gramps still under center?"

"Danny," Sawchuck said, "you're the one who wanted to give Ted one more year."

"No," Danny Wolf snapped at Sawchuck. "No, you and my father wanted to give him one more year and convinced me to go along." He put a hand to his heart. "All so we could win one for Joe."

"I thought that's what we all wanted."

"Get over it."

Sawchuck said he was going downstairs to watch the end of practice from the field. As soon as he was out the door, Danny's cell phone rang. He picked it up, saw who was calling.

"Talk to me."

"It's about Joe," the voice said.

FOUR

JACK WOLF WAS ABOUT to join the afternoon editorial meeting at the *San Francisco Tribune*. He'd decided to hold it in the middle of the city room, a choice he made just often enough to make them think he loved being a newspaperman—and the paper—the way his father had.

All bullshit.

The room had gotten smaller since Joe Wolf had named his second son to succeed him as publisher. But what newspaper outside the *New York Times* or the *Washington Post* hadn't gotten smaller? The *Tribune*'s print edition on some days looked less substantial than the wine list at Acquerello.

Jack didn't mind that the paper remained a conservative voice in the otherwise liberal city that Joe Wolf liked to call Pelosi-ville. Problem was, Jack Wolf just didn't think it was conservative *enough*. Or loud enough. Or angry enough. Or nearly down and dirty enough. When he and his father fought—and they fought a lot—it was mostly about that. His father kept saying that as long as he was alive, the paper was still going to have standards.

"Whose?" Jack would ask. "Ronald Reagan's?"

Now Jack Wolf turned his chair and put his feet up on

the desk closest to him in what they called the bullpen. His managing editor, Megan Callahan, was standing next to him. The other top editors were in a circle in front of them.

"So what do we got?" Jack said.

The Metro editor raised a hand. Rob something. One more kid Jack had hired on the cheap.

"I might have something pretty fresh; check it out." He handed his phone over to Megan Callahan, who looked down at it and said, "You have *got* to be shitting me."

She turned back to Rob.

"Is that who I think it is?"

The kid nodded. "In the flesh." He grinned. "So to speak."

Megan said, "I didn't know guys still wore tracksuits like those."

"They're like Lululemon for geezers."

Megan handed Jack the phone. And smiled. On the screen, big as life, was the mayor of San Francisco, Charlie Spooner. Getting ready to step down next year because of term limits and well into his seventies now.

And here he was, big as life, coming out the front door of Precious Orchard massage parlor, on Geary Street.

Jack Wolf's smile grew.

"God is good."

"Isn't the mayor your friend?" Megan said.

"Things change. And by the way, what's that got to do with anything?"

"Seriously, what do we do with this?"

"What we do," Jack said, "is put that picture on the front page, underneath type that will make people think the Russians just blew up the Bay Bridge."

"Don't you think you should at least run this by your father?"

"You're right. I should."

Jack pulled out his phone, punched out a number, waited, put the phone back in his pocket. Smile getting bigger by the moment.

"Oops. Straight to voice mail."

He stood up now and said to the group, "And if I see this on Twitter before the story goes up on our site later, every one of you is fired. Understood?"

In six months, half the people in the room were going to be gone anyway during the next round of buyouts. Joe Wolf used to dread having to tell people they were being let go. Not his middle son.

"It's still his paper," Megan said.

"Not today," Jack Wolf said.

Ten minutes later, Megan Callahan was bursting into his office. Behind her he could see everybody in the city room staring at the big television set near the bullpen.

"Your father died."

She told him how and said, "I guess Charlie just got saved from death by front page."

"Like hell he did," Jack said.

FIVE

BECAUSE OF THE LOCATION where they'd found his boat and the time when his body ended up at Crissy Field East Beach, the assumption was that the tide had carried him in.

After a thorough search of *The Sea Wolf*, the police could find no signs of foul play and reported drowning as the official cause of death—even though the autopsy showed that Joe Wolf had died with a blood alcohol level almost twice the legal limit and suffered a massive heart attack sometime after he'd gone into the water.

We'd been informed by the lead detective, a guy named Ben Cantor, that the case was still very much open.

And that we'd all be hearing from him as he continued his investigation.

The manager of the St. Francis Yacht Club said that night when he'd yelled over and asked if he had any passengers with him, Joe Wolf clearly didn't hear the question. As we all knew, it had been a long time since Dad could hear worth a damn.

"Go, Wolves!" was his answer.

It was the last anybody had heard from Joseph Thomas Wolf.

Now I was in his suite overlooking the fifty yard line at Wolves Stadium. Though calling it a suite didn't do it justice and really never had. I'd always thought of it as one of the city's great luxury apartments, with a football view instead of water and bridges and the little cable cars that my father liked to sing about when he had enough vodka in him, the ones going halfway to the stars.

It wasn't a wake today. The memorial service would be held at the end of the week, the day before the Wolves' next game. It was what had been billed as a "gathering" to celebrate Joe Wolf's life, organized, mostly for show, by his second wife, Rachel, who'd been living apart from my father for months. The first Mrs. Joe Wolf, Elise, mother to my brothers and me, was also in attendance, keeping her usual healthy distance from the second Mrs. Wolf.

Joe Wolf had met Rachel, thirty years his junior, when she sold him the house he bought after he left my mother.

I thought both the house and Rachel had been impulse buys on his part.

"She ended up waiving her commission," he told me after they had separated. "I should have paid it—might have saved me a boatload of money on the back end."

My three brothers were involved in three different and intense conversations throughout the room. Danny, I saw, seemed surgically attached to the NFL commissioner. Jack Wolf was in a heavy exchange with the governor, who, I noted, was almost as pretty as Jack was.

My younger brother, Thomas, vice president of the Wolves and just back from his most recent trip to Cabo, was chatting up a female bartender, nonalcoholic beer in hand.

Thomas was my favorite, the funniest of all of us and the one who did his best to hide how much he knew about football and cared about the Wolves. After spending too much of his adult life drugging and partying, he was six months out of rehab, even more fun clear-eyed and sober than he'd ever been under the influence.

The mayor was noticeably absent. But both of California's US senators were in attendance. The owners of the Warriors and the Giants. Station managers and anchor monsters from their stations. Jim Nantz was here, and Tony Romo, and so was the owner of the Horseshoe Tavern, my father's favorite bar. The archbishop had just arrived. So had my ex-husband, bless his heart. He waved when he saw me. I acted as if I hadn't seen him.

"It's like a scene out of *Succession*," I heard from behind me. "Just without any good actors."

I turned to see that the voice belonged to Seth Dowd, the one-man investigative unit in the *Tribune*'s sports department and someone I trusted about as far as I could throw the buffet table.

"I forgot how much I didn't miss this," I said. "It's like the Tournament of Ass Kissers Parade, without floats."

"May I quote you on that?"

"Hell, no."

He smiled.

"Everybody always says you're the one most like him."

"You didn't know him, and you don't know me. But thanks for sharing."

"Why *are* you here?" he said.

"I finally decided I'd make more trouble for myself with guys like you if I was marked absent."

"I'm not guys like me."

"Sure. Go with that."

There was a reason why I'd stopped watching Wolves games up here long ago. Not hanging out with a lot of the people standing around this suite was worth not watching the games with my father anymore.

"I kept waiting to hear that the governor washed up, too," Dowd said, "as a show of solidarity."

Then Dowd said he was going off to work the room. I told him to knock himself out—I'd had about as much fun as I could handle for one day and needed a drink.

Just not here.

I was starting to ease my way toward the door when I felt someone tap me on the shoulder and turned around to see John Gallo.

He was tall and silver-haired and far more tanned than San Franciscans were supposed to be at this time of year. Or any time of year. He was also rich as shit—if not Silicon Valley rich, then close enough. Gallo had been the sworn enemy of Joe Wolf for as long as I had been alive, from the time my father—and not Gallo—had been awarded the right to put the NFL franchise that became the Wolves in downtown San Francisco.

My father had always told me that the biggest reason was the unproved rumor that John Gallo might have been more mobbed up when he was starting out building East Coast shopping malls than a boxed set of *The Sopranos*.

And probably still was.

"What are you doing here?" I said.

"Paying my respects, of course."

"No, you're not."

"You're right," he said, and smiled. "I'm not. But I'm too well-bred to have ignored Rachel's invitation."

"Bullshit."

"She did invite me. You can ask her."

"I was actually calling bullshit on the well-bred part, John."

He let that go. Maybe he was worried about the two of us making a scene.

As bad as things had gotten between my father and me,

blood was still blood. Sometimes I couldn't keep myself from looking for a good fight, and I felt myself spoiling for one with this slick bastard who had never stopped trying to screw my father over every chance he got.

During the past two years he had been doing everything humanly possible with the politicians we knew he had in his pocket to prevent the Wolves from getting the new stadium the team badly needed. Gallo had even wildly overpaid for a local sports radio station, one built around Wolves programming, to keep Joe Wolf from getting it.

"Funny how things work out, if you really think about it," Gallo said. "Your father once told me that the only way I'd ever end up with his team was over his dead body."

"Now you'll end up with it over my dead body."

"What, the little high school teacher is now speaking for the whole family?"

We stood staring at each other, as if waiting to see which one of us would end up with the last word.

"Listen," I said. "We really need to stop talking now."

"And why is that, Ms. Wolf?"

"Because if I don't walk away, people might start to think that I'm the asshole."

He smiled.

"Ah, your father's daughter."

"You're happy about this, aren't you?"

"You want me to lie?"

I said, "My dad always told me that you lied to stay in practice."

"Your dad always said the last goal he had was to outlive me. Catch me up: How did that work out for him?"

"You really do still think you're going to end up with the Wolves, don't you?"

"What makes you think I'm going to stop with the Wolves?" he said.

Then he put his hand on my shoulder, quickly leaned over, already whispering in my ear before I could back away from him.

"Did he fall?" Gallo said. "Or was he pushed?"

Before I could answer, he was the one to walk away first, smiling at me one last time over his shoulder.

Shit, I thought.

The asshole had gotten the last word after all.

SIX

JOHN GALLO SAT IN the back seat of his limousine as it pulled away from the VIP entrance to Wolves Stadium.

Usually he liked the kind of scrap he'd just had with Jenny Wolf. Lord knew he'd had enough of them with her father, going all the way back to the time when they'd had an agreement to go in on the Wolves together, until somehow Joe and his brother, the drunk, had found enough money to go it alone.

It really is true, Gallo thought. *In the end you really do forget everything except the grudges.*

But something bothered him about the girl. Teaching and coaching, even though she had a law degree from Stanford. How adorable. Even the other paper in town, the *Chronicle,* had done a big story on her a couple of weeks ago. Joe Wolf's daughter, coaching Hunters Point High. They acted like it was going to end up being a TV movie.

People might start to think that I'm the asshole, she'd had the nerve to say to him.

The only person who'd ever talked to him that way and gotten away with it had just washed up on Crissy Field East Beach.

Gallo picked up the phone on the console next to him, punched in a number that by now he knew by heart. Made sure to push a button and raise the window between him and his driver. John Gallo hadn't made it this far by being a careless man.

He could hear the noise of the party—he thought of it as a party, anyway—in the background behind him.

"Is your sister going to be a problem?" Gallo said.

He didn't wait for an answer, just ended the call right there. They both knew it wasn't a question, it was an order. Make sure she wasn't a problem.

Gallo hadn't gotten this close to the prize—for all of them—by not sensing trouble. Somehow he knew this girl was trouble. And might eventually have to be taught some manners.

There was something about her that bothered John Gallo. He didn't just hear her father in her voice. It was also in her attitude. Something in her eyes, the way she looked at him with contempt.

The father's daughter.

He picked up the phone again and called a man he knew didn't like surprises of any kind.

"We need to put somebody on the daughter," Gallo said.

SEVEN

DAD'S FUNERAL, WITH ALL the trimmings, had been the day before, at the Cathedral of Saint Mary of the Assumption. Now it was game day, the Wolves' opener, against the Browns. I was using only one of the two season tickets on the forty yard line that I'd secretly bought after my last argument with my father, during which he told me for the last time what a disappointment I'd been to him.

I was happy sitting by myself, not having to listen to somebody who wanted to impress me with how much football he knew. I could focus on the game, take notes when I saw a play I thought might help my high school team, test myself to see how many plays I knew were coming just by the formation the Wolves were in.

Joe Wolf had always said that I was the best football man in the family.

Including himself.

By now we'd gone through all the phony pageantry of a death in sports, the moment of silence before the kickoff and the flags at half-staff and the video tribute at halftime. I was hoping that wherever my father was today he was laughing his Irish ass off at the spectacle of the whole stadium being practically overwrought, wanting the Wolves to win one for Joe today.

And we *were* winning in the fourth quarter. Our quarterback hadn't been great today, hadn't been great for a while. But Ted Skyler, that horse's ass, had managed to throw a couple of touchdown passes, and when he did throw a bad interception, the way he just had, the defense covered for him and held the Browns to a field goal and kept us in the lead, 23–20.

All we needed to do when we got the ball back with two minutes to go was run out the clock, if we could.

Ted handed the ball off twice. Third and four now. The Browns called their last time-out. We needed just one first down.

This time I did know what was coming from our formation: Ted was going to throw a quick slant pass to DeLavarious Harmon, our star rookie receiver.

The kid ran a perfect pattern, Ted hit him in stride, DeLavarious was brought down immediately: first down, game as good as over.

DeLavarious popped right up, handed the ball to the ref, pointed in a showy way indicating that he had in fact made the first down, started walking back to the huddle.

I don't know why my eyes were still on him. But they were. So I was looking directly at the kid, right there in front of me on the forty, when his left leg buckled underneath him, and he spun around as if suddenly dizzy, then fell face-forward to the turf.

And stopped moving.

EIGHT

THEY DIDN'T BRING OUT the kind of flatbed cart they used to transfer an injured player off the field, calling for an ambulance instead while players from both teams knelt and formed a circle around DeLavarious Harmon.

Who still hadn't moved.

Wolves Stadium was as quiet as it had been during the pregame moment of silence for Joe Wolf. Our offense didn't even line up for one more snap in what would have been the last minute. The refs waited until the ambulance had left the field, then the lead official went to midfield and waved his arms, indicating that the game was over.

In my life, I'd never seen a game called before the clock officially ran out.

I was moving up through the stands then, pulling out the all-access pass I kept in my bag, taking the closest elevator down to the field level and the Wolves' locker room, on my side of the stadium.

By the time I got to the runway, the ambulance was already gone. It was thirty minutes, maybe, since DeLavarious Harmon had collapsed. Some of our players were standing outside the locker room door, many still wearing their helmets. One of them was Ted Skyler, who looked at me and shook his head.

Danny Wolf was leaning against the wall next to the door, alone, eyes vacant, ashen-faced, phone in his hand.

I walked over to him.

"What happened?"

He turned and stared at me, almost as if he didn't recognize me at first.

"What?"

"Danny, how is he?"

"He's dead, is how he is," my brother said.

Now I stared at him. My father had told me one time that in the history of the NFL, only one player had ever died during a game. Back in the 1970s. I don't know why I knew his name in that moment, but for some reason I did. Chuck Hughes of the Lions. A heart condition nobody knew he had. The things you remember.

"How?" I said to my brother.

"How? He stopped breathing. That's how."

"A perfectly healthy twenty-two-year-old kid just dropped dead? He didn't even get hit that hard on the last play."

"Doc said he was dead before they got him into the ambulance."

"Where's his wife?"

"In the ambulance," Danny said.

He turned to me, keeping his voice low.

"This is a terrible optic for us," he said.

I looked at him.

"A terrible *optic*? For *us*? The kid was one of ours, Danny. And now he's dead, not a goddamn public relations problem."

He started to walk away. The media had been roped off, about twenty yards from where we were standing.

I grabbed my brother's arm.

"Don't make a scene," he said.

"Everybody keeps telling me that."

"What do you want from me?"

"You always wanted to be Dad," I said. "Well, here's your chance."

"What does that even mean?"

I talked to him then as if he were one of my players.

"Do your job," I said.

NINE

MY THREE BROTHERS, my father's two wives, and I were gathered in the office of Dad's longtime attorney, Harris Crawford, for the reading of his will. It was a big office but one that felt as small as a boxing ring once we'd been seated by Mr. Crawford's assistant.

The atmosphere while we waited for him to finish up a conference call reminded me of family dinners when my brothers and I were growing up, today with an extra wife getting a seat at the table. It was fitting that the room really did feel to me like a ring, because my father had once described those dinners as boxing without blood.

Rachel sat on one side of the room. If my mother had moved her chair any farther away from Rachel Wolf's, she would have been sitting outside the Museum of Modern Art, next door.

Danny turned to me.

"Two straight appearances with the family. Nice of you to wait until Dad was dead."

"She's here for the parting gifts," Jack Wolf said.

"I'm not on the payroll, Jack. What's your story?"

"At least we didn't turn our backs on him," Danny said.

"Only because you were afraid you might slip and fall off the gravy train?"

My two older brothers had rarely been aligned, even as kids, except when they aligned against me.

Danny was the one sitting closest to me. I angled my chair closer to his. He reflexively leaned back slightly as I did. When he was twelve and I was ten, he tripped me as I was about to score the winning basket in a driveway basketball game. After I got up, I punched him in the face.

When he went crying to dad, Joe Wolf said, "Good Lord, how many daughters do I have?"

It wouldn't be the last time we'd hear a version of that line from him. And it wouldn't be the last time I'd slug one of my brothers.

Now I said to Danny, "Do I need to break your nose again?"

"Grow up, Jenny."

"You first."

I wasn't there because I expected some great windfall from my father. In all ways, *that* was the boat of his I felt had sailed, at least for me. It wasn't just that I had walked away from him. It was that I had never shown any interest in the family business, even after graduating from law school. He told me I was the smartest one of his children. I told him that wasn't my problem, it was his. Then we'd had our last argument, the granddaddy of them all. There had been no contact since. He was stubborn, and so was I. I told myself I didn't hold grudges the way he did. But I knew it was close.

From behind me Thomas Wolf said, "Is there going to be cake?"

"All of you hush," Elise Wolf said, in a tone of voice that always reminded me of the crack of a whip.

"Does that include me?" Rachel said from the other side of the office.

My mother, who had ignored her to this point, looked

at her with enough fire and brimstone to turn her into a pillar of salt.

Mercifully, the office door opened then, and Harris Crawford walked in. He had been my father's lawyer and best friend for all my time on earth. Tall, flowing white hair, one of the three-piece suits that I knew he had made in London. I'd always thought that if Morgan Freeman hadn't played God, Harris Crawford could easily have gotten the part.

He sat behind his desk, made a sweeping gesture with one hand that took in the room, and said, "Still one big happy dysfunctional family, I see."

My mother sighed with such force that I was surprised it didn't send ripples through the curtains behind him.

"You have no idea."

"Why do we even have to do it this way?" Danny asked.

"Because that's the way Joe wanted it," Harris Crawford said.

"He *still* won't let go," Danny muttered.

"Shall we begin?" Crawford inquired, looking out at us over his reading glasses.

"The sooner we do," Danny said, "the sooner we get this over with."

Harris Crawford started reading. Mom got the Nob Hill house on Jones Street in which we'd all grown up along with an extremely generous amount of money, which I knew was guilt money from my father because of the way he'd hurt her. I looked for a change of expression. But there wasn't one. She'd always been the toughest one of all of us. The real alpha Wolf.

Rachel Wolf got the house in which she was living, the one in Presidio Heights she'd sold to Dad before they began the affair that became his second marriage, a marriage that included a prenup that my dad once said would have survived the earthquake of '89 far better than the Bay Bridge had.

She smiled, waiting for Harris Crawford to say something else. But he didn't.

"That's it?" she said.

I was watching her.

Rachel Wolf began to color slightly.

"Just this additional note from Joe, directed at you, Rachel," Crawford said, reading now. "'If you're looking for more, sell the place to another sucker. Or your boyfriend the tennis pro.'"

At this point Rachel Wolf looked as if she might have just swallowed a hamster.

"This is bullshit," she said.

And walked out of the room.

"Nevertheless," Harris Crawford said in a voice as dry as the papers on his desk.

My mother was always a lady, no matter what the circumstances, with an almost regal bearing. She turned to me now, smiling, and said, "I wasn't watching, sweetheart. Did the door hit her in that remade ass on the way out?"

Thomas Wolf II was the next order of business. He retained his position as vice president of the Wolves and inherited a modest amount of money. According to Mr. Crawford, there was a lot more set up in a trust if he made it to the age of forty.

Thomas had just turned thirty-five. We all knew that our uncle Tommy, his namesake, had died at thirty-nine in a drunk-driving accident.

Thomas nodded.

"Everyone needs goals. Guess Dad missed the memo that I'm clean and sober now."

Harris Crawford told Danny the amount of money he was receiving.

"You're kidding, right?"

Crawford peered at Danny over his reading glasses.

"Have I ever struck you as a big kidder, son?"

"It's not enough," Danny said.

"Nevertheless."

Crawford looked out at Danny and said, "But you maintain your quarter share of the Wolves, as do all Joe's children. I'm sure you saw that *Forbes* recently established the value of the team at three billion dollars. Do the math on what your shares are worth."

"What about being president of the team?"

"You retain that title," Crawford said, "as Jack maintains his title as publisher of the *San Francisco Tribune*."

Jack nodded.

"So are we done here?"

"Not quite," Harris Crawford said.

He looked at me over the reading glasses now.

"As for Jenny."

Crawford took a deep breath.

"I'll read this as it's written. 'It is so stipulated that my only daughter, Jennifer Elise Wolf, assumes the role of chairman of the board of Wolf, Inc.'"

As that news sunk in, the air suddenly changed in the office even as I felt most of the air leaving my body. "The majority of the voting shares on the board are now transferred to her," Crawford continued.

Not everyone immediately processed what he'd just said.

As someone who'd briefly practiced law myself, I certainly did. When my father and I were still on speaking terms, he explained to me one time that voting shares are what give you the hammer in business.

A hammer he had just handed to me, even as I honestly did struggle to catch my breath.

Nobody spoke until Danny Wolf said, "Wait . . . *what*?"

"Chairman of the *board*?" Jack said. "She's barely still a member of the *family*."

Danny was shaking his head, like a horse being bothered by a fly.

"What's he saying here? The only vote on the goddamn board that mattered was *his*."

Crawford took his glasses off, placed them on the desk in front of him, and stared at my older brother.

"Was there something in there that you didn't understand, Daniel? I feel as if the language is self-explanatory."

Danny opened his mouth and closed it.

"What your father is saying," the lawyer continued, "is that the control of both the football team and the newspaper now belongs to your sister."

Danny was the one who stood now, nearly knocking over his chair as he did.

"This is bullshit."

I was about to tell him that line was already taken, but he was already gone.

TEN

"I NEED TO GET with my team," I said to my mother. Just the two of us were left in Harris Crawford's office.

"Don't you think it's a little premature to address the Wolves?" she said.

"I meant the Hunters Point Bears, Mother."

"Your little high school team?"

"It's nice to see that you understand me as well as you ever did."

I'd already canceled my afternoon class that day because of the reading of Dad's will. But I hadn't canceled practice. By now I knew full well what a good place, and even a safe place, those two hours were for my players every day after school. I had no idea that it would be a safe place for me, too, now that Joe Wolf thought he could run my life from the grave.

He'd always told us when we were growing up that winners would do anything to win the fight, even when the other guy was already out of the room. Now he was the one out of the room but still trying to win the fight between us, which had been going on for most of my life.

Thinking about it that way made me smile as I sat in my car in the parking lot a half hour before practice was scheduled to begin.

Once a controlling SOB, I thought, *always a controlling SOB.*

So this is the way he thought he could win the argument about my having a role in the running of the Wolves.

You want to know how the world really works? he'd always said. *Here's how: kill or be killed.*

I stopped home briefly to change into a hoodie and jeans and sneakers. As I was coming out of my house in Bayview, I saw a television truck making the turn at the corner and heading in my direction.

News travels fast in the modern world. This time the news was about me. I got into my Prius and headed the other way.

So it begins.

I drove around aimlessly for a while, trying to clear my head, trying to wrap my mind around what had just happened to me, the family, the team, the newspaper. In the space of a few minutes, I'd gone from a high school coach and teacher to chairman of the board of my father's business empire.

And I knew it was more than sudden change that was making my head spin. If I accepted my new role, with the football team especially, I would be claiming the identity I had most come to hate.

Being a Wolf.

By the time I made it to the school parking lot, I'd shut off my phone, having discovered that the only media outlet that didn't seem to have my cell number was *Pravda.* Before I did turn off my phone, though, I'd gotten a call from my next-door neighbor and friend, Rashida McCoy, who ran a small day-care center in Bayview.

"You rob a bank, girl?" she asked, then told me about the two TV trucks parked in front of our houses.

"In a manner of speaking." I told her what had happened.

"I haven't checked Twitter or any of the other feeds lately!" she yelled into the phone. "Girl, you must be *trippin'*!"

"I feel like I am."

The players already knew by the time we were all on the field together.

"Do we still call you Coach?" linebacker Carlos Quintera said. "Or Madame President?"

"Or Your Highness?" Deuce Stiles, our best safety, said.

"Have your fun. But it's going to cost all you great wits when we start practice."

"Wait," quarterback Chris Tinelli said. "Aren't you hanging with the wrong team?"

"Nope. I'm right where I'm supposed to be."

I smiled. They had no idea how happy I was to see them today. The only place I really did feel safe—feel *normal,* at least for the time being—was right here.

Davontae Lillis, star wide receiver, maybe the funniest kid on the team, stepped forward now.

"Okay, who should we fire first, the coach or the quarterback?"

"As you know, D, it would be a little complicated with this particular quarterback."

"Straight up? Not if you want to win."

He was right, but I didn't tell him that.

"Hey, let's pump the brakes here. I haven't even decided if I want to do this."

Carlos started banging his palm against the side of his helmet, as if he hadn't heard correctly.

"Say *what*? Are you the only person in America who *doesn't* want to run their own NFL team?"

"Coach," Chris said, "do you know how few women have *ever* run an NFL franchise?"

"Actually, I do."

Davontae said, "You *got* to do this."

"I don't *got* to do anything I don't *want* to."

"You're saying you *don't* want to do this?" Deuce asked.

"What I'm saying is that I got a blind-side hit on this a couple of hours ago. I need a little time to make up my mind."

"Let us make it up for you," Carlos said. *"Of course you're doing this!"*

. "Can you get us one of those suites?" Davontae said.

"I'm gonna need one of those passes to go stand on the sideline," Deuce said. "Hundred percent."

"Locker room pass for me to go with it," Carlos said. "Hang with my boys after the game. So I know how to act when I'm in the pros."

He high-fived Davontae and Deuce.

"Why wouldn't you do this?" Chris Tinelli said. "Your dad obviously wants you to do this or he wouldn't have left you control of the team."

Chris was one of those kids. He just looked the part of high school hero. I imagined this is what Ted Skyler was like when he was a senior in high school.

"I didn't do what my dad wanted me to do when he was alive," I said. "I'm getting my head wrapped around the idea that he still thinks he can tell me what to do."

Chris grinned.

"You like to be the one tells people what to do."

"Kind of."

"So why don't you want to tell the Wolves what to do same as you tell us?" he said. "Isn't football your family business?"

"Love the football business. Hate the family."

Carlos said, "Is that why you had that big fight with your father?"

"I never told you about that."

Now he grinned. "There's this thing called the internet, Coach Jenny. And it pretty much knows everything."

We practiced then, and practiced hard, but then these kids always practiced hard, because their season mattered as much to them as the pro season meant to the Wolves. And maybe even more.

Damn, I do love this game as much as these kids do. This is my favorite time of day, the same as it is theirs.

No wonder they acted as if they didn't want to live in a world where somebody got handed an NFL team and was even considering handing it back.

At one point during a water break, Carlos came over to me and said, "If you do take over the Wolves, you gonna leave us?"

"The only time I leave this team is if you guys tell me you don't want me around anymore."

He lowered his voice.

"Promise?"

"I promise."

Practice ended a few minutes later with Carlos reading Chris's eyes perfectly and breaking up what looked to be a perfect pass to Davontae. As soon as he did, he looked over at me and shook his fist. I smiled and shook mine back.

Maybe the Hunters Point Bears *had* made up my mind for me.

When I got back in my car, I decided to turn my phone back on, just to see if it had blown up yet.

The last text message I'd gotten was from Rashida.

Check out the Trib.

ELEVEN

I SAT WITH MY ex-husband at a table near the wall at the Horseshoe Tavern on Chestnut Street, once my father's favorite hole-in-the-wall bar. Fascinating that Joe Wolf, the guy who had such a taste for the finer things in life, also loved places like this.

Just not as fascinating, in the whole grand scheme of things, as my once being married to the quarterback of the Wolves.

Ted Skyler had his navy cap imprinted with the white wolf logo pulled down low.

My phone was in front of him next to his mug of beer. The screen was filled with a headline in end-of-the-world type on the *Tribune's* home page:

SHE WOLF

Now my ex tipped his cap back and grinned.

"What did you expect? That your brothers were going to fight fair?"

"I didn't do this to them," I said. "Dad did."

"You should have heard your brother Danny in the locker room after practice today," he said. "He's pacing up and down and yelling that hell would freeze over before his sister was going to take over *his* football team. And his imagery got even more colorful after that."

"Jack probably feels the same way about the paper," I said. I pointed at the phone. "Hence the hit piece."

"You have to know it's only the beginning."

He clinked his mug against mine.

"Well, cheers."

"Easy for you to say."

We both drank.

There were only half a dozen customers at the bar. All guys. They'd made Ted Skyler the moment he walked in. I had called him from the car after I'd seen the *Tribune*, then driven around a little more before arriving at the decision that drinking with my ex was better than drinking alone. There had been a time when we'd only spoken to each other through our lawyers. My position had softened, at least slightly, over time. He wasn't a better person now. But he hadn't gotten any worse, either.

Low bar, I thought.

We'd married in his second year with the Wolves. It had been treated in San Francisco like a royal fairy tale, a Wolf marrying the team's star quarterback. The marriage had lasted until his fifth year. He swore he still loved me. It just turned out that before very long he liked the sports anchor at one of the local network affiliates more.

He was thirty-seven and still looked remarkably like the golden boy he'd been at USC. Somebody had once written that when Ted Skyler walked into a room, all the women—and half the guys—wanted him.

"I didn't ask for this," I said.

"Nobody knows that better than I do," he said. "You spent

your whole life running away from the team. Even when you were married to me."

"It had nothing to do with the team. Everything to do with them. And being afraid I'd turn into them."

He checked his own phone. I didn't know if he was seeing anyone at the moment. But the night was young. And he was still Touchdown Ted Skyler. God's gift.

All you had to do was ask him.

"You are going to do this, right?" he said.

"No."

He had the mug halfway to his lips.

"You're joking."

I didn't say anything, just gave him a look he probably felt he knew as well as he did the deferred money he had coming to him when he retired.

"Okay. You're not joking."

"I had spent most of the day talking myself into it," I said. "That somehow I owed it to Dad to honor his dying wish, or whatever you want to call it, and make things right between us even though he's gone."

I drank more beer.

"Then I saw that headline and I knew I was kidding myself. That I couldn't hold on to the life I've made for myself and go back to the life of being a Wolf."

"She Wolf," he said.

"Don't start with me."

He waved at the bartender, who came over and took Ted's order for a Scotch. I didn't say anything, but almost by reflex he said, "I've got a driver."

"Of course you do."

"This is some serious shit here. I need a real drink."

He waited until the bartender came back with a glass of

Johnnie Walker. He told me he'd read once that Joe Namath used to drink Johnnie Walker.

He toasted me, drank, and said, "You have to do this."

"Why? Because you think I'd give you a better chance of holding on to your job?"

The grin disappeared, but only briefly. "Maybe you're more like them than you think."

"Sorry. I *did* call *you*."

"So you did," Ted said. "But you sound as if you've already made up your mind. So why *did* you call me?"

"I wanted to see if maybe you could un–make up my mind." I grinned. "Other than on the subject of that TV twink, you were always pretty honest with me."

"I think you should do it," he said. "You'd be good at it. A lot better than your brother is."

"Any random member of the grounds crew would be."

"Look at what Jeanie Buss has done with the Lakers."

"She didn't mind having a public fight with her brother over control of her team," I said. "But that's not me."

"You sure? And what fight are we really talking about? Sounds like you got all the power you need today."

"Dad used to talk about being famous. He said it was like living in a Macy's window. That's not me."

"I was under the impression everybody wants to be famous," he said.

"I had my taste just being married to the quarterback of the team. And found out I didn't like that particular taste."

He leaned forward. He was still cute as hell, even though I could see him getting older around the eyes.

"If you quit, they win. You get that, right?"

"Or maybe I win, by holding on to the things that really matter to me."

41

"Forget the paper for the moment," he said. "This is an NFL team we're talking about, Jennifer. You need to think about this, because your father obviously gave it a hell of a lot of thought."

"Maybe he just wanted to screw Danny over."

"Or maybe he wanted to save the Wolves." He gave me another one of his lopsided grins. "Though now that I think about it, they might be the same thing."

"I'd be walking right back into everything I walked away from," I said.

"When you broke your father's heart."

"He sure found an interesting way to get even. And what heart, by the way?"

"Whoa," he said, and then I told him I'd stolen that line from the second Mrs. Joe Wolf.

We sat there in silence. He'd shown me something tonight, I had to admit. He'd been engaged for ten long minutes in a conversation that wasn't about him.

"I've been thinking about something since Joe died," Ted said. "After the last preseason game, I went up to have a drink with him in the suite. We used to do that a lot. Anyway, he and Danny were arguing when I came in. And your father said something like the worst mistake he ever made was putting Danny in charge of the Wolves, and the second biggest was leaving him in charge. And Danny said, 'So take the team away.' And Joe said, 'You think I won't?' And then Danny said, 'And you think I won't end up with it anyway?'"

"What did that mean?"

"No clue," Ted said.

"You ever ask him?"

"Sounded like a Danny problem, not a Ted problem."

"For now," I said, "Dad has taken the team away from him."

"Has he ever." Ted finished his Scotch. "Sleep on this."

"I don't need to."

"You're really going to walk away."

"Kind of my thing. I'm going to call a press conference tomorrow." I shrugged. "I've come to the conclusion that I already have the only team I need."

We walked out together. He signed a couple of napkins for the guys at the bar. By the time he got into the back seat of his car, he was already talking on his phone, most likely setting up a date or confirming one.

By the time I got back to Bayview, the television trucks were gone.

But someone was waiting for me on my front steps.

TWELVE

I'D THOUGHT ABOUT ISSUING a statement about my plans but decided that would look as if I were hiding. So I told the public relations people that we'd hold the press conference on the field. Nobody could say Joe Wolf's daughter was hiding if she was standing there at the fifty yard line.

The *Tribune* had published a longer news story in this morning's print edition, the paper I still had delivered to my house, today headlined:

QUEEN PASSES ON BEING KING

The byline on the story amending the one published on the website about my having been given control of the Wolves was Seth Dowd's. It even included what I'd said to Ted moments before he got into his car about how I already had my team. My ex-husband, bless his heart, wasn't calling one of his girlfriends. He was calling Seth Dowd. Probably a practical matter for Ted. Maybe he thought that if I couldn't help him hold on to his job, the media could.

Dad always said that if you were born round, you didn't die square.

My three brothers sat behind me. Mike Sawchuck and the Wolves' coach, Rich Kopka, were in the row of chairs behind them. A sizable number of reporters vied for position in front of the podium set up on the Wolves' logo at midfield, a platform for the TV cameras behind them.

Not exactly like addressing my poli-sci class.

When it was time for Danny to introduce me, he leaned down as he passed me and said, "This is for the best."

"Trust me. I know that now."

Danny kept his remarks short, thanking everybody for coming on short notice, saying that because there had been so much speculation over the past twenty-four hours about the family and the team and our father's will, we'd decided this was the best way to speak directly to what he called "Wolves Nation."

A country, I thought, *constantly at war.*

Then he introduced me.

I was wearing my favorite Michael Kors dress—pricey for a teacher's salary, but not for a Wolf—and heels just high enough to make me look taller than my older brother.

I opened by saying, "You all may have read about me. I'm the She Wolf." I shrugged. "In this family, we'll do anything to boost circulation."

Some laughter rippled through the crowd.

I turned around and said, "Thanks for that, Jack."

Got another polite laugh, just not from Jack Wolf. At some point the two of us were going to have a long talk about the paper. But not today. Today was about football. Joe Wolf used to say it wasn't just Sundays and Mondays—every day was a football day.

"I'll try to keep my remarks brief."

From behind me Danny Wolf said, "That will be a first."

He got a laugh, too, the people in front of us clearly not aware that Danny was generally as funny as back spasms.

"My family, as you can probably tell, has always been a tough room."

Then I told them I *was* briefly going to act like the teacher that I was, proceeding to explain what had happened yesterday, the difference between the shares in the Wolves my brothers and I had all inherited, and the voting shares that came with being chairman, the majority of which now belonged to me.

"The aforementioned She Wolf," I said, turning and staring at Jack Wolf again.

He shifted slightly in his chair, looking as happy to be here as he used to be in church.

"Anyway, Danny's right: there has been much speculation in the media about what the family is going to do. I'm sure you all read Seth Dowd's very fine exclusive this morning in the Wolf family newspaper."

I took a deep breath and let it out, then smiled at him and the rest of the audience stretched out in front of me.

"But to bring back an oldie but goodie, it turns out that story is fake news."

I had everybody's full attention now.

"Because as of today, I am taking over full control of both the Wolves and the *Tribune*."

There were already questions being shouted. Just for my own amusement, I took one, from Seth Dowd.

"You can't possibly be serious about actually doing this," he said.

"*So* serious. *So* doing it."

Danny Wolf was closest to me behind the podium.

"I will bury you," he hissed.

"You're repeating yourself. That's what you told me when you came to my house last night."

"You lied," he said.

"And you never learn."

"What's that mean?"

"Threatening to beat me up didn't work when we were kids. And it sure as shit doesn't work now."

I could still hear questions being shouted at me as I disappeared into the runway.

It was already good being king.

Or queen.

Either way.

THIRTEEN

"WE NEED TO TALK," Danny said to me.

I'd moved into a vacant office down the hall from his. It looked like a broom closet compared to Danny's and had belonged to an assistant general manager he'd fired a few weeks before. If you followed the Wolves, you occasionally got the idea that Danny Wolf fired people every time he got bored.

That's the way people thought of them in town. Not the San Francisco Wolves.

Just the Wolves.

I looked at him over my laptop.

"Unless you're here with the Wi-Fi password, I'm thinking we're kind of talked out at this point."

"Still the great wit of the family," he said.

"Low bar."

There was no point in asking him to sit. Even if there had been more than one chair, asking him to sit would have been the same as asking him to stay. And I had work to do before heading down to speak to the Wolves players before practice.

After that I was heading to Hunters Point High, having

told the principal that even though I was taking a leave from teaching, I was going to continue to coach my team.

"I just wanted to give you a heads-up that you're going to be hearing from the commissioner," Danny said.

"To welcome me to the old boys' club?"

"There are women, too," he said.

"Occasionally seen. Rarely heard."

Danny sighed. It sounded sadder than if he'd blown a blue note on a trumpet.

"He is going to tell you that you need to give this up now. Because there's no way you're going to get approved by three-quarters of the owners."

"And why is that?"

Danny said, "I'm sure he'll explain."

"Is that what you came here to tell me?"

"No, as a matter of fact it isn't."

He put his hands on my desk and leaned forward.

"What I came here to tell you is that all football decisions in this organization still run through me."

"Maybe by you," I said. "But not *through* you."

"Why don't you just go ahead and fire me?"

"I have no plans to fire you unless you give me no other choice. Imagine how much fun all my new friends in the media would have with that. And I was hoping we might find a way to work together."

"Not happening."

"Your call."

Today was all about the Wolves. I'd already decided I would deal with my brother Jack and the *Tribune* later—starting with this morning's front-page headline:

CELEBRITY FAMILY FEUD

"You can't possibly want to do this," Danny said.

The feud was on.

"And why is that? Because I'm a woman?"

"Because you have no experience!" he snapped. "Because coaching your little high school team doesn't qualify you to run a pro football team! Because you're out of your goddamn depth, and the only person in San Francisco who doesn't appear to grasp that is you."

Splotches of red were showing on his face. That had been happening to him since he was a little boy, every time he got upset. Or didn't get his way.

"You've done everything possible to avoid being around this team or part of it," he said. "But now you suddenly love it— and dear departed Daddy—so much that you're going to be a boss?" He snorted. "The only people you ever wanted to boss around were Jack and Tommy and me."

"Who knew things would come full circle like this?" I said, putting my hands out helplessly.

"Keep making jokes."

"Who's joking?"

"This is my team, goddamn it!"

"Dad's team."

"Maybe you heard," Danny said. "He died. It was in all the papers, including yours."

I stood up now and came around the small desk. I was suddenly tired of him looking down at me. Even in running shoes, I was the same height as he was. So we were eye to eye. It just felt more like toe-to-toe. An old-fashioned stare-down between the two of us.

Yeah, I thought, *things really have come full circle.*

"If he'd wanted it to be your team after he died, it would be," I said in a quiet voice. He'd always been the shouter. "He didn't want it to be. So it's not."

"Enjoy this while you can," he said.

We really weren't in each other's personal space. It just felt that way.

When I didn't say anything, he said, "This is going to be a disaster."

"We'll see about that."

"Why *don't* you fire me?"

"Because I'm not going to make a martyr out of you. Unless you leave me no choice."

He stared at me. His face was now almost entirely red.

"You know what the real joke is?" he said. "People always thought you were the smart one in this family. On top of that, they thought you were the nice one. But those of us who really know you know you're more like Dad than Jack and Tommy and me combined."

"And that's a bad thing?"

"You lousy, stinking hypocrite," he said. "You didn't run away because you were afraid you'd be like us. You were afraid you'd end up like *him*."

He slowly shook his head from side to side, smirking.

"And now you have."

He walked toward the door.

"One more thing," I said.

"No. We're done."

"How did DeLavarious Harmon die?" I asked.

He turned back to me and hesitated a couple of beats too long before responding.

"How the hell would I know? I'm waiting for the autopsy report along with everybody else."

"Could he have been taking something that you knew he shouldn't have been?"

"Why are you asking me?"

I wondered if he knew how defensive he sounded in that moment.

"You just told me it was your team," I said.

He cursed at me before walking out, leaving the door open behind him.

"Good talk," I said to myself.

Then texted Thomas Wolf.

FOURTEEN

MY COACH, RICH KOPKA, was looking at me as if I'd come down to his office to steal his playbook. Or his wallet. I was as fascinated as always by his nose, which seemed to make a hard right turn about halfway down.

I got right to it, told him what I wanted to do in a few minutes, when the players were on the field, and that I didn't want him out there with us.

"It's my team," he said, peering at me over his reading glasses and trying to look fierce.

"Yeah, no."

Then I explained to him that I wouldn't want the players present when I was having a private conversation with him, but that if I went past the time when practice was supposed to start, he could fine me.

So a few minutes later I was standing on the big Wolves' logo at midfield, suddenly feeling the way I had the first time I ever stood in front of a class. Genuinely surprised at how nervous I felt.

I had rehearsed what I wanted to say. I just wanted to let them know that I knew football but had no intention of trying to sound as if I had invented it, the way their coach did just about every time I saw him interviewed on television.

Some of the players in front of me were kneeling. Some were standing. I was wearing jeans and my Hunters Point hoodie. Like I was one of the boys, even though they were all staring at me as sullenly as if I'd just shown up from human resources.

Just like that, I threw out my prepared remarks.

Read the room, Joe Wolf had always taught us when we were kids. And I just had. I realized they didn't need to hear from me as much as I needed to hear from them.

"You guys know who I am by now. Sometimes I feel as if people in outer space know who I am, at least if there are football fans up there. So ask me anything."

They looked at each other before Andre DeWitt, our free safety, stepped forward, grinning.

"Which conference did you play in?" he said. "Big Ten or ACC?"

"The Joe Wolf conference. Three brothers and me. Everybody needed to wear a helmet."

Got no reaction. But then I wasn't out here to get laughs.

"By the way?" I said to DeWitt. "That pass interference call against Cleveland was total BS. The other guy was the one who pushed off."

"Just one more ref acting like Boo Boo the fool."

"Hear you."

I thought, *Maybe one guy on my side. Or at least not against me. A start.*

Just make sure you don't end up sounding like Boo Boo the fool.

Caleb Crowder, our best running back, with the longest man braid I'd ever seen, was the next to step forward, hand raised. Maybe this was like class after all.

"Is this where you say you want to win so bad it hurts?"

I grinned. "The only time you hear about how much an owner wants to win is when a team isn't."

He nodded.

"And Caleb? You need to get more touches. We don't run the damn ball nearly enough."

He turned around, stretched out his arms, and yelled at his teammates, *"Thank you!"*

I looked into the crowd. They all had their helmets in their hands. Football players don't put on their helmets until it's time to go to work. I was struck by how young so many of them were, not all that much older than my players at Hunters Point.

"What else?"

Ron Sadowski, the tight end, said, "Are you going to be one of those owners who wants to be on the sideline during games? I hate that shit."

"Same," I said, and grinned. "I'll be watching games from where I always have, the seats I bought for myself on the forty before I ever thought about running this team. That way I'm not tempted to listen to the announcers explaining football to me. A long time ago, I used to watch in my father's suite. But I grew out of it."

"How do we know you're not just acting this way to make a good first impression?" Sadowski, a giant, ham-faced young guy out of Iowa, said.

"Not that guy," I said. "If you don't know it yet, you will."

I looked up at the clock on top of the scoreboard at the other end of the field. I only had a few more minutes.

I saw Ted Skyler in back, standing behind his offensive linemen. Or hiding behind them. Gave him a good long look. We both knew that he'd tried to sell me out with Seth Dowd. It was why I hadn't taken any of his calls since the Horseshoe

Tavern. But I wasn't going to call him out in front of the team. I had no standing to do that, not after a few minutes. And he was still our quarterback.

At least for the time being.

Quindlen Moore, the Wolves' All-Pro left tackle, the guy known as the blind-side tackle, called out to me from where he was standing in front of my ex-husband.

"Tell us why we should trust you."

We were getting to it now.

"I can't."

"Say what?"

"Nothing I say today is ever going to convince you of that. So here's the deal: I earn your trust, and you earn mine."

"Talk's cheap," Quindlen said.

I smiled at him.

"But you're not."

I heard some chuckles from his teammates.

"Never had me a woman boss," he said.

"Neither did LeBron before he got to the Lakers."

I waved him up to where I was standing. He slowly made his way through his teammates. When he got to me, so tall and so wide I felt as if he were blocking out the sun, I simply reached up and bumped him some fist.

I knew I hadn't won them over today. Might never win them over. But I hadn't expected to. And hoped it hadn't seemed as if I were trying too hard to sound like one of the boys. It was a start—nothing more. I hadn't made a fool out of myself or looked weak. Joe Wolf had always taught us that weakness isn't a condition; it's a choice. It was one of the things he was right about.

My heart had been pounding like a jackhammer the entire time I was standing in front of them. But it was getting back to normal as I walked toward the tunnel.

That was when I yelled at the Wolves over my shoulder, knowing they were all still watching me.

"One more thing?"

I stopped then and turned to face them.

"You guys want to make a good impression on *me*? Win on Sunday. That will impress the holy hell out of me."

FIFTEEN

DANNY WATCHED FROM HIS window, wanting to punch a fist through it as he saw *her* fist-bump Quindlen Moore. Then she said something to them before she left the field, and Danny could see them nodding, almost in approval.

She's going to ruin everything.

He had everything lined up. *They* had everything lined up. His father was dead, so Danny Wolf no longer had *him* looking over his shoulder, the way he had been for Danny's whole life, second-guessing everything he did. Danny didn't have him constantly in his ear, even after he'd sworn up and down that he was going to be hands-off with the football operation, that it was Danny's show now.

Same as he told Jack he could run the newspaper any way he wanted to.

Always with this one qualifier: as long as you don't muck things up. Right before one or both of them would hear for maybe the ten thousandth time from Mr. Hands-Off about everything he'd built with those two hands.

It's time for you to run things your way, he'd told Danny when he made the announcement that he was stepping back from the Wolves, at a press conference that was supposed to be about Danny and turned out to be all about Joe Wolf.

It had taken hardly any time at all for Danny to be reminded, as if he needed reminding, that there had only ever been one way in the Wolf family.

His father's.

Only now it was his *sister* in the way.

She had crushed their father by walking away from him the way she did. From the time he was a kid, Danny had never thought anybody or anything could hurt Joe Wolf. But she had. It almost made Danny jealous—that she mattered that much to him.

Danny clenched his fists, still picturing himself punching a hole through the glass in front of him. Feeling like a grenade with the pin already pulled. But then he'd been feeling that way since the reading of the will.

His sister had spent just about her entire adult life acting as if the family wasn't worthy of her. Somehow, though, she'd remained the fair-haired child up until she told their father she was leaving and not coming back. The one who'd been the smartest. The one who'd been the best athlete in the family. The one Joe Wolf had loved the most, even though she was the one who told him she didn't want to end up like the rest of us.

Including him.

Especially him.

How many times had they all heard that one?

A pack of wolves, she'd always called the men in the family.

Only now she was the one he'd rewarded.

He took his phone out of his pocket, walked across the room to make sure the door was closed, and made the call.

His brother answered right away. He was the type. He'd always acted like if he waited until the second ring, the phone might explode in his hand.

"We need to go after her now," Danny said. "You're the best one to do it, and we don't have a lot of time before the league meetings."

"Understood."

"I need you on this," Danny said.

I've always needed you when I want something.

"By the time we finish with her, she will be begging us to take it all back, starting with her precious voting shares."

Danny walked back to the window. How many people in sports had a view like this? Owning everything he saw down there? No wonder guys like Gallo were willing to do anything to get it.

"You know how to do this."

"I do," Jack said to his brother. "And I know exactly where to start."

"Where?"

"Her past," Jack said.

"Any particular part?"

"How about all of it?"

SIXTEEN

BEN CANTOR, THE DETECTIVE investigating Joe Wolf's death, was waiting for me in the parking lot at Hunters Point after practice, leaning against my car.

"I'm unarmed," I said.

"I'm not. Got a few minutes to chat?"

"That's not really a request, is it?"

"Nobody ever *has* to talk to the police," Cantor said. "But when they don't, it's been my experience that they generally have something to hide."

He's not here to screw around.

"I have nothing to hide."

"Then no reason why we can't have a nice chat."

"Haven't you already asked all the questions you need to ask about Dad's death?"

"Wouldn't be here if I had."

"Am I a suspect?"

"Seems like that's for you to know and me to find out," Cantor said.

He was tall, curly hair the color of ink sprinkled with some gray, probably around my age, good-looking, blazer, no tie, jeans, ancient penny loafers. He actually reminded me a little of

Jack Wolf, the dark knight of the Wolf family. Cantor was probably in his early forties, as Jack was. Danny and Thomas were more fair, favoring our mother. Cantor wasn't as good-looking as Thomas Wolf was, I thought. But good-looking enough.

"I thought my father's death was an accident," I said.

"Maybe it was. Unless you know something I don't know."

I stared at him.

"Let me ask you again. Are you actually looking at me as a suspect?"

He stared back at me. His eyes were so dark they looked navy blue.

"Don't take it personally. I'm a suspicious type of person, especially when it comes to what we classify as an unattended death."

He grinned.

"And I figured I better have a sit-down with you before one of your brothers turns *you* into an unattended death."

He held up a hand.

"Kidding."

Sure you are.

"Do you know something *I* don't?"

"Depends on the subject matter."

I nodded back toward the field. We walked down the sideline and sat in the bleachers on the home side. I wasn't sure why he made me feel uneasy. Or maybe *uneasy* wasn't the word. Maybe *alert* was. I told myself to treat him as if he were a reporter. Anything I said could, and would, be used against me.

"Have you had this kind of chat with my brothers?"

"You gonna let me ask the questions or not?"

"Must be the teacher in me."

"Or the lawyer."

He stared out at the field.

"I played football at Oakland Tech," he said. "Wide receiver. Thought I was on my way to Cal before I blew out my knee."

Guys always have to tell you.

I waited.

"Soooooo, the conventional wisdom on your father's death is that he got sloppy drunk enough to go over the rail. And that because there's no fixed ladder on that particular boat, and because there was no reason why he would have dropped down the swim ladder that night, he realized he was screwed once he was in the water and started to swim for it, at least until his heart exploded."

"Or?"

"Or," Cantor said, stepping on the word, "somebody snuck on his beloved boat that night and waited until it was far enough out in the water and threw him over the side when he wasn't looking. Maybe even watched him until he went under."

"How would that person get back to shore, since the boat was *still* out in the water when my father's body washed up?"

"Well, I've certainly considered that," Cantor said, "because that would be some swim in currents like there were that night. Wouldn't it?"

"You checked the currents."

"Why not?"

He took his phone out of his pocket, looked at it, put it away.

"I know he used to be a swimmer. And, all due respect, I know he was a boozer, more of one as he got older. So my question to you is, could he have gotten so hammered that night that even the fact that he had been a decent swimmer couldn't save him once he was in the water?"

I took some time before I answered him.

"I haven't seen him since January, as I'm sure you know. But even before that, I could see that his tolerance for vodka had started to weaken once he was up into his seventies, along with everything else that was getting weaker, including his memory, even though he would have killed *himself* before admitting that."

Cantor was one row below me. He turned and smiled up at me now. Not a bad smile, all things considered. He probably knew that. The cool guys always did. My ex-husband sure as hell always had.

"Did you know what was in his will before the reading?" Cantor said.

Where did that come from?

"My father knew. And the lawyer knew."

"He could have mentioned it," Cantor said.

"My father or his lawyer?"

"Either way."

"Are you calling me a liar, Detective?"

"Just chatting, like I said."

"I just told you that my father and I hadn't spoken to each other in quite some time."

"Doesn't mean you couldn't have reconciled and not told anybody."

"That sounds like another way to suggest I'm lying," I said.

"I'm just doing my job. Sorry if I've offended you."

"Are you?"

"In my job, you keep pulling on strings."

"Wouldn't 'jerking chains' be more accurate?"

"You're aware you're starting to sound a little defensive, right?"

"Wonder why."

"The point is, your father dies suddenly and the big winner turns out to be you," Cantor said.

In the distance I saw some of my players in the parking lot, staring out at us. They waved. I waved. I could feel Cantor's dark eyes still on me.

"Do you have any reason, other than an inheritance that I didn't know was coming, for making me feel like a suspect? Or at least a person of interest?"

He smiled. "Well, you are an extremely interesting person."

Good cop, bad cop. Same guy.

"I believe we're done here." I stood.

"For now," he said. Still smiling.

I walked with him back to the car because I thought it would make me seem defensive if I simply walked away from him. As I opened the door he said, "One more thing?"

"Who are you, Columbo?"

I was behind the wheel, but the door was still open. Cantor leaned in, one arm on the roof of the car.

"You were a champion swimmer, right?"

SEVENTEEN

THE NEXT AFTERNOON I was seated across from Joel Abrams, the NFL commissioner, at a table big enough to serve as a helipad. We were in the dining room of the presidential suite at the Mark Hopkins Hotel. I had told him we could meet at the stadium, but I could tell he wanted this to be a command performance and on his own turf.

I had already gotten an earful about his having gone back to New York after my father's funeral and now having had to fly back here.

I wanted to tell him that I knew he had a Learjet at his disposal. Joe Wolf had habitually referred to him as a glorified bean counter, a world-class ass kisser, and one of the phoniest people he'd ever met.

He was short and round and balding and had always reminded me of a dumpling. He nodded now at the liquor cart at the other end of the table and almost proudly said, "Dedicated concierge service."

"Good to know," I said. "Better to have."

He asked if I wanted something. I said I was fine. He got up and poured himself a Chivas on the rocks, drank some on the way back to his seat.

"You can't possibly want to do this," he said when he sat back down.

"This?"

"Run the team."

"And why is that?"

"Because you have never spent a day of your life being part of the football operation," he said. "Because being a high school football coach doesn't make you a Glazer or a Kraft or a Rooney or a Mara. And mostly because a family controversy over the team couldn't come at a worse time."

"And why is *that*?"

"We're starting to make some progress on getting the Wolves a deal on the new stadium," Abrams said.

It had become the longest-running sports drama in town. The city had been fighting my father on a new stadium for the past few years, putting up one roadblock after another, even as he kept telling them and anybody who would listen that he just wanted the same kind of new-stadium deal that other owners in other cities had gotten. But the board of supervisors had fought him every step of the way, getting more dug in as time went on, continuing to raise the amount they expected him to kick in to get the thing done. They said they were looking out for the taxpayers. Joe Wolf called it a shakedown. So there had been no movement from either side for months, even though everybody knew that a new stadium, once built, would mean a Super Bowl for San Francisco.

In pro football, that was the Holy Grail.

"What does this have to do with me running the Wolves?"

"Your brother can get this done," Abrams said. "He's quietly repairing bridges your father burned."

"Golden Gate?" I asked. "Or Bay?"

Abrams sighed.

"How does my brother plan to come up with the money my father said he couldn't afford?"

"Ask him."

"Asking you, Commissioner."

"Let's just say he's more amenable to outside assistance," Abrams said. "Being transactional, so to speak."

"It's still a shakedown."

"You sound just like him," Abrams said. I could see him starting to get exasperated, as if he were conditioned to getting his own way. "He stopped negotiating in good faith a while ago, even though he knew better than anybody else how much the Wolves need a new stadium."

"But at what price?"

He drank some Scotch.

"At whatever price it takes to get the deal done."

"There has to be another angle here. With all due respect, of course."

I thought something might have changed in his eyes. But only briefly.

"What makes you say that?"

"Because there's always another angle with guys like you."

"I'll take that as a compliment."

"I can't imagine why in the world you would."

"You need to give this up," he said. "It will save you the embarrassment of not getting approved by my other owners."

My other owners.

I wanted to tell the little jerk, *You're the dedicated concierge.*

"I don't have to be approved," I said. "The team is staying in the family. Nobody had to approve John Mara with the Giants when his father died or Steve Tisch when *his* father died. We both know the list of children inheriting teams is longer than that."

He gave me a smug look.

"They told me you think you know everything about everything," he said. "But your father must have neglected to inform you that we added some language to the bylaws about inherited teams a few years ago. It was after the software guy bought the Saints. Remember that? His idiot son inherited the team, hired all his frat buddies, then thought it would be cute to let fans call plays over the internet."

The kid in New Orleans ended up selling the team, under what I recalled was rather massive pressure from the league. Keegan something. He'd still made a couple of billion dollars from the sale.

"Now it doesn't matter whether it's a son or daughter or widow," Abrams continued. "If the person inheriting the team hasn't had any previous role in the football operation, he or she has to be approved the way an outside owner would. By a three-quarters vote."

He looked so pleased with himself that I felt as if I should give him a treat.

"Maybe your father was drunk the day the ownership committee changed the rules," Abrams said. "Or was off bad-mouthing me to somebody from ESPN."

"I'm not quitting."

"You don't have to quit. You can keep some kind of title. Just step aside, for the good of the team and the city and the league."

It sounded as if he'd been practicing that part.

I shook my head.

"I'll take my chances with the other owners. I'm a lawyer, I'm a teacher, I'm even a coach. And I'm a woman, Commissioner. Hear me roar. And take your best shot."

It was as if he hadn't heard me.

"You don't even have to call a press conference," he said. "All you have to do is issue a statement that this is what's best for all concerned. We can even write it for you, if you'd rather."

"My father always told me how often you forgot that you worked for him and not the other way around."

"He earned the right to think that way, honey."

I tilted my head just slightly and smiled. "Honey?"

"Oh, don't start with that MeToo shit," he said. "Are you really going to fight me on this?"

"I thought we were getting to know each other. But you already seem to have made up your mind about me."

"Like father, like daughter."

He slammed his glass down on the table.

"You have to know that if you fight me on this, I will crush you."

"You sound an awful lot like my brother."

"The league meetings are in a month or so in Los Angeles," he said. "That gives you plenty of time to change your mind and get on the right side of this."

We sat there in silence for what felt like a long time, until I finally said, "You know what? You're the one who's right."

I got up then, walked down to the liquor cart, saw that it held a bottle of Grey Goose. Joe Wolf's drink of choice. I put some ice cubes in the glass, poured just enough vodka, walked back down to him, and said, "I just thought about it."

I touched my glass with his.

"Here's to the National Football League," I said, and drank.

So did he.

"So we're good," the commissioner said.

I laughed.

"Of course not."

EIGHTEEN

DANNY SAT ACROSS THE desk from John Gallo in Gallo's office, on the top floor of the Salesforce Tower. Joel Abrams sat next to him.

"I don't care how stubborn she is," Abrams was saying now. "I don't care if she's more stubborn than Joe was. There is no way she can get the votes."

"I was told the Democrats couldn't win Georgia that time," Gallo said, "after I spent a vulgar amount of money on the other side."

Danny started to say something. Gallo silenced him with a finger to his lips.

"You both told me it would never even make it this far," Gallo said. He looked at Danny. "First you told me it would be handled." He turned to Abrams. "And then you told me the same damn thing."

"I thought I had handled it when I went to her house that night. How did I know she was lying to me?"

"Perhaps because she's a Wolf."

"We could go through the list of owners," Abrams said. "One by one. I can predict how they're going to vote right now."

"When's the vote?" Gallo said.

"Next month."

"You can't move it up?"

"The dates for the meetings are locked in," he said. "And even though this is an emergency for all of us, it's not for them. We don't want to look as if we're panicking here."

Gallo turned back to Danny.

"You tell me you will get something on her that we can use."

"That's exactly what I'm telling you," Danny said. "We're going to throw everything at her we can."

Gallo turned his attention back to the commissioner. "You have far more resources than he does. Just so you're ready the next time one of your players gets arrested for a gun or drugs or a wife."

"On it, Mr. Gallo," Joel Abrams said.

"Mr." Gallo, Danny thought.

As deferential as if John Gallo were the commissioner.

"Your brother Jack has skin in this game, too," Gallo said to Danny Wolf. "Do I need to have another conversation with him? He knows what everybody in this room knows, about how much money I am willing to invest in this process and the control I exert over the board of supervisors."

"Jack is highly motivated, trust me. We all know what the stakes are, for everyone involved."

Gallo looked at him. Or through him. Danny started to say something. Gallo gave a slight shake of his head.

"I didn't get to where I am—or accumulate the kind of wealth and power I have—playing by somebody else's rules. And here is rule number one: I am *always* the last one in the room."

They only know what I want them to know, Gallo thought. *They have no idea how much is riding on this for me.*

"Everybody always talks about throwing everything except the kitchen sink. You throw that at her, too."

He smiled.

"Or drop one on the poor girl," John Gallo said. "I frankly don't care. Just stop her."

He slammed his hand down, making both Danny Wolf and the commissioner of the National Football League jump.

"Now."

NINETEEN

THOMAS WOLF'S SECRETARY TOLD Ben Cantor that Thomas was on his way to the yacht club and might be planning to spend the night on *The Sea Wolf*.

Cantor had released the boat back to the family by then, after having gone over it again, still finding no evidence that someone had been on it that night with Joe Wolf. Cantor had no idea whether the youngest son had inherited it or just grabbed it for himself, being a Wolf. Frankly, Cantor didn't care. He had just decided it was time to make a more serious run at the boy prince, put him in the same barrel he'd put his sister in the other day.

After just one conversation with Thomas Wolf at the stadium, Cantor had already gotten the idea that you had to Taser him to shut him up once he picked up a good head of steam.

Thomas was on the top deck when Cantor came walking up the dock.

"Permission to come aboard," Cantor called out, grinning up at him.

"I was hopeful that my only company tonight would be my date," Thomas said. "Blair. Or maybe it's Blaine."

"This shouldn't take long," Cantor said.

"Bullshit."

They ended up in the stateroom. Thomas Wolf had a bottle of Heineken Zero in his hand. Nonalcoholic, Cantor knew. He'd heard the guy had been on the wagon for a while, but who the hell ever knew for sure?

"Should I have a lawyer present?" Thomas said.

"Do you need one?"

Everybody talked about Thomas Wolf as if he were an aging frat boy. Cantor thought it was a pose, especially after the first time they'd spoken. There was intelligence in his eyes, an almost cool sort of irony to his general attitude, as if the joke was on you. Cantor had already decided he would not make the mistake of underestimating him.

Or believing him.

"Is this where you ask if Daddy loved me?" Thomas said. "Spoiler alert—he didn't. One night I overheard him and a friend getting sloshed in the study. And the friend wanted to know how many sons Joe Wolf had wanted.

"'Two' was his answer."

"Something like that would sure piss the hell out of me."

"You mean, enough to throw him over the side?" Thomas shook his head. "Nah. As much fun as it sounds like, and as many times as I thought about it, I decided a long time ago that I wouldn't do well in prison."

"Hardly anybody does."

"So what do you want to talk about, really?"

"Your brothers and your sister."

Thomas grinned. "Oh. You want me to throw *them* over the side."

He likes having an audience. Cantor imagined him as the kid at the family dinner table who didn't get to talk and had been making up for lost time ever since.

"Things certainly worked out great for Jenny. She just turned into the wealthiest and most powerful schoolteacher in America."

"Smartest, too. She asked me to be her right-hand man with the Wolves."

"Sounds like more responsibility than your father ever gave you with the team," Cantor said.

"He didn't want me to have any real responsibility. Behind my back, he told his friends he just needed me to have an office to go to. He didn't believe I'd turned my life around even when I had."

None of them needs much encouragement to talk about their daddy issues.

"Is there any way your sister could have known he was going to leave the store to her? Two stores, actually."

"I was in the room that day," Thomas said. "She sure looked as if the news shocked the shit out of her."

"Maybe she's a good actress."

"Aren't they all?"

Cantor waited.

"You really think somebody might have killed him?"

"I didn't say that."

"Didn't have to," Thomas said. He took another sip of fake beer. "Well, if you're asking me, if one of them finally decided they'd had enough, it wouldn't have been her. What did she have to gain if she didn't know how *much* she had to gain beforehand?"

Let him think you're leaving him out of it.

"But if one of your brothers, or both, knew how much they had to lose, it could have thrown them into a rage, am I right?" Cantor said.

Thomas shrugged.

"Danny's too weak, as much of a tough guy as he likes to think he is. Jack never had any use for Danny, to tell you the truth. Or for the rest of us, for that matter. He thinks he's one of those strongman types. But now he wants Danny's help, and mine, to take down Jenny."

"You pick a lane yet?" Cantor said.

"Not until I have to."

"Even though she just upgraded you?"

"Even though."

Cantor walked over to the drinks setup and grabbed one of those small bottles of soda water.

"It sounds like you think Jack could have done it, especially if he knew your father was going to put Jenny in charge of the newspaper."

"From the time we were kids," Thomas said, "Jack was the one who would do anything, and I mean *anydamnthing*, to win whatever competition Dad had set up for us. If he needed Danny on his side, he'd get Danny. Same with me. The only one who wouldn't ever go along was Jenny."

"Kill or be killed," Cantor said.

"So you know the family motto."

"Sounds like an interesting way to grow up."

"Interesting would be one way to describe it," Thomas said. "Boot camp would be another. Or military school. Or reform school."

Cantor said, "Say somebody did do it. They'd have to swim back to shore, correct?"

"Unless they rowed out, climbed up the ladder, got it done, pulled up the ladder, and jumped back down into the boat."

"Who said the ladder was up?"

Thomas didn't hesitate. "The world's greatest detective agency. *TMZ*."

"Your brother Jack was on the rowing team at Stanford," Cantor said.

"Wasn't he, though?"

There was another silence. But they never lasted very long with Thomas Wolf. Cantor got the idea that if Thomas went too long without saying something, his whole body might begin to cramp up.

"Who would *your* money be on?" Thomas said to Cantor.

"Maybe you."

With that, he stood up and headed back up the stairs. Thomas followed him.

"How come you didn't take any notes?"

"Trust me," Cantor said. "I'll remember this conversation just fine without them."

TWENTY

I FELT LIKE I had a very weird, very split football personality going. My kids on the Bears, they wouldn't lose. The Wolves? They just refused to get me a win.

We lost to the Seahawks as badly as we did—as if they'd thrown us down a flight of stairs—because our coach decided to bench Ted Skyler and replace him with his rookie backup, Chase Charles, who proceeded to throw three interceptions. By the end of the game, Charles had me wondering from my seat in the stands if it might be time for him to consider a change in vocation.

I waited an hour after the game had ended before I made my way down to Coach Rich Kopka's office, adjacent to our locker room.

He was alone in there when I walked in. I didn't waste any time, since my coach was constantly reminding me what an extremely busy guy he was.

"What do you think you're doing?"

He peered over his reading glasses at me. They were perched at the break in his nose, one he'd suffered at the hands of his best assistant coach a few years ago, after Kopka had fired him—mostly because the guy, Ryan Morrissey, was smarter than Kopka and a much better football coach. Morrissey was also tired of taking the blame for the boneheaded play-calling decisions that Kopka kept making.

"What does it look like I'm doing? I'm working."

"What I *meant* was what were you doing putting that scared little boy in at quarterback today?"

"He's six four," Kopka said. "Maybe a little scared today. Definitely not little."

"Question remains the same."

"I needed to find out what we've got with him."

"That's what training camp is for," I said.

"It's not as if your boyfriend was lighting things up before I sat his ass down."

"Ex-husband. Not boyfriend. And irrelevant to this conversation. We're talking about you, Coach. Not him."

Kopka leaned back in his chair and laced his fingers behind his head and said, "Let's just say I'm tired of him doing to the Wolves what he used to do to you."

I knew he was trying to get a rise out of me. But I let it go. At least Joe Wolf had raised us to never punch down. My father hadn't given us a lot of positive life lessons. But that was one of them.

"The only person who thought that kid was worth drafting was you."

"I'm gonna make a pro quarterback out of him," Kopka said. "It's just gonna take a little time."

"You could take until the end of time and not make an NFL quarterback out of him."

"If you came down here to second-guess decisions *I* make about *my* team, you best get out of my office now, lady."

My team.

They all think it's theirs.

"Ted gives us the best chance to win this season," I said.

"Your father didn't tell me who to play. So I'm certainly not going to let you do that."

"Who do you plan to start at quarterback next week?"

"Not that it's any of your goddamn business," he said, "but I'm gonna announce on Wednesday that I'm going with the kid."

"No, you're not."

He smiled, calmly took off his reading glasses, folded them and placed them on his desk.

Then he stood up, as if the simple act of doing that would terrify me.

"This meeting is over."

"Sit down."

"Ex*cuse* me?"

"This meeting is over when I say it's over," I said, my eyes locked on his. The girl who'd grown up with three brothers and never taken any shit from any of them. "Now sit *your* ass down."

He glared at me for a moment longer. But sat his ass back down.

"Have it your way, leastways as long as you get to have your way around here."

"I'm not going anywhere."

Kopka smiled. "Not what I'm hearing."

"Just so we're clear," I said. "It is your intention to bench Ted and start that kid, is that right?"

"We're not making the playoffs with your boyfriend under center."

"So that's it. You're writing the season off."

"I'm writing the season off because our aging quarterback already looks older than the Golden Gate Bridge. Good a time to turn the page as any," he said.

"Well, you're right. About turning the page, I mean."

"Finally."

"You're fired," I said.

"What did you say?"

"You heard me."

He jumped out of his chair again, knocking it backward into the wall behind him, face as red as it got during cold-weather games in the East near the end of the season, when he looked like somebody had stuck a Wolves cap on a tomato.

"Fire me?" he shouted. *"You can't fire me. Your father told me I have a lifetime contract."*

"His lifetime. Not yours."

TWENTY-ONE

I WAS SITTING WITH the Wolves' former offensive coordinator, Ryan Morrissey, in my living room much later that night.

He had been the hottest assistant in the league until he had dropped Rich Kopka with that one punch the day after the Wolves had lost their last playoff game. Kopka had blamed the loss on Morrissey's play calling even as the team's defense was in the process of blowing a 28–3 halftime lead.

The league had suspended Ryan for two years. When the suspension was lifted, nobody would touch him.

"You're really offering me the job," he said.

"I am. My father should have kept you and gotten rid of him. That loss to the Packers was his fault, not yours."

"No kidding."

He grinned. We were drinking beer out of bottles. Ryan Morrissey was younger than Ted Skyler and better-looking, not that I was ever going to mention that to him. I probably shouldn't have been thinking it. He had never been good enough to make it as a starting quarterback in the league himself, despite getting drafted out of Texas Tech by the Rams and being a backup for five years before going into coaching.

"How did old Dick take it, by the way?"

After his firing, Ryan had always referred to Rich Kopka as Dick. Combine that with the punch heard round the football world, and he might have been my favorite coach ever. One I was about to hire.

"He took it badly. The general manager took it even worse. So I fired him, too."

"Seriously?"

"He had it coming, too."

Then I listed all the bad decisions Mike Sawchuck had made over the last few years, involving trades and free agency and draft choices, one by one.

"Just off the top of my head."

He was smiling at me with his eyes. "Right. Couple of dozen names. Just off the top of your head. You have the dates, too?"

"I like football," I said.

"I can tell. Who's going to be the new general manager?"

"My brother Thomas. And the team will be a lot better off, frankly."

"How's Danny going to respond to all these bombs you're dropping?"

"I'm hoping badly."

"I bet Danny as team president would like to install himself as acting general manager," Ryan said.

"Don't bet on football."

We were both sitting on the floor, on either side of my coffee table.

"We're really going to do this?" he said.

"If you accept."

He reached across the table. We shook hands.

"I accept," he said.

"You want to talk about money?"

"We'll figure it out."

"How about a dollar more than Dick was making?"

We shook again. He was sitting with his legs crossed and somehow stood up without effort. I asked if he needed a playbook. He said he'd refused to give his old one back after Kopka fired him.

He asked if Kopka was actually planning to start Chase Charles next week.

"He was."

"At least he's consistent," Ryan said. "A meathead until the end."

Then he said it was going to be a long night. I asked him what his wife was going to say about all this. He said he'd be sure to ask her if he ever made it back to Maui.

"Divorce?"

"She got custody of her trainer."

I walked him to the door.

"Well, this isn't going to be dull."

"For as long as it lasts."

He smiled.

"Somewhat like a kamikaze mission."

TWENTY-TWO

THE NEXT MORNING, the front page of the *San Francisco Tribune*, the paper delivered to my doorstep nice and early, wasn't nice at all.

The front-page headline was set in the biggest type yet, at least as far as I was concerned:

WHAT AN ASS

Unfortunately, those three words didn't just refer to my firing my coach and my general manager the night before and replacing them with Ryan Morrissey and Thomas Wolf. And it wasn't an editorial opinion about my abilities as an owner, my judgment, or my qualifications for my current position.

Oh, those subjects were covered in the front-page commentary, all right, in one of the stories that ran below the fold.

But the headline had so much more to do with the photograph of the bare-assed woman that went with it.

The woman was me.

The nineteen-year-old me, in a ridiculous pose, my back—and backside—to the camera, a Wolves cap on my head, smiling and trying to look sexy. It was a picture that I had completely forgotten, taken one drunken night by my boy-friend when I was a freshman at Cal.

One of many he'd taken that night, as I now recalled, even though he swore he'd deleted them all after we'd broken up.

Now here was the money shot, on the front page of the *San Francisco Tribune*.

I sat at the kitchen table staring at it and my younger self. What was that thing people always ask you? If you could go back in time, what would you say to your teenage self?

I knew the answer now.

I could hear my phone buzzing from my bedroom nonstop, as if it were on the verge of blowing up. I left it where it was, got up and walked into the front room, pulled the drapes back just slightly, and saw the first television truck pull up out front.

Eventually I'd have to go outside. I decided to do it now. I changed into my sweat pants and a Wolves T-shirt and my ancient Cal baseball cap and went for a run. As I passed the TV reporter and her cameraman, I didn't wait for her to shout a question at me.

I asked her a question of my own.

"Anything interesting in the papers today?"

Then I took off.

Showing them my best side one more time today before I disappeared around the corner of 3rd Street.

TWENTY-THREE

JACK AND DANNY WOLF were having breakfast at the Park Grill, on Battery Street. The *Tribune* was on the table between them, like a centerpiece.

"How did you find him?" Danny said to Jack.

"Let's just say I had help."

"From who I think?"

"A good newspaperman never reveals his sources," Jack said.

He was seated with his back to the wall. Danny's back was to the room. Danny looked over his shoulder now, as if wondering to whom his brother was speaking.

"Good newspaperman? Where?"

Jack sipped green tea. "Today I am."

"You hear from our sister yet?" Danny said. He was in workout clothes, having come here straight from the gym.

"I haven't spoken to her since the reading of the will. You know Jenny. She likes to keep you off balance."

"Only now she's the one off balance," Danny said. "Or maybe down for the count. Bare-assed on the front page of the paper. I wonder what Mom thinks."

"She's not happy."

"With her darling daughter?"

"Are you serious?" Jack said. "With me. She called first thing. How could I have done such a thing?"

Jack turned slightly in his chair. A waiter appeared with a fresh pot of tea at what Jack thought might have been world-record speed.

"How much did you have to pay the boyfriend?" Danny said.

The boyfriend's name was Josh Bauer, from Jenny's girls-gone-wild period. He'd sworn to her that he'd deleted the pictures from his phone. She believed him. And Joe Wolf had always thought she was the smart one.

"Let's just say his life didn't turn out the way he'd hoped it might after sitting next to Jenny in class," Jack said. "He's living in Vegas now, in what appears to be a constant state of debt. He said he hated doing this to her."

"But he took the money."

"Like the whore that he is."

Danny grinned. "Imagine such a thing in a family paper."

"Well, it is *our* family."

"How does she keep her job at the high school?" Danny said.

"I'm already thinking about tomorrow's front page after they fire her ass. No pun intended."

"She deserves it, just for firing Kopka and Sawchuck," Danny said.

"You were going to do the same damn thing when the season was over."

"Hey, try to remember that we're in this together."

How could I ever forget such a thing?

They were at their usual corner table, no one close to them, plenty of privacy.

"The pictures just kind of fell into my lap," Jack said. "We're going to run a couple every day." He smiled. "But you have to say that the timing of all this couldn't have worked out better.

As a circulation booster, our sister is the gift that just keeps on giving."

There was, they both agreed, no possible way now that the other owners would give her the votes she needed to keep control of the team.

They sat in silence for a few minutes, eating the last of their breakfasts. It was Danny who finally spoke.

"Now we have to figure out how to deal with Thomas. I still can't believe he turned around and better-dealed me."

"*I'll* deal with Thomas when the time comes," Jack said as he waved for the check.

He handed the waiter his credit card. When the kid was gone, Jack leaned across the table, smiling again, and said in a soft voice, "Don't you sometimes wish we could just kill them both?"

TWENTY-FOUR

"YOU CAN'T HIDE UP here forever," Thomas said to me.

We were in what had been our father's suite in the late morning. Thomas had picked me up at the back door to my house and sent his assistant back to get my car. The field below us was empty, practice not starting for another hour or so.

"I'm not hiding," I said, and managed to smile. "My life is pretty much an open book at this point."

"Everybody was young and stupid once," Thomas said. "Holy hell, I sure was. And when I got older, I was still stupid, until I went off and got what Dad still called 'the cure.'"

"You know what else Dad said."

"Dad said a lot of things."

"Ignorance isn't an excuse," I said.

Now Thomas smiled. "At least there are no pictures of *my* you-know-what out there. Not that I know about, anyway."

"Is that what passes for good news today?"

"Either way," Thomas said, "you were going to get crushed."

"When I saw the paper, I thought about quitting, no lie. Just to put myself out of my misery. Like a mercy killing."

He pulled his sneakers off the railing in front of us and turned to face me. Somehow, no matter how much older Thomas got, I still saw him as the charming little boy he used to be.

"You can't quit," he said. "Not when I'm going good."

"Josh Bauer," I said. "I hadn't even thought of him in years. But I was right about one thing, even when I was young and stupid: he turned out to have all of the qualities of a dog except loyalty."

"You want me to find him and beat him up? That's how we would have handled it when we were kids."

"If anybody's going to do that, it will be me."

"So what do we do about our present circumstances?" Thomas said.

"You mean me going viral?"

"Yeah. That. And in the flesh."

I thanked him for that.

"The first thing I have to do is head over to Hunters Point and quit there before they fire me. They don't deserve this."

Thomas said. "The one who doesn't deserve any of this is you, Sis."

I looked down at the field. A couple of players were out early, jogging up and down the sidelines. Then I noticed the photographer behind the Wolves' bench pointing his camera directly at Thomas and me. I fought the impulse to turn around and moon him, just to keep with the theme of the day.

We got up from the terrace seats and went back inside.

"I certainly made things easy for all those old dude owners who act like old ladies," I said.

Thomas laughed.

"Are you joking? How about the one who got caught with the hooker a couple of years ago? This isn't even a misdemeanor compared to that."

"Danny and Jack are just going to keep coming if I *don't* quit. With everything they've got."

"You let me worry about our brothers," Thomas said. "Danny

told me that everybody's got a past. Well, guess what? That includes them."

"They don't seem to have much interest in fighting fair," I said.

"Now I don't, either," Thomas said.

He kissed me on top of my head.

"They got stuff on you? You think I don't have stuff on them? I've been waiting to take both of them down my whole life."

TWENTY-FIVE

I'D GOTTEN THE EMAIL from the principal at Hunters Point, Joey Rubino, around one o'clock. He said he wanted to see me after school let out to discuss my "situation." To the best of my knowledge, it was the first time I'd ever heard my exposed rear end described quite that way.

I emailed him back and said I was on my way, knowing I had enough time to make one stop.

Jack Wolf was standing in the middle of the *Tribune* city room when I arrived, talking to an attractive red-haired woman. It had to be his managing editor. Megan somebody. Thomas said he couldn't remember whether Jack was still sleeping with her or not.

"Just in case you need a little extra ammo when you get there," Thomas had told me.

"Don't worry. I won't."

I walked down the middle of the room, past reporters at their desks, feeling every single eye in the place on me. Apparently they all recognized me just fine with my clothes on.

"Jenny," Jack said when I got to him, not acting remotely surprised to see me.

"Jack."

The room had gone quiet.

"This is Megan Callahan, our managing editor," he said.

"I know who she is," I said, keeping my eyes on my brother.

"If you want to talk, we should really go to my office."

"I'm fine here."

"Have it your way."

"That was some front page today," I said. "What's the London tabloid with naked women on page 3? I always forget."

"The *Sun*," he said.

"Well, you beat them by two pages, didn't you?"

"We don't make the news. You did that all by yourself. We just try to present it in an interesting way."

He sat down on the edge of the nearest desk. He wore a vest, no jacket, tie pulled down from his collar, more for effect than comfort, I was sure. He seemed to enjoy playing the part of editor, even though I was fairly certain he would have gone into a dead faint if he were asked to lay out pages himself.

"If you came to have a scene," Jack said, "then have at it."

"I came to ask you a question."

"And what's that?"

I waited, then smiled.

"Is that all you got?"

I walked out the way I'd come, without looking back.

TWENTY-SIX

MY BOSS AT HUNTERS POINT was younger than I was.

Joey Rubino came from the neighborhood, lived a couple of blocks from where I did. He was a good guy and had made it clear, from our first meeting, what a huge Wolves fan he was. I liked him a lot and realized now how much I was going to miss working for him.

"Quite a day," he said when I was in his office, door closed.

Then he grinned.

"I'm talking about me, not you."

It was three thirty. Practice normally began at four. I was going to miss that most of all. It was the teacher in me. I liked practices better than games.

"You don't have to explain anything to me, Joey," I said. "*You* didn't do anything. *The kids* didn't do anything. This is all on me. I talk to my players all the time about making good choices."

"Who puts a picture like that on the front page of a newspaper?"

"My brother."

"To sell papers?"

"To sell me out is more like it."

In addition to being smart and funny and someone who, I was told, had been a great English teacher, Joey Rubino loved the school from which he had graduated. I thought it was his best quality.

"Got a lot of calls today, as you might imagine," he said.

I smiled now. *"Might?"*

"The cancel culture. Full speed ahead."

There were pictures on the table behind him of his wife and children, three beautiful little girls. I sat there across from him and wondered what it was like for them, growing up in a normal family and having a normal childhood, with a father who didn't constantly pit them against one another.

"I did my best to explain to the parents that I thought we had to do better than handing out some sort of death sentence for the worst moment of someone's public life," he said.

"It's funny, Joey. Until a couple of weeks ago I hadn't had a public life since I was married to Ted Skyler."

He was taking his time with this, I could see, wanting to let me down gently. It wasn't my place to rush him. He had to do this his own way, even though we both knew how this particular movie was going to end.

When we finally did make our way there, I was just going to ask him if I could meet with the players before cleaning out my office.

"Unfortunately, the parents didn't want to hear it. They already had the scarlet letter on you."

I smiled again. "I bet I know where, too."

As awkward as this was for both of us, that got a chuckle out of him.

"For what it's worth, I never got fired before."

Joey Rubino looked confused.

"Who said anything about firing you?"

TWENTY-SEVEN

OVER THE NEXT FEW DAYS, I knew people wanted me to issue some kind of statement. Beg for forgiveness in the court of public opinion. But I wasn't playing that game, especially over something that had happened when I was a freshman in college. I certainly wasn't going to stand in front of the cameras and say that if I offended anybody, I wanted to apologize.

Every time I saw one of those press conferences, I found myself screaming at the television.

You did *offend us, you moron. It's* why *you're apologizing!*

Everybody except Supreme Court justices had weighed in by now, from the commissioner to my fellow owners to every exploding head in sports television. But my favorite comment had come from one of my own players, Andre DeWitt, who simply said, "We already knew she was badass. We didn't need no damn pictures to convince us."

Every day I drove past crowds of reporters when I left the parking lot at the stadium and past reporters when I got home. I smiled and waved. And said nothing. There was a crowd of reporters waiting for me at Hunters Point on Saturday after the kids won again. When it was time for me to leave the school grounds, my players—the ones who had gone to their principal and said they'd all quit the season if he even thought about firing me—formed a circle around me as I walked to my car.

The only difference for me when I took my usual seats for the Wolves game—Joey Rubino was my guest—was the two security guys stationed at the top of section F to keep the media away while we watched Ryan Morrissey win his first game as head coach.

When the game ended, the security guys walked me over to the elevator and stayed with me while I went downstairs to see Ryan in the office that used to belong to Rich Kopka.

"You did good, Coach," I said.

"It's a players' game, even if the former inhabitant of this office frequently forgot that."

"He forgot it as soon as he stopped being a player," I said.

"They played hard. All I can ask."

I walked over and bumped him some fist.

"Look at you. You sound as boring as the other head coaches already."

I was home later, alone, having a glass of wine to celebrate, when my doorbell rang. I looked through the peephole and saw my ex-husband standing there.

I opened my door just to give myself the opportunity to close it in his face.

He got his foot down just in time.

"Honey, I'm home."

"My home," I said. "Go away."

"No 'Nice win'?"

"I have nothing to say to you. *We* have nothing to say to each other. Now that I think about it, I'm not sure that we ever really did."

"I came here to tell you that I'm on your side, whether you believe me or not," he said.

I couldn't help myself.

I laughed.

"I wouldn't believe you at this point if you told me water was wet."

He still had his foot preventing me from closing my front door.

"And as for 'Nice win'? We didn't win today because of anything special you did. We won because we went back to running the ball."

"You happen to be right," he said. "But I didn't come here to talk football."

"Then why did you come?"

"To tell you that as soon as your brother can get you out of the way, he's got a deal in place to sell the team to Gallo," Ted Skyler said. "Now can I come in?"

TWENTY-EIGHT

JACK WOLF KEPT HIS scull at the Bair Island Aquatic Center, in Redwood City. It was a couple of miles from the spot where he'd rented a small apartment for himself and Megan Callahan—under her name—when they were still together.

That was just another form of exercise, he thought, nothing more, just less rigorous and satisfying than single-sculling.

And he'd kept the apartment.

Win, win.

The Wolves had played a one o'clock game, which he'd used to entertain advertisers in his suite. Once the game was over, he'd driven over here and had been in the water ever since. He was still in his wet suit, on his way out of the boathouse, when he saw Seth Dowd standing by his car.

"Shouldn't you be off writing me a column about how winning one game doesn't change what a Dumpster fire the Wolves have become?" Jack said.

"Isn't that what you told me to write?" Dowd said. "Written, sent, probably already up on the website."

"Who told you I was here?"

"Trained reporter."

"At least you're not resting on your laurels after finding that weasel my sister used to date."

"I told you, boss," Dowd said. "We're just getting started."

Jack took a long look at him.

"You've got something. I know that look."

"Now who's acting like a trained reporter?" Dowd said.

He reached into the inside pocket of his jacket and came out with a folded piece of paper.

"What's this?" Jack said.

"*This*," Dowd said, "is the toxicology report on DeLavarious Harmon."

"Isn't it too soon for that to be released?"

He sometimes felt the urge to smack Dowd, just to wipe the smug look off his face, one that was there a lot. But Dowd was far too useful, especially now, and he was the most widely read writer on the paper.

"It *hasn't* been released."

"Where did you get it?"

There was the look again.

"Does it really matter?"

Jack took the report out of his hand, leaning back against the driver's-side door of the Porsche. The heading read "Post-mortem Toxicology."

Jack's eyes scanned it.

"What does this all mean?"

"What it *means*," Dowd said, "is that the kid was suffering from cardiomyopathy, a heart thing that can legit kill young athletes. But his heart only gave out because he was juiced to the gills the day he collapsed."

"I'm listening."

"I'm not gonna give you the tutorial that the doc gave me," Dowd said. "But he had this new designer testosterone that still doesn't show up on league drug tests in his system, along with a legal pain pill called tramadol."

"And that combo can kill you?"

"When you mix in fentanyl, it can."

"Fentanyl?"

Dowd nodded.

"Even I know it's an opiate," Jack Wolf said. "We've written enough about kids OD'ing."

"Guys in the league know when their next drug test is coming, even though they're not supposed to. All they need is a heads-up," Dowd said. "So if they're in a lot of pain, they get a little boost from fentanyl the day of, to get them through the game."

Jack was thinking about calling Megan for old times' sake. He could use the toxicology report as a way of getting her over to the apartment, since it was looking like a slow night.

"I understand why this is a good story," Jack said, "but how does it help Danny and me with my sister?"

"It doesn't."

"So why did you come all the way over here to show it to me?"

"You've got two brothers," Seth Dowd said. "And I happen to know that the younger one was with the late DeLavarious Harmon in the trainer's room before the game on the day Harmon died."

Dowd paused and added, "Alone."

Then he paused again, just briefly.

"That doesn't mean he gave him the fentanyl, of course."

Jack Wolf smiled broadly at Seth Dowd.

"But then who gives a shit?" Jack said.

TWENTY-NINE

"THIS ISN'T EXACTLY OUR house in Pacific Heights," Ted Skyler said.

"I've discovered I'm much happier here," I said.

"Without me, you mean."

I sipped some wine. I hadn't offered him anything to drink.

"You sold me out to that cockroach Seth Dowd. And for a story that wasn't even about you."

"I am here to try to make that right."

"Why? Because I'm your boss now and have the ability to trade you to Cincinnati?"

He gestured at the sofa. I shrugged and sat down across from him in one of the Perigold armchairs my mother, in a rare display of maternal instinct, had bought for me as a housewarming present.

"Because I feel shitty about what I did, and because I don't like what your brothers are trying to do to you."

"Theodore, I've got to hand it to you. No one fakes sincerity better than you do."

I was almost certain that not even his parents still called him that.

"Is there any Scotch?" he said.

"No. Tell me about the sale. Who told *you* about it?"

"I honestly can't say."

"You're not Seth Dowd," I said. "You don't have to protect your source."

"In this case I do. You've got to trust me on that."

"Trust *you*?"

"I know I deserve that. I'm just here to tell you that this shit was always about to get real once your dad was out of the way."

"And Danny was going to sell us all out to the person my father hated the most?"

Ted nodded. "You always said that Danny was the one who hated Joe the most."

"And what better way to get even?"

"But now his problem is that he needs control of the team back," Ted said.

"Which he gets if I don't get the votes at the league meetings."

"It's why he and Jack are coming at you this hard."

"I don't get what's in it for Jack. The Wolves are completely separate from the newspaper."

"The person who told me this also told me that Danny and Jack might have some bigger play going with Gallo," Ted said.

"Bigger than Gallo getting the San Francisco football team he's lusted after for his entire lousy life?"

Ted got up off the sofa, went into the kitchen, came back a minute later with a glass of Scotch.

"I knew you were lying."

I sighed. "Learned from the master."

"I've told you everything I know. But I admit there's a lot I don't know."

"Tell me about it."

He smiled. He used to describe it as his cover-boy smile back when people still read magazines.

"You know you love me."

"I just wish like hell that I liked you."

He had only poured himself a small drink. I'd seen his car out front when I'd let him in. He drained the last of the Scotch and gave a quick look at his Omega watch—Omega being one of his endorsements.

"I have to be somewhere."

"I'll bet."

"But before I go," he said, ignoring that one, "I have to ask you something, because I *am* on your side, whether you trust me or not."

I don't know who to trust anymore.

Ted said, "You see what they're like. Why put yourself through this if you're going to lose the team in the end? Why not quit now?"

"I don't quit."

"You quit on us."

"No," I said, "that was all you."

He stood up. "For what it's worth, you did a good thing with the coach."

"I know."

"Man, you're tough."

"I'll get the votes," I said.

"How do you figure?"

"Don't worry your pretty little head about it."

When he was gone, I made a call that I'd hesitated to make before this.

"I've been expecting to hear from you," he said, in a voice even more gravelly than I remembered. "You finally ready to fight?"

THIRTY

RYAN MORRISSEY AND I were in my office, late. It had quickly become a habit for me, sometimes staying at Wolves Stadium as long as he did, almost like a contest to see which one of us could outlast the other and work longer hours.

"I don't mind putting in the time," he said. "But so you know? I'm never going to be one of those coaches who sleeps in his office."

"That's because you don't sleep."

"I'll sleep when I'm dead," he said.

I grinned.

"Warren Zevon."

Now he grinned. "He also wrote 'Disorder in the House.'"

"It could have been about *this* house."

I had spent the past few days immersing myself in the job, doing as much as I could to block out the noise. I had even managed to stay off the front page of the *San Francisco Tribune* for the time being, even though I was pretty sure *that* wasn't going to last.

Every morning I would check the injury lists around the league to see which players had been released and which ones had been brought in for tryouts. Including quarterbacks. Ryan and I had been talking a lot about quarterbacks the past couple of days.

"We still need a backup to Ted," he said now, "since you may have noticed that we don't exactly have a future Tom Brady behind your former husband at the present time."

"Wait a second. Chase Charles *is* Brady's height."

We had ordered in Chinese food from Fang, on Howard Street. The cartons were still scattered around my desk. I mentioned to Ryan Morrissey, not for the first time, that this was the glam part of pro football that I hadn't known existed, even when my father was still the big boss around here.

"Nothing glam about cutting players, either," I said to Ryan.

"Maybe we don't have to cut the kid until after the season, even though we'd be delaying the inevitable. Just send him down to the practice squad and keep him around for emergencies."

He speared a dumpling out of the container closest to me.

"Listen, I know this could get complicated with you and Ted, but he's nothing more than a JAG at this point in his career. You know what a JAG is?"

"Bill Parcells's acronym for 'just another guy.'"

"Very good."

"Because I knew about Parcells or his acronym?"

"Both," Ryan said.

"Let me ask you something. Can we make the playoffs with Ted as our quarterback?"

"Maybe. But only if I don't ask him to do too much and only if he can remember not to throw it to guys wearing a different-colored uniform than his." He blew out some air. "The problem isn't that he's too old. There's a lot of aging quarterbacks in the league. The problem is that he plays older than all of them. And can't still make the throws he needs to make."

"But he looks in the mirror and *does* see Brady, just without all the Super Bowl rings."

Ryan said, "He needs to stop looking in that mirror."

"Are you joking? He likes *all* mirrors."

"He can't throw the ball down the field with anything on it."

"I've noticed."

"So has the other team."

"So what do we do, Coach?"

"I may have a guy. But it might be kind of a tough sell."

"You mean like hiring a head coach who punched out the previous head coach?" I said. "That kind of tough sell?"

"Compared to the guy I'm thinking about," Ryan said, "I'm a Cub Scout."

He shrugged.

"But we're trying to win now, correct?"

"That would be extremely helpful."

When he told me who it was, I laughed.

"You think I'm joking?"

"No. I was thinking that just when I was off the front page, here I am, being pulled back in."

Then we called Thomas and put him on speakerphone and told him who we wanted to bring in for a tryout.

"Wait," my brother said. "He's out of prison?"

THIRTY-ONE

HIS SISTER HAD JUST walked right into his office a little before nine in the morning, not caring if he might be in a meeting or on some kind of important call—not that he was making or taking any calls like that these days, at least as they related to the Wolves.

She acts as if she's always had the run of the place, Danny thought.

But she'd find out soon enough that she was only renting here, as if her office, down the hall, were an Airbnb. The only surprise, considering what they'd thrown at her so far, was that she wasn't gone already.

"You never knocked when we were kids, either," Danny said to his sister.

"I believe," Jenny said, "that's how I walked in on you and Peggy Brooks playing doctor that time."

"I've got nothing to say to you," Danny said.

"Well, I've got something I want to say to you."

"Don't care."

But he could see she was dug in. When she got like that, Danny knew, it was like trying to stop the ocean.

"Is it true that you started the process of selling this football team to John Gallo before the reading of the will?"

"No," he said.

"Liar."

"Prove it."

"If I could prove it, I wouldn't be in here asking you. And hoping to get an honest answer out of you for once in your life."

"You just asked," he said. "I just told you. Now beat it."

"If it's true, I'll find out."

"You know what you should do?" Danny said. "Ask Gallo if it's true."

He smiled then.

"And let's just say, for the sake of conversation, that it *is* true. What are you going to do about it? Fire me? If you were going to do that, you would have done it already."

"Did you really hate Dad that much?" she said.

Danny leaned forward and put his chin in his hand, trying to look curious.

"Still assuming it's true," he said. "This Gallo thing."

"Only because I know what a sneaky bastard you are and always have been."

"This isn't any of your business."

"Now it is, whether you like it or not."

"I forget," Danny said. "Who was the one who walked away from our father, and this team, and this family? Was that your idea of family honor?"

"And what's your idea of honor, Danny? Getting into bed with a cockroach like Gallo?"

"Why are we still having this conversation?" Danny said. "You're the one in charge. Do what you have to do."

"While my two older brothers do everything in their power to crush me."

"But you've got Thomas now," Danny said. "The legendary

football executive, for as long as he stays clean and sober. Two against two. Fair fight, right?"

"You never fought fair," Jenny said. "Neither did Jack."

"You should know as well as anyone that's how we were all raised," Danny said to her. "When it's all over, nobody cares how you won. They just remember that you won."

"You're taking this team away over my dead body," she said.

"Isn't that what Dad always used to say?"

"I'll tell you what I told Jack," Jenny said. "Take your best shot."

"You want some brotherly advice?"

"From *you*? Hard pass."

"Stop being delusional. No shit, Sis. You think you're the one respecting our dead father's wishes? What you're really doing is embarrassing him, embarrassing this team, and embarrassing a family that you've suddenly decided you care so much about."

Jenny turned and walked out of his office, leaving the door open behind her. Danny was about to walk over and shut it when she appeared back in the doorway.

"I'll tell you one more thing, and then you can pass it on to Jack."

He waited.

"I haven't taken *my* best shot yet," Jenny said.

Then she was gone.

THIRTY-TWO

"WHEN WAS THE LAST time you played in an actual game?" I said to Billy McGee, who'd been the bad boy of professional football when he was still allowed to play professional football and before he really did do six months of prison time.

He smirked. After only ten minutes, it already seemed like his default look. Or attitude. Or both. Somehow he seemed to be slouching even when he wasn't.

"Blackjack or football?"

"Come on, Money," Ryan said.

It had been Billy McGee's nickname from the time he'd scored his first college touchdown, off a thirty-yard scramble, as a freshman at Arizona State. He'd pulled up his jersey when he was in the end zone that day and shown off the tattoo of a dollar sign on his chest, right under his shoulder pads.

He won the Heisman Trophy that year, came out of college two years later as the number one pick in the entire NFL draft, for the Lions. He was rookie of the year, got the Lions to the NFC championship game in his second season. After that it seemed that football was a sideline for him—that his full-time job was drinking and drugging and partying and casino hopping in Vegas every chance he got. And crashing cars. One columnist wrote that he'd had more wrecks than NASCAR. And he got into an endless series of fights in clubs. But two major events finally put him out of the league.

The single-car wreck of his Porsche on the Pacific Coast Highway was an accident—if not the fault of the liquor, pain pills, and Ambien in his system.

Within six months, he entered his former agent's living room, accused him of stealing millions of dollars from him, pulled a gun, and threatened to shoot him. The whole thing was streamed live on YouTube.

That incident, two years ago, had earned him his prison time.

"You guys count the Canadian league as me playing?" McGee said. "I wasn't there long, but if you count that, the last real game I played was a year and a half ago. That was before they found the 'drug paraphernalia' in my glove compartment after they pulled me over for nothing."

He put air quotes around "drug paraphernalia."

"For going twice the speed limit on a stretch of road outside Montreal," Ryan said. "Hundred and forty kilometers, as I recall."

Money McGee smirked again.

"Whatever."

I had sent a plane to pick him up in Las Vegas, not wanting anybody to see him walking through the concourse at SFO, then had a car pick him up at the private field in Hayward. Now Billy "Money" McGee and Ryan and me were in my living room. McGee wore a Nas T-shirt, Mohawk haircut, earrings. He also had a small dollar sign, another one, tattooed underneath his left ear. Somehow he was still only twenty-six years old. Everything about his physical self reminded me of Eminem.

"Was appreciating Canada before all that," he said. "Wide-open game, everybody in motion at once. Dudes, it was like being in a *video* game. Dope place to live, Montreal." He grinned. "No pun intended, right? The dope part?"

Ryan sighed. "We get it."

"Then I get into one beef with the cops, and they haul off and cut me."

Ryan said, "The whole league cut you, Money. It was like the whole *country* cut you."

"Plus, there was another positive drug test," I said.

"How many times I got to say I thought it was a supplement?"

"Pretty sure it's what they all say," I said.

"Hey, lady. *You* called *me*."

"Okay, let's cut through all the bull," Ryan said, "if that's all right with you. If we give you a legit shot, which I guarantee you will be the last shot anybody is going to give you, do we have any reasonable expectation that you can behave yourself?"

The smirk again.

"Says the dude who punched out the other dude."

I said, "Says the dude who might have thrown away a hundred million dollars or so."

"What do you want to hear from me?" he said, slouching so much into my couch I thought he might slip down to the floor and end up under the coffee table.

"That you're still a football player," I said. "That you might be willing to stop throwing your talent away."

"That you're ready to be a quarterback and not a punch line," Ryan said.

"I don't have to listen to this shit," he said.

I smiled.

"Sure you do."

"Why is that?"

"Because you've been famous since high school, and you were

on your way to being great in the pros before you turned into a career slob," I said, "and an all-around punk-ass bitch."

He came out of his slouch then and off the couch, on fire.

"I want to play!" he said. *"Okay? I…want…to…play."*

We all let that settle.

Billy McGee realized he was standing and sat back down.

But now everybody in the room seemed to have everybody else's attention.

"We'd be drug-testing you every other day," Ryan said. "Minimum. That would be just one of the rules of the road. Along with the league testing you whenever it damn well pleases."

"Test away," McGee said. "I've been clean for six months." He shrugged. "My wife got me into a program. Did the full twenty-eight. Now I go to a meeting a day."

It was all there in the reading I'd done on him. His wife, Amanda, who'd been his college sweetheart, had gotten him to go to Betty Ford, in Rancho Mirage. Somehow, through it all, she had stayed with him. Having now been in his presence for an hour, I thought it seemed like a love that passed all understanding. But they really were still together. And here we all were.

"You know we'd be taking all the risk here," Ryan said.

Billy McGee looked at him and in a quiet voice said, "Dude, I don't just want to play. I *need* to play."

Bad-boy pose completely gone, at least for the moment.

"Well, then," I said. "Let's see what you got."

My bag was on a table inside the front door. I walked over to it, threw my phone inside, took out my car keys, opened my front door, made a motion for him to come along.

"We going somewhere?" Money McGee said.

"We are."

"And where's that?"

"High school."

THIRTY-THREE

I'D GOTTEN PERMISSION FROM Joey Rubino to pull half a dozen of my players out of lunch and work them out with Billy McGee.

"I don't expect to keep this quiet for very long," I said. "But for now, I'll just have Billy waiting at the far end of the field when the kids get out there. And worry about my dear friends in the media later."

"With friends like those..." Joey said.

He said all six of the players were in the same history class. He'd meet them when it let out and walk them down to the locker room himself, then out onto the field.

"Only one condition," Joey said.

"Name it."

"I get to come watch," he said.

Now we were all down at the far end of the field, Ryan and Joey Rubino and my four best wide receivers and two defenders, just to make things interesting. And me. By now the kids had finally stopped losing their minds that they were on the same field and using the same football—even breathing the same air— as the infamous Money McGee. It really was as if their favorite rapper had suddenly appeared and asked them to hang out.

And they had all realized, quickly, the receivers especially, that they better get the stars out of their damn eyes or risk one of his passes hitting them in the face.

Davontae Lillis came over to me after he'd managed to hold on to half a dozen passes and whispered, "Coach, I can't tell you how much my hands hurt. Just no way I'm letting *him* know that."

Tayshawn Pratt was there, too.

"I thought Chris's passes were *tight*," he said. "What we got goin' out here? That is what you call a whole different situation."

Then McGee was motioning to them and telling them to get their asses back out there, as Caleb Mortimer was taking a break, his eyes big.

He was the one keeping his voice low now, as if afraid Money McGee might hear him.

"You see that ball I dropped a couple of minutes ago?" he said. "When I ran back to where he was throwing from, he told me that if I dropped another one on him he was gonna follow me home after school."

He looked at me. "He was kidding, right, Coach?"

I shrugged.

"Why don't you hold on to the ball from now on, just to be on the safe side?"

Billy McGee sent out two receivers at a time, telling them what patterns he wanted them to run against the two defenders. Most of the time he had at least one guy open. Even when he didn't, even when he had to put a little extra on the ball, the pass would end up in increasingly sore hands.

The whole time, Billy McGee was trash-talking a bunch of high school kids, almost like he was still one of them, like he was having more fun than any of them.

When the ball wasn't in the air, McGee spent a lot of time talking about the kids' mamas.

"We didn't bring him in to be a role model," Ryan Morrissey said to me.

Billy McGee heard him. At which point he turned around, tugged his jeans about halfway down his butt, pointed at it, and, grinning, said to Ryan, "Kiss this if you brought me in here to act like I'm running to be these dudes' class president."

The Hunters Point Bears out there with him howled with delight.

When we finished, after one last fifty-yard strike to Davontae, my players crowded around their man Money McGee for a selfie festival. He still seemed to be enjoying himself more than anyone. But I was aware that he'd been full of good intentions before.

Ryan pulled me aside.

"What do you think?"

I grinned. "He looks like he'd be able to kill it if he was starting for us against Galileo next Saturday. Now we need to see how he acts when he's back on the field with grown-ups."

I saw his head whip around. I'd figured out by now that Billy McGee had almost mutantlike hearing.

He called over to us and said, "I plan to treat those grown-ass players y'all have the way I always did."

"How?" I called back.

"Like the bitches that they are."

THIRTY-FOUR

EVEN I HAD TO admit the next morning that the *Tribune*'s front page was inspired. There was Billy McGee bending over and pointing to the half of his back end hanging out of his faded jeans at Hunters Point High under the headline:

ANOTHER ASS

The feature was accompanied by other photographs shot at Hunters Point High School of Billy McGee working out on the field there with some of my receivers and running backs.

The pictures had to have been taken either by a student or a faculty member, but the column had been written by Seth Dowd. McGee's previous transgressions, Dowd said, included just about everything except storming the US Capitol that time.

Dowd also quoted Ted Skyler as saying, "Apparently Money really lit it up with the prison team in its big game against Alcatraz."

I watched from my office at Wolves Stadium now as Ryan Morrissey put McGee through one passing drill after another with a handful of our wide receivers and defensive backs.

They'd only been out there for about thirty minutes when Ryan turned, knowing I was watching, and gave me a thumbs-up.

But we'd really decided to sign him, and offer him one of those contracts loaded with incentives to get him back on the field and keep him there, after watching him throw to the kids at Hunters Point.

The commissioner hadn't called me when he saw the story on the *Tribune*'s website about us working out McGee. He'd called Thomas instead, sounding as if he'd gone into labor, according to my brother, threatening to suspend Money McGee all over again and maybe the whole Wolf family along with him.

"For what?" Thomas said. "Regularly attending AA meetings? Hell, that could get me suspended, too."

Somehow, Thomas said, the conversation devolved from there, finally ending with Joel Abrams yelling, "Tell her to keep digging!"

On the field, Billy McGee rolled out to his right, chased by Andre DeWitt, stopped right before he reached the sideline, then threw a ball fifty yards to Calvin Robeson, our best and fastest wide receiver.

Thomas had come in by then and was standing next to me.

"Just so you know, we're getting creamed all over again on social media."

"Kind of our thing at this point."

"I think we did better with your badass self on the front page," he said.

"Thank you for that."

"Just saying."

"I trust our coach," I said. "You know the real badass around here is him."

"I trust him, too," Thomas said. "But he better be right about this guy. *We* better be right."

121

"If you look at this strictly as a football decision, which is all it is for the time being, we have just made a significant upgrade at backup quarterback."

"Is that really all we've done?" Thomas said.

"What's that mean?"

"It means that you don't trust Ted and I don't trust Ted and neither does Ryan," my brother said. "We're not signing this guy just to back up Ted Skyler. We're signing him because you guys think he gives us a better chance to win before the season is over, provided we can keep him out of the lockup."

"First we need to get him into a game. That would be helpful."

"Obviously Ryan thinks he can still play," Thomas said.

"He *always* thought that. And he's convinced that the guy is more motivated than he's been since he first got to the pros."

"Because this probably is his last lifeline?" Thomas said.

"Because he's dead broke."

"What happened to all the money he made?"

I looked at him. "Rhetorical question?"

"He didn't have a rainy-day plan?"

"You spoke with him downstairs. What do you think?"

There was a rap on my door then. The intern who'd become my full-time assistant, Andy Chen, poked his head in.

"Somebody here to see Mr. Wolf."

Ben Cantor didn't wait to be announced. He just slipped past Andy Chen and into my office and looked at Thomas, giving him a little two-fingered salute before firing off a question.

"How come you didn't tell me you were at the yacht club the day your father died?"

THIRTY-FIVE

THOMAS CASUALLY TOLD JENNY, "I got this," and told Cantor that the two of them should take a walk.

They walked down the flight of stairs closest to Jenny's office and then outside into the stands and made their way all the way down close to the field, where Billy McGee had just concluded his workout, finally sitting down behind the end zone at the west end of Wolves Stadium.

"You guys really thinking of signing that little criminal?" Cantor said.

"In person," Thomas said, "he's much bigger than he looks on TV."

Thomas turned to Cantor, wanting to get right to it, and said, "This thing with the yacht club—it's not what you think."

"You being there or you not telling me you were there?" Cantor said.

"Both."

"And I thought we were buddies," Ben Cantor said.

"You didn't think that for one minute."

"Why'd you lie to me?"

"I didn't lie," Thomas said.

"But you didn't tell the whole truth and nothing but, now, did you?" Cantor said.

He explained to Thomas that the regular harbormaster had just returned from racing down the coast to Catalina and back. He'd been gone since the day after Joe Wolf died. The first time Cantor had talked to him had been that morning.

"I honestly didn't think it mattered," Thomas said.

"Yeah, you being there does matter."

"Not if 'there' means the boat."

"Why were you there at all," Cantor said, "on this visit that wasn't even worth mentioning to me?"

Definitely not my buddy.

"I'd spent the night before there," Thomas said. "They've got rooms that members can use. I go over sometimes for—well, you know."

"If you mean for a night of unbridled passion," Cantor said, "then yeah, I do know."

Thomas grinned. "The heart wants what the heart wants."

"But why were you still there in the afternoon? That's when the harbormaster saw you."

Thomas told himself not to sound defensive or as if he had something to hide. Even though the cop already thought he *had* been hiding something. Thomas was used to lying to women. Considered it almost an art form that could evolve over time. Not something he could do with this guy. This guy just kept coming.

"I went *back* there in the afternoon," he said to Cantor. "The lady in question had left a bracelet behind. One her husband had given her."

Thomas grinned. "Now you know everything."

"Not quite yet. You still could have gone aboard and stayed aboard until you threw your father overboard and then swam for it yourself."

"But I didn't go aboard. If Lou told you he saw me do that, he's lying."

"He said that the last time he saw you, you were standing on the end of the dock in the rain," Cantor said. "He just doesn't remember seeing you leave."

"Check my phone calls. I kept trying the lady in question until I told her I had the bracelet."

"You could have called from the boat," Cantor said.

"But I didn't."

"Where'd you go after you say you left the yacht club?" Cantor said.

After you say *you left.*

"I went home. And stayed home all night. I told you that."

"No other lady to back that up?"

"I try to pace myself," Thomas said. "You know how it goes. All play and no work."

He shifted slightly in his chair in the stands and took a closer look. Cantor hadn't changed expression. He'd never changed his tone. They could have been talking about last Sunday's game or next Sunday's.

"Maybe the reason he didn't see me leave," Thomas said, "is because I left my car on the other side of the club. If I'd known my father was going to end up dead in the water, I would have done a better job getting myself an alibi."

Cantor just sat there, feet up on the railing in front of him, squinting slightly because of the sun but keeping his cop eyes on Thomas.

"Come on. You don't really think I snuck on that boat and did him."

"Just processing new information as it comes in."

Cantor got up then and headed up the aisle. Then he held up a hand, as if stopping himself, and walked back down the aisle to where Thomas was still in his seat.

"One more question, buddy."

Thomas was getting tired of Cantor trying to trip him up, but he wasn't going to show him that. Or show annoyance.

"What can you possibly ask me at this point about my sister that you haven't asked me already?"

"It's about your mother," Cantor said.

THIRTY-SIX

I HAD GONE to Hunters Point for practice after Thomas and Cantor had left my office.

Cantor couldn't have been in my office for more than a minute. But I'd gotten the same feeling I'd gotten before when he was in my presence—a certain attraction to the cool vibe he gave off, almost like he was playing a part. But I was wary of him at the same time. As if he had something on me. Or Thomas. Or all of us.

As if he was just waiting for one of us to make a mistake.

But once I was on the field with my high school players, I was back at my safe place, practicing them even harder than usual, almost as if I was more worried about losing my edge than I was about them losing theirs. And we could all see the work paying off, could see that they were playing better than they thought they would when they found out they were going to have a woman coaching them.

The best part of it was that the kids hadn't lost a game yet.

No, I thought.

That isn't quite right.

The very best part of it was that every afternoon of the school week, and then on Saturday afternoon, I got to remember what football was like without constant drama. It was what my whole life used to be like without constant drama.

When I left school after practice, I went straight home, thinking this would be another night when I ate dinner alone. Occasionally my neighbor and friend Rashida would invite me over. But most times I would cook for one or lean on Uber Eats and look at Ryan Morrissey's game plan, the draft reports, or the grades the assistant coaches were giving the Wolves players week by week, sometimes even from practice to practice.

But on this night, on the spur of the moment, I decided to surprise my mother—maybe have an early dinner with her, act like a better daughter to her than the mother she'd been to me. I didn't know whose side she was on right now, mine or Danny and Jack's. Probably theirs. But I knew from experience that it was better to have her on mine, if I could somehow get her there.

Maybe I'd even splurge and take her to Venticello, on Taylor Street, my favorite Italian restaurant in the neighborhood.

It was six thirty by the time I made it across town to the big, complicated, unhappy home in which I had grown up. I had just pulled around the corner of Sacramento and Jones, hoping to find a parking space in front of the house, knowing that the garage would have my mother's car in it as well as the housekeeper's.

I was making my way slowly up Jones when I saw our front door open and John Gallo walk out.

And I slammed on the brakes, just far enough from the house to ensure that there was no way they could spot me as I pulled up next to a double-parked SUV.

I sat and watched then as John Gallo took my mother's hand and kissed it. They stood there, just a few feet apart, until he turned around and headed down the walk. She watched him go, leaning against the door frame, as beautiful and imperious as ever. Even from this distance, I could see her smiling.

Smiling at John Gallo.

Elise Wolf stood there until Gallo's driver got out and opened the back door to his Mercedes. I ducked down behind my steering wheel as the car went past me.

I'd gone there thinking I'd surprise her tonight. Only it had turned out to be the other way around.

And I had maybe found out whose side Elise Wolf was on after all.

THIRTY-SEVEN

THEY WERE IN THE Celentano Room at Che Fico, on Divisadero, having come unseen through the back entrance, which the owner allowed them to use, giving them their privacy before they were even in their own private room.

Their usual table was set in a corner, near a white brick wall. The wall next to it, directly behind John Gallo, was covered with old album covers and movie posters, just about all of them featuring Italian singers and actors both living and dead. Mayor Charlie Spooner was seated to Gallo's right, bowls of pasta and meatballs and baskets of freshly baked bread in front of them along with a bottle of Gallo's favorite Chianti. When Jack Wolf arrived, he apologized to Gallo for being late.

"Nice to see you, Jack," Spooner said, "you sonofabitch."

"Come on, Charlie," Jack said as he sat down. "We've gone over this. You know why I had to run that story. And it will provide us with cover later on when John puts everything into play."

"And," Gallo said, "you know how quickly that particular controversy went away."

"Later on, no one will be able to say that I rolled over for you before we ended up in business together."

"I'd still like to know who sold me out with those pictures," Charlie said.

The mayor was looking at Jack Wolf, so only Jack saw the smile that crossed Gallo's face, there and gone, as if a shade had opened and closed.

"Just see if you can manage to keep it in your pants going forward," Gallo said to the outgoing mayor of San Francisco.

Then he raised his glass and said, *"Alla nostra salute."*

They all drank.

"Where's Danny tonight?" Spooner said to Gallo.

"Running a little errand for me."

"I worry sometimes that he's a loose cannon."

Gallo smiled more fully now. "Only because he is. What *I* worry about sometimes is that he doesn't fully grasp that this is about so much more than football."

They ate in silence for the next few minutes, until they heard a knock on the door. The waiter's head appeared. "How are we doing with the wine, Mr. Gallo?"

Gallo told him they were fine for now.

When the waiter had left, Jack said to Gallo, "My mother said you stopped by the house tonight."

"Strictly a social call."

"Is there really any such thing with you?" Spooner said.

Jack said, "She wouldn't say what the two of you discussed."

"Because that is our business and not yours," Gallo said as evenly as if he'd asked Jack to pass the bread basket.

"No worries. We're all on the same team here."

"A team I own," Gallo said without the slightest change of inflection or tone. "The way I will eventually own the Wolves."

"We understand that, John," Spooner said. "We've understood that from the start."

"The way we understand that the current mission remains destroying Jack's sister," Gallo said, "as a way of arriving at our ultimate goal."

"I'm frankly not sure we can totally accomplish that in the media," Jack said. "And I'm *in* the media."

John Gallo said, "Oh, yes, we can."

"So far, so good," Jack said.

"Just not quite good enough, you cocky bastard," Gallo said.

Something about him had changed, but neither one of the men with him at the table noticed.

Jack Wolf said, "Relax, John."

Gallo's fury was sudden then. He slammed his hand down on the table, making their bowls jump, causing Charlie Spooner's wineglass to fall and shatter on the floor, the sound like a gun going off.

"Don't you tell me to relax."

Jack Wolf and Charlie Spooner stared at him.

"Pretty good isn't *good enough!"* Gallo snapped at Jack. *"Do better!"*

The waiter appeared then, Charlie directing him to the shattered glass. The waiter cleaned it up, went away, and came back with a new one. He poured Charlie a fresh glass of wine and left.

When he was gone, Gallo turned to Jack, his voice not much above a whisper, and said, "If I don't get everything I want, and I mean everything, remember that you end up with nothing. Not even your newspaper."

"I'm aware of that," Jack said. "I was just trying to say that we've still got time to beat her up a little more before the vote."

"I don't want you to just beat her up. I want you to finish the bitch."

He smiled, as if the last couple of minutes hadn't happened.

"Is that understood?"

"Understood," Jack said.

Then John Gallo slapped his palms together and said, "What about some dessert?"

THIRTY-EIGHT

DANNY HAD JUST GOTTEN off the phone—again—with the commissioner, explaining to Joel Abrams that because he was no longer calling the shots with the Wolves, there was nothing he could do to prevent Billy McGee from suiting up on Sunday, and to keep suiting up.

"First she brings in an ultimate fighter to be her coach," Joel Abrams screamed at him. "Now she hires this skid-row bum to be one of her quarterbacks. What's next—she tries to find out if O.J.'s got any life left in his legs?"

"There're three weeks or so until the league meetings," Danny said. "Her signing McGee actually helps us. She just drove one more nail into her own coffin."

There was a pause then. When Abrams started speaking again, he seemed to have calmed down.

"When does your brother drop the story about the tox screen?" Abrams said. "He's got to do it before the medical examiner releases it."

"He says soon. Right now, he just wants to ride Money McGee's rap sheet for a couple more days."

"And what about Thomas being in the trainer's room with Harmon that day? Is that true?"

"It is."

Danny had turned his chair around to look at the way the stadium appeared when it was empty at night. It would be all his again soon enough. This and a lot more.

Jack thought he had his plans?

Danny had his.

I'm through being pushed around by my father. I'm certainly not going to get pushed around by my brother. And I'm not going to get pushed around by my sister for much longer.

"Hey, you still there?" Abrams said.

"Sorry. What did you say?"

"I said that just because your brother was alone with him before the game doesn't make him some kind of pusher."

Danny felt a brilliant smile cross his face.

"And it doesn't mean he's not," he said.

He spun his chair back around.

"And that's not even the best part," Danny said. "The best part is that Jack has a couple of sources who will say that Jenny knew about Thomas being alone with the kid that day before she made Thomas general manager."

"Is *that* true?" Danny could hear the excitement in Abrams's voice.

"All due respect, Commissioner?" Danny said to him. "Who really gives a shit?"

"I thought your brother Thomas was off drugs," Abrams said, "and everything else except girls."

"All guys like my brother are off until they're back on. So it will look as if a guy who used to hook himself up was hooking up one of our players."

Danny ended the call and walked down the hall. For a change, Jenny wasn't working late tonight. Sometimes he wondered if she stayed around as long as she did just to show off. He occasionally wondered what her life was like when she wasn't here or off coaching her little high school team.

But Danny knew who'd still be here.

He took the elevator down to the field level and walked down the silent runway toward the Wolves' locker room. He went inside and made his way across a space twice as big as it once had been—and about a hundred times more lush—after he'd spent a small fortune improving it.

Just to let the players know how much he cared about them, of course.

He saw that the door at the other end of the room was open.

Danny walked down there and gave a slight rap on the outside wall and said to Ryan Morrissey, "We need to talk."

Ryan pointed the remote at the flat screen on the wall opposite him and froze the coaches' film of the Wolves' defense.

"What's up?"

"I've got a proposition for you," Danny said.

THIRTY-NINE

I SAT THERE IN front of the house for a long time after John Gallo's car was gone.

I knew enough about him to know that he had been a widower for more than ten years. I knew that he had briefly pursued my mother after my parents' divorce. My father had believed she'd merely gone out with him a few times to get even, knowing my father would find out about it. All I knew is that their relationship—Gallo and my mother's, if you could even call it a relationship—had gone nowhere, at least at the time.

Until he'd come to the house tonight and kissed her hand in an old-fashioned way before he got into his car and then disappeared into the night.

I would ask her about the visit eventually.

Just not tonight.

I called ahead to Venticello, just a few blocks away, and ordered a pizza and salad and circled back to pick it up. I brought it home and reheated the pizza and poured myself a glass of red wine and ate at the counter in my kitchen while trying to educate myself about the Wolves' salary cap situation, which was about as easy to understand as the federal tax code.

The trick in pro football is to spend as much money as you

can while managing to stay under the salary cap so as not to get killed with penalties if you spend too much. It's why all teams now employ a SWAT team of what are known as capologists, people whose understanding of the numbers is as important as the coaches' understanding of *X*'s and *O*'s.

I already knew that Thomas wanted to trade for anyone and everyone he thought might help us. But I needed to know which transactions we could manage, within reason. I also needed to know which available players might make sense for us and which ones were too expensive, even in the short run.

Thomas, I thought.

The one member of my family I knew I could trust, now that I had proof that I couldn't trust my mother. If I ever really could trust my mother. But even though Thomas would have my back in the end, if for no other reason than how much he hated Danny and Jack, I didn't know exactly how *much* I could trust my kid brother. And how far.

So who could I count on the most these days?

The answer to that one was easy.

I could count on my coach. I wanted him in the foxhole with me.

I read up on the salary cap for as long as I could. Tried to watch a movie, but by the time I was half an hour into it I couldn't follow the story, about a rivalry between two sisters.

So against my better judgment I turned the television to the West Coast edition of *SportsCenter* on ESPN and watched and listened to various NFL insiders and pundits pundit away until they were blue in the face—*Wolves blue?* I asked myself—about our signing of Billy "Money" McGee, most of them acting as if his coming back to the NFL, even in a backup role, was the end of everything good and decent.

I was about to go to bed when the doorbell rang.

As late as it was, and not expecting company this close to midnight, I smiled when I looked through the peephole and saw who it was on the front porch.

"We need to talk," Ryan Morrissey said.

"Any subject in particular?"

"I need to quit."

FORTY

DANNY WOLF SAT ACROSS the dining-room table that, when he was growing up, he always thought should have been covered by a steel cage. This rare breakfast together hadn't been an invitation—more like a command performance.

It wasn't yet eight in the morning, but his mother was already dressed as if for some kind of photo shoot at one of the ladies' lunches she seemed to attend on a daily basis. This woman, bless her heart, still treated getting dressed up, and dining out, like full-time jobs.

Elise Wolf thought nothing of changing her outfits yet gave no thought to, or acknowledgment of, her advancing age. "I always wonder what it will be like when I'm old," Danny heard her say from time to time, playing her imagined role as the queen in her own version of *The Crown*.

Except she's queen of the House of Wolves, Danny thought, *not the House of Windsor*.

"You're sure this will work?" Elise Wolf said to him now, sipping some of her special tea. "I assured John that you had assured *me* that it would work to our mutual benefit."

"I presented things to our coach in a way that I'm sure John Gallo would appreciate," Danny said. "One of those offers I frankly don't think he can refuse."

She gave him one of her withering looks, one he didn't have the heart to tell her didn't scare him the way it had when he was a little boy.

Well, maybe still just a little bit.

"I certainly hope you don't make your *Godfather* jokes in his presence. John is a legitimate businessman."

Sure he is.

"You need to give me more credit."

She sighed theatrically.

"I try, Daniel. Lord knows I try my goddamn ass off."

If only, he thought, the rest of the world could hear how the queen of the manor really talks, especially to him. He'd heard much worse language, of course, from both his parents, especially when they'd start to go at each other. Had heard it his whole life. The Wolf children joked that if they'd had a swear pot for their parents when they were growing up, they wouldn't have had to wait to inherit their share of the family fortune.

"Jenny won't let this happen to her handpicked coach," Danny said. "I thought about going to her first. I decided to go to him instead. Told him that either he quits or I go public. He asked if there was a third option. I told him to ask my sister—she knows everything."

"That would be the option of her giving up control of the team," his mother said. She sipped more tea. It was a habit her "holistic adviser" had convinced her would extend her longevity, even though all her children were convinced she was going to outlive the earth. "Is there any point in me asking if these allegations against the coach are true?"

"Doesn't matter whether they are or they're not," Danny said. "If they get out there, he's through. That's how it works with MeToo. And he's already got that assault rap on his résumé."

"I worry that we keep underestimating Jenny. Because it turns out that she has even more of her sonofabitch father in her than she ever let on."

It almost made him laugh.

"Don't you mean she's got more of you in her, Mother?"

"Oh, spare me," she said dismissively, always her default tone with him. "Are we going to start up with all that old happy horseshit about how I was your father's Nancy Reagan? That is, as they say, such false news."

He could have corrected her, but doing that always pissed her off even more.

"All I know," she continued, "is that your plan better work. Things can't continue this way for the family." She shook her head. "Your sonofabitch of a father is gone now, but I'm somehow still cleaning up his messes."

"Sonofabitch? Is the mourning period officially over?"

"There was never going to be a period of mourning once he married that whore," she said.

Danny let that one hang in the air for a moment. *Whore.* He'd heard worse about Rachel, too.

Much worse.

"I did exactly what John Gallo instructed me to do," Danny said. "I raised the stakes a little more by showing I'm willing to take down the coach right along with her."

"How long did you give him to make up his mind?"

"I told him he had a couple of days," Danny said. "But I can't believe it will take that long to resolve itself. She won't let him take the fall for her."

"Even if it means giving up the team?"

"If she doesn't, she watches Ryan Morrissey sail off to Weinstein Island," Danny said.

"Where?"

"It's like the lost island of Atlantis. Named after the movie guy. It's the place well-known men get exiled to after they get accused of forcing themselves on women."

They sat in silence. The housekeeper brought a fresh pot of tea. She asked if Danny wanted more coffee. He said he was fine. Mostly he wanted to leave. He never wanted to be here, at least not for very long. But then Danny wasn't sure he'd *ever* wanted to be here.

"Are you sure you didn't know what was in that will?"

"What is that supposed to mean?"

"Sometimes I wonder if you're still playing us all off against each other," Danny said, "the same as he always did."

"To what end?"

"You tell me."

"Don't you give me that shit!" she snapped. "I'm doing what I've always done, which means protecting this family."

"Aren't Jenny and Thomas part of the family, too?" Danny said.

"Not if they won't get out of the way."

She took her lace napkin out of her lap and placed it next to her plate. He was being dismissed.

"We can't allow our secrets to get out."

"No," Danny said, "we can't have that, can we, Mother?"

FORTY-ONE

"I DIDN'T EXPECT TO still be here for breakfast," Ryan Morrissey said.

"When you told me why you were here, I didn't expect you to, either," I said.

He looked as if he'd slept in his clothes because he had, even though there were a few moments around two in the morning, after we were both all talked out, when I thought it might be touch and go where he'd end up sleeping. And whether he'd be alone.

"It's like the line in that television commercial," I said. "Life comes at you fast."

"Like a blitzing linebacker."

"You had a lot to drink," I said.

"We both had a lot to drink."

We were having coffee in the kitchen. I asked if there was anything else I could get him. He said more coffee. He said the last couch he'd slept on had been the one in his old office at Wolves Stadium, the couch on which he was being accused of forcing himself on one of the secretaries there when he still worked for Rich Kopka.

"I didn't know they'd play this dirty," Ryan said.

"Unfortunately, that makes just one of us."

"I didn't do anything that woman says I did."

"I like you, Ryan. And I listened to you for a long time last night before we got solidly into the wine. But you have to know that's what all men say."

"But you know me."

"I've known men longer. Including the ones in my own family. There was something with Jack about ten years ago that my father magically made disappear."

"Was it true?"

"He said at the time that he didn't do anything the woman said he did."

"How did it go away?"

"How do you think? Money changed hands."

"That won't work with this," Ryan Morrissey said.

"It won't come to that," I said.

"How can you be sure?"

"Leave that to me."

"Jenny, for the last time, he made the whole thing up and got her to go along with it."

"And for the last time, I'm the defense attorney, not the prosecutor, remember?"

"Money must have changed hands with *her*," Ryan said.

"Gee, you *think*?"

Her. Donna Kilgore. She'd been the secretary for all the assistant coaches before Ryan had punched out the head coach. I'd met her a couple of times. Smart, pretty, ambitious as hell—you figured that out in five minutes. I always suspected she'd had something going with my brother Danny, not that I could ever prove it.

Two years ago, she left the team. Suddenly and without explanation. I hadn't heard a word about her until Ryan

Morrissey showed up last night and told me about his meeting with Danny, who'd said he had a sworn statement from Donna and one of her best friends that Ryan had sexually assaulted her after hours, and on more than one occasion.

Her leaving the Wolves synced up quite nicely with her version of things. Danny told Ryan she was living in Las Vegas now, working as a casino hostess. But she had decided she had to come forward after she saw that Ryan Morrissey was back with the Wolves.

"He's not after you," I said. "He's after me."

"It's why I still think I need to walk away," he said. "Don't put the team through this; don't put you through this."

"What about you?"

"I've had practice at getting kicked out of football, remember?" Ryan said.

"It won't matter. If I'm not the one who walks away, he'll give you up to the media anyway without a second thought."

We both *did* have a lot to drink, starting with wine and then switching to Irish whiskey. We knew we weren't going to solve anything last night. So we drank, and kept drinking, until I made up the couch for him and went to bed alone.

But there really had been a point, right before that, one of those sliding-door moments, when I wasn't sure that's how the night would end.

"Thanks for letting me stay," he said.

"Nobody who ever slept on that particular piece of furniture ever thanked me before."

I poured us both more coffee.

Ryan said, "He gave me until tomorrow to give him an answer."

"What a guy."

He stared at me now across the table. He'd been looking at

me just as intently about two this morning, from a much closer distance, after we'd run out of things to say to each other.

"I'll figure it out while you get to work," I said.

"How?"

"Because I'm Joe Wolf's daughter, that's how."

FORTY-TWO

I DROVE TO MY office right after I waved goodbye to Ryan and didn't leave my desk until it was time for practice at Hunters Point, which I shortened so I could get right back to my office at Wolves Stadium. I had told Thomas what was going on and how I was trying to fix things, and I told him I would let him know when it was resolved.

If I could get it resolved to my satisfaction.

"Two can play this game," I said to Thomas.

"Which one is that?"

"Well, not a game, exactly. More like a knife fight."

Ryan Morrissey had done the same thing I'd done today: coached his team. There had been a couple of times when I'd been tempted to go down to Danny's office and tell him what I thought about what he was trying to do. But there was no point. He already knew what I thought about him and what a gutter move this really was. Let him wonder what I would do next—if I could find a way out of this particular jam. He had to know that I would come at him with everything I had. He was the one who used to call dinner at the house on Jones Street— an occasion when Joe Wolf would find increasingly creative ways to pit us all against one another—a blood sport.

Now I felt like it was a blood sport against my two older brothers every single day. And Danny, with Jack's blessing, I was sure, had brought Ryan Morrissey into it. Get at me through him.

I remember a dinner one night when we were kids. Jack had talked back to my father about something—all these years later I can't remember what. At which point my father reached over from where he always sat at the head of the table and slapped Danny on the shoulder, hard enough so it sounded like a whip being snapped. And hard enough to make Danny cry.

"What did I do?" Danny wailed.

Joe Wolf shrugged.

"I couldn't reach Jack," he said.

Now they were willing to hit Ryan, even though they were taking another swing at me.

I was still trying to go about my business, reading through the file of clippings from around the league that Andy Chen put on my desk every afternoon, along with injury reports and the previous day's player transactions. But I kept staring at my cell phone, waiting to hear the old-fashioned ringtone and see a familiar name pop up on the screen.

First I got a text from Ryan.

Anything?

I texted him right back, knowing that he was as anxious as I was.

Not yet

The phone finally rang a few minutes after seven o'clock. Uncle on the screen.

I took a deep breath and picked it up.

"It's been handled," the familiar gravelly voice said.

No greeting. No preamble. There never was. Then he told me how it had been handled.

"I'm still working on the other."

"Believe me," I said, "this will do fine for now. Thank you so much."

"You don't have to thank me. It's what family does."

"I love you," I said.

"Ti amo anch'io."

I love you, too.

There was a pause.

"Check your email," he said.

I did.

Then I walked down the hall to Danny's office, folder in my hand, hoping that he was still there and that I wouldn't have to drive over to his house to have the face-to-face with him for which I was very much spoiling.

His assistant, Molly, was at her desk.

"He in?" I said.

"Let me tell him you're here," she said, reaching for the phone on her desk.

"No," I said, and went through the door.

"Now I've got a proposition for you," I said to my brother.

FORTY-THREE

THEY SAT AT A window table at the Top of the Mark bar, at what was now officially known as the InterContinental Mark Hopkins.

From Cantor's youth, he remembered the expression "dressed to the nines." But the woman across from him was clearly into much higher numbers than that. Pearl necklace. A diamond ring that looked as big as a golf ball. He assumed that the black sequined cocktail dress she was wearing cost more than his car. Even in the dim light of the bar, he suspected that she'd had some work done, especially around the eyes. But he could see, as a trained detective, that it had been artfully done. Maybe a tuck under the chin as well.

She was sipping on a martini. Cantor didn't usually drink when he was working, but he had ordered an Anchor Steam beer to be polite.

"Thank you for meeting me," he said to the second Mrs. Joe Wolf.

"Please call me Rachel. I stopped thinking of myself as the second Mrs. Joe Wolf after the reading of the will."

"Well, then, thank you for meeting me, *Rachel*," Cantor

said, and clinked his bottle of beer against her stemmed cocktail glass.

He had looked her up online and knew that if she wasn't lying, she'd been half Joe Wolf's age when she married him. It made her slightly older than Jenny. She was tall, a couple of inches taller than Cantor even in low heels, and pretty. Not in the same way as Jenny, who didn't appear to have to work at it, ever, and whose fair-haired beauty somehow made *her* look younger than she actually was. If Cantor hadn't known better, he would have thought Jenny and her brother Thomas could have been twins—they looked that much alike.

Rachel Wolf, though—Cantor could see she worked like hell at maintenance. She wasn't going to give in to getting older without a fight. She looked to have the size and figure of a beach volleyball player. The cleavage showing from the black dress, Cantor thought, was rather epic.

"I was frankly wondering when you'd get around to looking me up."

Up and down, Cantor thought.

She picked her glass back up, raised an eyebrow, and smiled at him over it.

"Am I to believe I'm a suspect in my late husband's murder?"

"Why would you assume it was a murder?" Cantor said. "I'm still looking at it as an unattended death."

"A distinction," she said, "without a difference."

She took the tiniest sip of her drink. And smiled brilliantly.

"I'm quickly learning to watch what I say with you."

"I'm mostly trying to get a complete picture of the family dynamics at work here," Cantor said.

She laughed.

"The dynamics are simple in the Wolf family. They eat you if you let them."

She turned to look out at the lights of the city, which seemed to stretch forever. Maybe she wanted Cantor to see her in profile. Like she was moving from one pose to another.

"Why did your marriage end?" he said.

"Is that relevant to your investigation?"

"I try not to look at anything as irrelevant. Keeps me young."

She pushed her chair back slightly and crossed her long legs.

Then he said, "You had a pretty rock-solid prenup, correct?"

"My head is beginning to spin, Detective, with these sudden twists and turns in the conversation."

"Perhaps it's the altitude."

"I signed it willingly," Rachel Wolf said. "So he wouldn't think I was in it for the money, the way his children are."

Perish the thought.

"I had no idea that he would eventually treat me even worse in death than he did when he was still alive."

"He mistreated you in life how?" Cantor said.

"By constantly accusing me of cheating on him."

"Did you?"

"Never," she said emphatically.

"I hope this line of questioning doesn't offend you."

She recrossed her legs.

"They *all* thought I cheated on him, to the point where I started to feel as if I might as well have." She smiled again. "Just to have some fun in the bedroom again."

He didn't know what to say to that, so he said nothing. There was a lengthy silence between them until she finally said, "You can't possibly think I was the one who threw him off that boat, even as big a girl as I am."

"Just checking boxes," he said.

"Did you check one with the Iron Maiden?"

They both knew she was referring to the first Mrs. Joe Wolf.

"She's a tough old bird," Cantor said. "But I'm not sure she's tough enough at her age to get it done."

"Or maybe she waited a long time to get even with him for leaving her and had somebody do it for her." She gave a tiny shrug. "Perhaps another way of looking at things."

"I'm told you were pretty upset at the reading of the will," Cantor said.

"Damn right I was. I thought I deserved more, especially since I did *everything* for that man when we were still together."

"Then he screws you."

"Figuratively," she said. "Not literally."

He ate some peanuts. He'd been trying to pace himself, not wanting to empty the bowl in her presence.

"I keep wondering if there was a way somebody had gotten a look at that will beforehand," Cantor said. "And been in enough of a rage after seeing what was in it to take him out. With the exception of his daughter, of course."

"She was always Daddy's little girl," Rachel Wolf said. "No matter how badly she treated him."

She leaned forward in her chair.

Eyes up here, Cantor told himself.

"Are you now suggesting I knew what was in the will?" she said. "Ask anybody who was in the lawyer's office that day. Even I'm not that good an actress."

She suddenly reached into her purse and came out with her phone and said, "I need to go."

"Date?"

"Are you asking, Detective?" She gave a shake of her head. "Charity thing for the New Conservatory Theatre."

She stood up. She really was quite tall.

"One more question," he said. "If you had to put your

money on a member of the family who could have killed Joe Wolf, who would it be?"

"That's easy. The son who told me on multiple occasions that the whole family would be better off with Joe dead."

"Jack or Danny?" Cantor said.

"No, that would be the boy prince," Rachel Wolf said. "Thomas."

FORTY-FOUR

I OPENED THE FOLDER and removed the printouts of the email correspondence between Danny Wolf and Donna Kilgore on what was called ProtonMail, emails in which he laid out the terms of his deal with her—what she would be paid for accusing Ryan Morrissey, what she was supposed to say, and what her best friend, a woman named Barb Rubio, was supposed to say to back up Donna's account of things.

There were also some embarrassing dirty exchanges as Danny and Donna Kilgore took what sounded like a rather sweaty trip down memory lane.

"You know," I said to my brother, "your writing skills haven't improved with time."

He stared at the papers in front of him, then back at me, then back at the papers.

"This is an encrypted account."

"That's your response to what's sitting there in front of you?"

"How did you get these?" he said.

"Not important. What's important is that I did."

He put his hands out.

"You know what I'm thinking?" he said. "Now it's his word

156

against hers, because I've got sworn statements from her saying that the coach did it. Or did *her,* as the case may be."

"And I've got a sworn statement in which she recants everything in yours."

He opened his mouth and closed it.

"You paid her off."

"Somebody did. And paid a lot more than you did."

"I don't even need to guess who, do I?"

I shrugged.

"Our uncle," he said.

"Well, not yours," I said.

"Screw him. And screw you."

"He said that I should remind you that not everything that happens in Vegas stays in Vegas. Right before he called you the same schmuck you've always been."

"So now you're the one blackmailing *me*?" Danny said.

"Twist of the tale."

I sat down. Danny laced his fingers behind his head and leaned back in his chair.

"So you win this round."

"And the next one, if you ever try anything like this again. And the one after that."

I watched him and wondered, not for the first time, how I was possibly related to him.

"Let me ask you something, Danny. Did it ever occur to you to try to work with me? To make this a real family business?"

He snorted. "Oh, wait—you're serious."

Then he said, "So are you going to fire me?"

"Nope. I'm going to let you sit at this end of the hall and know that I'm doing your job at the other end."

"Not for much longer," he said. "Those league meetings fast approach."

"You're not invited."

"We'll see about that."

"I guess we will."

He shook his head, almost sadly. Or smugly. As if somehow I were the schmuck.

"You think you're so much better than us. And then you're willing to crawl right down into the mud with me."

"If that's what it takes to get the win," I said.

"Enjoy it while you can."

"I already am."

"You don't get it, do you?" Danny said.

"Get what?"

"A nick here, a nick there, and pretty soon you're bleeding to death."

Danny smiled then, as if he knew something I didn't. Or as if he was the one who'd won something tonight, though I couldn't imagine what.

"See you in the next news cycle."

As I headed down the hall, I heard him call out, "You and the coach."

FORTY-FIVE

I GAVE MY TICKETS to the Eagles game to my friend Rashida and her husband. On this day I watched from Thomas's suite, hoping that my football weekend might turn out to be a clean sweep, because my Hunters Point Bears had beaten Galileo 27–6 the day before.

It was 17–17, middle of the third quarter, when Ted Skyler was knocked out of the game with a concussion, and the next thing everybody saw at Wolves Stadium was Billy "Money" McGee running out onto the field to replace him.

The suite had been quite loud all afternoon but went quiet now.

"Okay," Thomas said. "This shit just got very real."

After Billy handed the ball off on first down, Joe Buck said to Troy Aikman on television, "So far so good. Nobody got arrested."

Second and ten. It went back to being so quiet in the suite that I thought I could hear my own breathing.

"It's a passing down," Troy Aikman said. "I expect they'll give him an easy one to get him into the flow of the game."

It was exactly what Ryan, who had taken over the play calling, tried to do. Billy was supposed to straighten up once he'd taken the snap from center, then throw quickly to Calvin

Robeson on the outside. In theory, the ball wouldn't even have to travel ten yards in the air.

But the Eagles cornerback was expecting the same kind of throw, reading Billy McGee's eyes the whole time, then stepping in front of Calvin and intercepting the ball and running sixty yards, untouched, for a touchdown.

Now it was all of Wolves Stadium that had gone into a stunned silence in response to how suddenly and disastrously the day had changed for the home team.

"Well," Thomas said, "at least everybody knows he's back."

I said, "Remind me of something. Who took that shot to the head—my ex-husband or Money?"

The next time we got the ball, Billy was nearly intercepted again. By the time the Wolves punted the ball away, he still hadn't completed a pass, at least not to anybody on our team.

I whispered to Thomas, "Plenty of time."

Thomas whispered back, "I'm starting to wish he was still *doing* time."

We were still behind 24–17 when we got the ball on our ten yard line with just under a minute left in the game. Billy's first-down pass was batted down at the line of scrimmage. The next one he threw wildly out-of-bounds.

Third and ten.

If we didn't get a first down, the game was over. The Eagles knew it, too, and blitzed Billy, chasing him back into the end zone. One guy nearly tackled him for a safety, but somehow Billy got away, running hard to his left.

Then a split second before he ran out of room and ran out-of-bounds, he stopped. And in that moment he seemed to remember the player he used to be. He had just enough time and room, before being hit from behind, to throw the ball as far as he could down the sideline to Calvin Robeson.

Who was wide open.

"Where'd everybody go?" Thomas said from the seat next to me.

We both watched then as Calvin, behind the defense by ten yards, caught the ball in stride and ran away from everybody for the ninety-yard pass-and-run play that brought us to within a point, 24–23.

Once we kicked the extra point, the game would go into overtime. Not quiet any longer at Wolves Stadium. Not even close.

Except that now there was a close-up on the huge television screen in Thomas's suite of Billy McGee up in Ryan Morrissey's face, pointing at his coach and then pointing back at the field, finally taking his helmet off as if he suddenly wanted to chuck it as far as he'd just thrown the ball to Calvin Robeson.

Billy's back was to the camera when something rather amazing happened, almost as amazing as the crazy touchdown play we'd just witnessed.

The head coach of the Wolves smiled. And nodded. And then waved the kicking team off the field and the offense back *on* it.

It meant we were about to try a do-or-die two-point conversion.

"He talked him into trying to win it right here," I said to Thomas.

"Or lose it."

What happened next seemed to happen fast in real time. Billy dropped back to take the snap. But the instant the ball was in his hands, he went running straight up the middle, taking off from around the two yard line and launching himself into the air and into the end zone as if he were flying.

When he landed, the score was Wolves 25, Eagles 24.

It was the way the game ended. I realized I hadn't moved from my chair since Billy McGee had run onto the field. But I did notice that I was breathing normally again.

I turned to my brother now and bumped him some fist.

"Money," I said.

FORTY-SIX

CANTOR SAT OUTSIDE THE VIP entrance to Wolves Stadium and waited. He had been a cop for twenty years and a detective for the last ten of that. He was good at waiting by now.

Another young detective had asked him one time for any advice he might have, and Cantor had said, "Hang around and hope something interesting develops."

Today he wanted something interesting to happen if he followed Jack Wolf.

He'd decided it was Jack's turn to go back into the barrel today. Jack, the rowing guy. The one Cantor thought was the real prick of the family. Cantor had interviewed him once already, seeing if he could get a rise out of him. But the second Wolf son had dismissed the idea that he could have rowed out to the boat that night, tossed his father into the water, made sure his father didn't come up, and rowed back to shore.

Wolf told him that he could go ask someone who'd been working at the Bair Island Aquatic Center if he'd taken his scull out that day—or night. Cantor didn't have to be told. He'd already called over there.

Another box he'd checked, even though it didn't mean Jack Wolf couldn't have gotten another scull somewhere else. Or swum out there. Or that he couldn't have been the one who stowed away.

No matter how hard he tried, Ben Cantor couldn't make Jenny Wolf for murder, even if she was a strong enough swimmer to make it to Oakland and back. He tried to tell himself that it wasn't just because he was attracted to her—it was that he honestly didn't believe she had it in her.

Could he ever see the two of them together when this was over? Maybe. Provided she wasn't the one; provided she and her kid brother weren't in on it together.

Could it be Thomas, who Rachel Wolf said had talked about wanting his father dead? Sure. Except nobody else he'd talked to had mentioned Thomas ever saying anything like that. Just wife number 2.

From the start, Cantor had been skeptical that Danny Wolf had the guts to do it, as much as he'd lost once the will was read. But Cantor knew better than to assume anything in cases like this, had learned the hard way not to always trust his gut. As far as he was concerned, at least for now, Danny was just a weasel with daddy issues.

Jack Wolf continued to be the one who interested Cantor the most. The one Cantor saw as being the lone wolf in all ways, even as he'd teamed up with Danny to ruin their sister's life.

Fifteen minutes later, maybe an hour after the game had ended, Jack came walking into the parking lot, the first in the family to leave the stadium. He had the space closest to the entrance. Cantor watched as he pointed his keys at a Mercedes SUV, saw the lights flash, saw him pull out of the lot that Cantor had badged his way into.

"Let's do this," Cantor said to himself.

He wasn't worried about Jack Wolf spotting him. Why would he even be looking for a tail? The way the *Tribune* was stalking Jenny, she was the one who needed to worry about being followed these days.

They eased their way onto King Street and then 280 South until it merged with the 101, then finally made their way onto Maple Street in Redwood City.

By now Cantor knew about the affair Jack had had with his managing editor, Megan Callahan, and the love nest he'd kept for them in Redwood City. Maybe they were back together.

What had Thomas Wolf said to Cantor that day?

The heart wants what the heart wants.

They passed the aquatic center, then Jack made a right turn past a sign that said BAIR VILLAS.

Where Jack and his editor did shack up once.

Jack Wolf pulled around to the back and up to a ground-floor villa that faced the swimming pool. There were two parking spaces in front. One was occupied by a sporty-looking silver Mercedes sedan. Cantor knew he could have run the plates, but he was busy right now, easing past Jack Wolf's car and turning his own around so he had a good look at the front door.

Ben Cantor smiled to himself as the door opened.

Standing there in a Wolves T-shirt and nothing else, a glass of white wine in one hand as she pulled Jack Wolf into a kiss with the other, was Rachel Wolf.

FORTY-SEVEN

RYAN MORRISSEY AND THOMAS and I were celebrating the victory over the Eagles at the Horseshoe Tavern.

Ryan had originally tried to beg off. He said that he wouldn't know until midweek, at the earliest, if Ted Skyler would be cleared to play, so he needed to draw up two game plans—one if Ted did play, one if Billy McGee was the starter.

But I told the coach he could take an hour and let Thomas and me buy him a drink at Joe Wolf's favorite bar.

"Your father brought me here one time," he said.

We were at the same table at which I'd sat not long ago with my ex-husband.

"Mr. Wolf told me that night I'd end up coaching the Wolves someday," Ryan said. "I thought he was full of it."

"Only because he generally was," Thomas said.

Thomas and I were on one side of the table, Ryan on the other. He smiled at us now. "I had no idea I'd get the job like this," he said.

I was drinking draft beer, along with Ryan. Thomas was drinking Diet Coke. I'd asked him once if he ever thought he'd drink again, and he'd said that his former dealer sure hoped so, because in the old days it only took a couple of drinks before he was off to the races.

"Okay," I said to Ryan. "I've waited long enough to hear what Billy McGee said to you before we went for the two points."

"Not sure I can repeat all of it in front of a lady," Ryan said.

"Trust me on something," Thomas said. "There's no language you can use that my sister didn't hear when we were all growing up. Sometimes at breakfast."

"Well," Ryan said, "doing my best to clean it up, he said that if I didn't have the balls to try to win the game right there, then I probably didn't have another body part, either."

The imagery made me laugh.

"You're telling me that's the sanitized version?"

"Well, there was one word that I'd never heard used as a noun, verb, and adjective in the same sentence," Ryan said.

The TV screen behind him, at this end of the bar, was showing highlights of the game. By now I'd seen Billy McGee's scramble and throw to Calvin Robeson about a dozen times. Fine with me. It came out the same way every time.

Ryan said, "He concluded by telling me that if he was willing to put his money where that particular body part was, then I should be, too." Ryan grinned. "And damned if he wasn't right."

We all drank to that.

It was a good night to end a good football weekend. I felt as relaxed and happy as I'd been since the reading of the will. This was, I thought, the way I'd hoped things would be before my older brothers had started throwing bombs at me.

Nearly midnight by now.

Thomas's phone was in front of him on the table and pinged with an incoming message. He picked it up and frowned as he stared at the screen, for much too long a time.

"Sonofabitch," he said.

Still staring at the phone in his hand.

"What's wrong?" I said.

There wasn't anything about the look on his face, and his sudden lack of color, that I liked.

"Tell me you're not looking at the *Tribune* website."

"Worse than that," he said.

"What can be worse than what they've been doing to us?"

"*TMZ*," Thomas said.

FORTY-EIGHT

TMZ HAD TIME-STAMPED video footage of Ryan Morrissey showing up at my house at 11:08 the night Danny had threatened him with those sworn statements.

And it had time-stamped video, every hour on the hour, of Ryan's car staying right where it was until he walked out my front door the next morning while I waved to him from the front porch, as if I were sending a hubby off to work.

Or a boyfriend.

See you in the next news cycle, Danny had said.

Death by news cycle.

Of course I wasn't spared by the *San Francisco Tribune's* front-page headline.

COACHES WITH BENEFITS

Underneath was the photograph, courtesy of *TMZ*, of Ryan and me.

"I'm telling you—this isn't that big a deal," I said to Thomas in my office the next morning.

The satellite trucks had been back in front of my house.

There was more media waiting for me when I got to Wolves Stadium. I'd shut off my phone by then, and when I got upstairs I told my assistant, Andy Chen, to hold my calls until the end of days.

I was at my desk. Thomas was behind me, staring down at the field.

"It's a big deal," Thomas said wearily.

"Wait a second," I said. "Jeanie Buss was engaged to Phil Jackson when he was winning championships coaching the Lakers. Even I know that, and I don't follow pro basketball all that closely."

"She wasn't running the team then," Thomas said.

"What difference does that make? Her family still *owned* the damn team."

"But she wasn't the big boss lady," Thomas said. "And she didn't fire one coach so she could hire her boyfriend."

"He's not my boyfriend!"

"You know that. And I know that. But the world thinks that you fired the previous coach and gave the job to the guy you are now having sleepovers with."

Rich Kopka, the coach I had fired, had already weighed in about that, and about *TMZ*.

"I didn't know that if I'd given her a little sugar," Kopka told Seth Dowd, "I could have kept my job."

Thomas kept staring down at the empty field, coffee mug in his hands.

"In the end," I said, "Danny managed to clip Ryan anyway. And me."

I slapped my desk hard, nearly spilling coffee out of my own mug.

"Seriously? Are people dumb enough to think Ryan screwed his way into his job?"

"You want the short answer?" Thomas said. "Yes. Same game plan they were going to use against Ryan with those women. He's the one who's totally screwed once the accusation is out there. How it works these days."

I angled my chair and took a closer look at Thomas. He looked the way Ryan had looked that morning at the house. As if he'd slept in his clothes.

I drank coffee that I wished had something stronger in it. It was the way my father used to drink it. I thought about reaching down for the bottle of Irish whiskey I'd taken out of the bottom drawer of his desk and put into mine.

"Somebody set Ryan up," I said.

"Or had your house staked out without your noticing it," Thomas said. "And guess what? It doesn't matter. They wanted you both to look bad, and now you do."

"Come on. Is it really worse than everything else they've hit me with?"

"Yeah, Sis, it is. You know why? Because it's one more thing. I kept hoping we could get to the league meetings without one more thing. But now this."

He turned and sat down on the windowsill.

"They're never going to stop."

"Well established," I said. "But so is something else: I'm not quitting." I managed a small smile. First of the day. "If we do, the terrorists win."

We kicked around some ideas about how to respond—if we even did respond. I wasn't on any social media platform. No Facebook. No Instagram. No Twitter. No TikTok. Somehow I'd managed to live my life to this point—even the life I'd now been thrown into—resisting the notion that having an unspoken thought was against the law.

Thomas, however, was all over social media, almost like it

was his new drug of choice. He even had a presence on some platforms that I hadn't previously known existed.

We finally decided to simply issue a statement on the Wolves' official Twitter account denying that Ryan Morrissey and I were involved in a romantic relationship.

"I've managed to not dignify any of this so far," I said.

"We're making an exception on this one," Thomas said.

So we kept it as simple as we could, without my sounding defensive in any way.

Ryan Morrissey and I are not now, and have never been, in any relationship other than the professional one we now share. Go Wolves.

Jenny Wolf

I had to be talked out of adding one additional sentence.

"But any personal relationship I do have is my business, and anyone who thinks otherwise can kiss my ass."

"Very powerful imagery, Sis," Thomas had said when I suggested adding the line. "But for now, let's keep that one between us."

Thomas went back to his office then and went to work on a couple of trades we were considering, one of them for another backup quarterback in case Ted couldn't play against the Broncos. I did the same. I considered watching today's Wolves' practice from the field but didn't want to turn it into another photo op for the masses.

The media gaggle was still in the parking lot when I came out and got into my car to drive over to practice at Hunters Point. They shouted questions. I smiled and waved and ignored them. There were more reporters waiting for me at the high school until the principal came out and told them that if they didn't leave the school grounds immediately, he was calling the police.

When my players were on the field, they wanted to know if the story about the coach and me was true. I told them it was not. Carlos Quintera couldn't resist telling me that it was a shame, because he thought we made kind of a cute couple.

I told him that was a very cute remark before making him run five long laps around the entire school property while I started practice without him.

There were no reporters left when I got back into my car. No reporters at the house. No stalkers with phones or cameras in parked cars on the street, at least not that I could see.

But I nearly had a heart attack when I walked through the door and saw Megan Callahan, managing editor of the *Tribune*, sitting on my couch.

"Sorry to frighten you," she said. "But your friend Rashida let me in. I told her it was sort of an emergency."

"Your being here can't possibly involve good news," I said, tossing my bag on a chair.

"Or any that's fit to print."

It was then that I noticed the laptop on the coffee table. Hers, not mine. She opened it.

"I can't do this anymore. This is a story I wouldn't poke with a stick."

I sat down next to her and began to read Seth Dowd's piece suggesting that Thomas gave drugs to DeLavarious Harmon the day he'd dropped dead on the field.

When I finished, I closed the screen.

"Who's seen this?"

"Seth, obviously. And Jack and me. That's it. Jack wanted to keep the circle tight until he decided to run it." She leaned back and sighed. "And now he's going to run it, the day after tomorrow. He wants to give you and the coach having your sleepover one more day of oxygen."

"Well, that's not happening."

"What's not happening?"

"The *San Francisco Tribune* running this piece-of-shit story."

"What are you going to do?"

"I'm going to call Dowd and then my brother and tell them that neither one of them has any further legal protection at the paper once Thomas sues them for libel," I said.

"How do you plan to do that?" Megan Callahan said.

"By firing them, that's how."

I turned to her and put out my hand for her to shake.

"Congratulations," I said. "In addition to retaining your position as managing editor, you're the new publisher of the *San Francisco Tribune*."

FORTY-NINE

AFTER MEGAN LEFT, I decided to call Jack myself. I thought about waiting until morning, even going over to the paper myself and doing it in person, giving myself the pleasure of seeing the look on his face when I told him to clean out his office. But I decided to get it over with and not to wait.

Either way, the pleasure would still be all mine.

I remembered a rare family dinner a few months after my father had turned over control of the paper to Jack. They'd both known by then, the newspaper business having just begun to shrink down to the size it is now, that they were going to have to start the process of cutting staff if they wanted to keep the *Tribune* afloat. First a little and then, if that didn't save enough money to keep the family newspaper viable, a whole lot more.

Joe Wolf said that he should be the one, as the owner of the paper, to tell people that they were being laid off and explain whatever kind of buyouts they were being offered, even though Jack was in charge.

I remembered Jack smiling that day as he listened to our father talking about people who had given their lives to our paper and to the newspaper business. And I remembered thinking that Jack looked in that moment like a real wolf.

Lowercase.

"No worries," he said, still smiling. "I've got this."

This was different, of course. My brother would never have to worry about money another day for the rest of his life. He wouldn't have to work again if he didn't want to, even though I knew him well enough to know how much he loved, and needed, to be a boss. How much power, and the fear that came with it, mattered to Jack Wolf.

He'd never been much of a drinker, even in college. The strongest drug he'd ever used, as far as I knew, was weed. No, the real drug to which he'd always been addicted was power, maybe over everybody except Joe Wolf when he was still alive. Thomas had at least wanted to kick his habit for hard drugs. But as a career bully, Jack didn't see any need to change. He liked himself just the way he was.

"This must be important," he said when he answered the phone.

I told him then, letting him know I'd read the story about Thomas and what garbage I thought it was and with whom I was replacing him. He didn't seem remotely surprised about Megan, just saying, "I always felt as if actually screwing me wasn't going to be enough for her."

There was a pause then at his end.

"You're really doing this."

"Not doing," I said. "Did. Done. Past tense. You're gone."

"And let's say I choose not to accept this decision because of the way my contract is written, and show up for work tomorrow morning."

"At that point, you will be escorted out of the building by security."

He laughed.

"Something funny here?"

"Just to me. But that happens a lot."

There was one more pause before my brother said to me, "What the hell took you so long, you silly cow?"

FIFTY

TWO DAYS LATER, I was in my office looking over the scouting reports for our Sunday game in Denver when Thomas came bursting in. He often treated Andy Chen's desk as nothing more than a speed bump—more manic sober than he was when he was still using.

"Remember how Dad always said that the most dangerous wolf was a wounded wolf?" he said. "Well, he was right."

He came around my desk and asked me to clear my laptop screen, which I did, then he leaned over and began hitting some keys.

"Any particular destination you're looking for on the old information highway?"

"Yeah," he said. "The gutter."

He stepped back and pointed. There, taking up most of my screen, was an image of a wolf, teeth bared, looking a lot more ferocious than the one we used for our team logo.

Underneath the illustration ran a few lines of jagged red type:

Welcome to Wolf.com, where you can come to find all the news that the rest of them don't want you to see. Starting now, the only ones

*who need to be afraid of wolves are the ones
who are afraid of telling you the truth.*

Thomas reached past me again and clicked on the arrow, and then we were in.

"Jack," I said to Thomas, as if that explained everything.

"Unleashed," Thomas said.

"Like he wasn't already?"

"Take a good look at the home page and decide for yourself," Thomas said.

He moved aside. I leaned closer to the screen, though I quickly realized I could have seen the two biggest headlines from my outer office, or maybe outer space.

One was about Thomas and DeLavarious Harmon. I clicked on it and saw it had been written by Seth Dowd, "Content Manager, Wolf.com." It was basically the same story for which I'd fired Jack and fired Dowd himself about an hour later. He'd told me over the phone that I hadn't heard the last of him. At least he'd been right about something.

The second one was about Ryan and Donna Kilgore, also written by Dowd. I read the first several paragraphs and saw that Dowd had placed her original allegations, and statement, up much higher in the story than her second statement, the one in which she'd denied everything after we'd confronted her.

This version included a quotation from Danny Wolf.

"It's pretty clear," he said, "that after I presented Donna's story to my sister, and our coach, money changed hands. I'm guessing quite a lot of it."

Donna Kilgore was unavailable for comment. Dowd had written that Ryan and I were, too, though he'd never reached out to me. I could check with Ryan but assumed that Dowd hadn't reached out to him, either. There were clearly about as many journalistic rules at play here as there would have been in dogfighting.

I looked briefly at the rest of the site. There was a story about a married city councilman and a teenage girl one year out of Convent & Stuart Hall—where she was a classmate of the councilman's youngest daughter—including a text-message exchange. There were naked pictures of one of the city's longest-tenured eleven o'clock anchors that someone had shot in her dressing room at the station.

And there was the promise of a message board, advertised as a page that would be required reading for all San Francisco once it was up and running by the end of the day.

I pointed to that and said to Thomas, "Another reason to live."

I reached over and closed my screen, feeling as if I still needed my bottle of Purell from back in the COVID days.

"In the end, they got these stories out there," I said to Thomas.

Thomas put a hand on my shoulder and said, "Like they took us both out with one shot."

FIFTY-ONE

CANTOR LIKED TO SURPRISE PEOPLE. Get them out of their comfort zone. Off their game, if he could manage, which he usually could. It's why he rarely set up appointments for interviews when he was working a case. Just show up and flash his badge, like he was shining a light into their eyes.

Like today.

He wanted to hit Jack Wolf with the affair with his step-mother—what else could Cantor call her, his nanny?—and see how he reacted, especially now that he was distracted by what had happened at the paper over the past forty-eight hours and by the new website, which Cantor thought was dumber than a bag of hammers.

He was saving the stepmother, what would be round 2 with her, until later. Rachel Wolf seemed to hate Joe Wolf—now that he was dead, anyway—as much as his sons had when their father was still alive. She'd clearly thought she was getting more in the will, even with their prenup and even though Cantor knew the house in which she was still living was worth plenty. But it was like a lot of things. It was worth plenty only if she put it on the market and decided to downsize her living situation, at least when she wasn't shacking up with her stepson.

Somehow Cantor didn't think she was the type.

But Rachel really was for later. The way another interview with Elise Wolf was. Somebody could be lying. Maybe somebody did know the contents of the will before the reading. Maybe they were all lying their asses off. Maybe Cantor would never know what happened to old Joe Wolf that night and give this up, move on. He just wasn't there yet. Not even close.

His focus today was on Jack Wolf out on the water, getting himself some after-work exercise. Maybe blowing off some steam after what his sister had done to him.

There were a lot of rowers out there, even in the early evening, some of them in the longer boats looking as if they belonged to school teams, to the point where sometimes Jack Wolf's boat looked like a solitary flyspeck in the distance. He had been out there awhile. Cantor waited. He really did believe he could teach a master class in waiting.

Seeing how far out Jack was, Cantor was considering a quick ride up the street to the Starbucks he'd passed on his way here when Jenny Wolf showed up, her car screeching to a halt on the other side of the parking lot.

FIFTY-TWO

I WAITED FOR HIM on the dock, having come straight here from our late practice at Hunters Point. I'd hoped that perhaps being on the field with the kids would make me less angry at my brother than I was.

It had not. I had been working up to this confrontation all day, from the time I'd entered the tedious portal for Wolf.com.

Jack pulled himself out of the water and then the scull, which he had on his shoulder when he saw me. He stopped where he was. I walked down to him.

"I can't believe it took you this long to come looking for me," he said.

"I still had *real* jobs to go to."

He laid the long, thin boat down next to him. I pointed to it.

"Shame that somebody couldn't fall out of one of these and drown."

"Where do you want to do this?" he said. "I've got somewhere I need to be."

"Hell?"

Then I added, "Right here is fine. All the privacy we need."

"And if I do mysteriously end up in the water like our father did, I'm pretty sure I can make it safely back to the dock," he said.

He sat down on the dock, cross-legged, and leaned back against the side of the scull. I stood over him, a few feet away. Already feeling the powerful urge to knock the smug look off his face. It was a feeling I'd largely, if not entirely, managed to keep under control our whole lives.

"Just out of curiosity," he said, "which story did you hate more?"

The story about Ryan and Donna Kilgore and me carried the headline GOING TO THE MATTRESS, giving him and Dowd the chance to revisit the story about Ryan Morrissey's coming to my house the night Danny had told him to resign.

"You know Donna Kilgore lied in that first statement," I said. "You know it; Danny knows it; I know it. The *New York Times* eventually blew it out of the water. So did ESPN.com. They treated it like the bullshit that it was."

Jack grinned up at me. "At Wolf.com, we prefer to let the readers, many, *many* of whom don't read the *Times,* decide." He whistled now. "And, oh, man, Sis, have they ever decided. Have you checked out the comments section in the last hour? I thought it would take a while for people to start weighing in. But it's a hotter platform than Reddit. Turns out they can't get enough of you."

"I'd check it out, but I haven't had my shots."

"I actually thought Thomas would be the one to show up," Jack said. "But it's just like it was when we were kids. He's still letting you fight his battles. Thomas never knew our little secret, did he, Jen? How scared you've always been of me."

"You wish."

"Bullshit."

"The bullshitter is you," I said. "You know Thomas doesn't go anywhere near drugs now."

"Do I?" he said in a singsong voice.

"You've done a lot of really lousy things in your life, Jack. But putting him out there as some kind of pusher might be the lousiest."

We had gone at each other like this, often to the delight of our father, for as long as I could remember. But Jack was right about something: there was a part of him that *did* scare me. Even as a kid, I knew he was the meanest one of all of us. I'd never considered Danny a true rival. I'd never thought of him as being smart enough or strong enough to beat me in any kind of fair fight. And even though Thomas and I had had our share of scraps, he'd always been, always would be, my baby brother.

Jack was different. In a way, I thought, Wolf.com was inevitable with him. He had always been a gutter fighter. He would always do anything to win, especially if he was competing with me. One time he'd stolen the start of my science project, and when I complained to my father, he said, "You should have done a better job hiding it."

So nothing had changed, not really. He was still willing to do anything to try to take me down. And when he'd gotten me down, as he'd at least temporarily done today, he was still looking to give me one more good kick to the head.

All in all, Thomas was more right than he knew about wounded wolves.

"Where'd you get the money for this website?" I asked. "I know you're opposed on religious grounds to laying out money of your own."

"Doesn't matter," he said. "What matters is that it's here. I'd originally seen this as being a spin-off from the *Tribune*. So now it's a competitor instead." He shrugged again, more theatrically than before. "And even though you think everything's about you, you had to see that there's a lot more going on on the site than just you and our baby brother."

He glanced at one of those underwater watches that looked as if it could do everything for you except check your cholesterol.

"What's your endgame here, Jack? It can't just be getting the newspaper back."

He closed his eyes and shook his head slowly back and forth.

"There's no end to this game, at least not for you."

"And no bottom for you."

"And in case you haven't noticed by now," Jack said, "this really isn't a game with me."

I looked past him, out at the water. There were still so many boats out there at twilight, set off against the last of the setting sun, the whole scene beautiful and peaceful, reminding me of a painting.

Things were peaceful everywhere except here, with Jack and me. Neither one of us willing to back up or back down.

"By the way?" he said. "If either one of you really is thinking about suing me, you ought to keep in mind that for the ones who *are* doing the suing, discovery can be a bitch."

He stood up now.

"Bitch," he added.

With that I took a step forward and punched him as hard as I could in the face, knocking him into the water.

As soon as I did, I heard a voice I recognized behind me, saying, "Smile."

I turned and saw Seth Dowd pointing his phone at me.

"Still rolling," he said.

FIFTY-THREE

BY THE TIME I got home and went online, I already had the home page of Wolf.com all to myself—the sequence of shots that showed me throwing the right-hander that put Jack in the water running right below the headline:

SUCKER PUNCH

I was beginning to think I should be starting a screenshot scrapbook.

The photos were accompanied by Seth Dowd's breathless first-person account of what had transpired on the dock, somehow making an argument between siblings read like the crime of the century.

I was also the lead story on the *Tribune's* site. I knew that one was coming because Megan had called to give me a heads-up. I was surprised I hadn't heard from her on the ride home from Redwood City.

"If we're going to maintain our credibility," she said, "I can't give you a pass on something like this."

"Wouldn't expect you to. Do what you have to do. I told you the ground rules when I hired you. I'm a big girl."

"With a pretty good right hand," she said. "Reminded me of Ali's daughter when she was still fighting."

"Thanks. I hope you know that means a lot."

"This isn't going to make you feel any better," Megan said, "but you are once again the number one trending topic for the entire city of San Francisco."

Then she asked if I had any comment for the story about Jack and me that would run in the print edition.

"Just one. Here goes: 'My only regret was when I discovered that I hadn't broken my brother's nose.'"

Megan's call had been followed, almost immediately, by one from Thomas.

"I know what you're going to say," I said.

"No, you don't."

"Try me."

"We can't go on like this, Jenny," he said. "And this is coming from someone on your side."

I told him he was right, but we'd talk in the morning. I was talked out for now. "Don't you mean punched out?" he said. Then he asked if I could manage to stay out of any more fights until then. I told him I'd try my hardest and was about to turn off my phone when Ryan Morrissey weighed in, as if the three of them had slotted their calls.

But Ryan actually got a smile out of me.

"We're now in a pretty exclusive club," he said. "Members of the Wolves football organization with first-round knockouts."

"I should have known better."

"Wait," Ryan said, "you mean I *shouldn't* have known better?"

He asked if I wanted him to stop by or meet him somewhere for a beer.

I told him I'd had quite enough photo ops for one night, thank you.

Then he said he'd almost forgotten something and asked if I'd seen the statement from the commissioner.

I told him I had not.

He paraphrased it, saying that the league office was taking both the allegations against Thomas and the ones against Ryan very seriously and that Joel Abrams was authorizing dual investigations involving the Wolves to begin immediately.

"You know who feels as if they're under water right now?" I asked. *"Me."*

The team was leaving for Denver in the morning. I told him I'd try to stop by his office before he left. He asked if it was too soon to start comparing my behavior to Money McGee's. I laughed and cursed him out like a true Wolf and ended the call.

Jack had won today. I'd taken the bait, and that meant I'd lost. And somehow managed, by being a hothead, to make things worse for myself than they already were, if something like that was even possible at this point.

Less than three weeks from the vote by the other owners.

Jenny Wolf, trending again.

Viral again.

Now being investigated by the league. Such a dream. I was about to finally fall into bed when the phone rang one last time, but only because I'd forgotten to turn it off.

Uncle on the screen.

I'd been expecting this one all night.

He got right to it, even though his voice sounded even more hoarse than usual. It was what he did. Another reason why he was who he was, always had been, and always would be. And why I loved him the way I did, in a way I wished I had loved my father.

"Taglia la merda."

Because of him, I knew enough Italian to know exactly what that meant. What he was telling me to cut.

I asked him about his voice, if he was feeling all right. He chuckled but didn't respond. Then he told me to stop talking and listen as he laid out what he thought we had to do going forward—not just at the league meetings in Los Angeles but also even before I got there—if I wanted to hold on to the Wolves.

Finally, he said, "At least there is one good thing to come out of today."

"What's that?"

"We seem to have identified who the real enemy is," he said.

"And who might that be?"

"You, *cara*."

FIFTY-FOUR

IT TOOK UNTIL SUNDAY MORNING, a few hours before the Wolves-Broncos game, to set up the meeting my uncle had referenced when we'd spoken on the phone.

Thomas and me and Bobby Erlich, who ran a crisis management firm that was not just the biggest in San Francisco but also one of the biggest anywhere in the country.

As Erlich said, "You don't say no to your uncle."

"You knew him before this?" Thomas said.

"He did me a favor once," Erlich said.

"I believe everyone owes him some kind of favor except Warren Buffett," I said.

"You sure about Buffett?" Erlich said.

We were on the top floor of the town house at Fisherman's Wharf that he'd turned into his personal office building. I had suggested that all of us meet for breakfast, but Erlich said that it didn't help anybody for me to be seen with him in public, at least for now.

Thomas had spent the beginning of the meeting sounding like Bobby Erlich's advance man. When he finally stopped to take a breath, Erlich smiled.

"I can't lie. Everything your brother just said about me is true."

However old Erlich was, he was trying hard to look younger, like an eternal boy. He was on the smallish side, maybe five foot six. He'd given in to his baldness, I had to give him that, somehow making it look cool. White T-shirt, khakis, white tennis shoes.

"Basically," Thomas said, "Bobby's specialty is getting people out of big shit."

Erlich tried to smile modestly. Missed by a lot.

"I like to think of myself as an emergency-room doctor."

"My situation isn't quite that bad," Jenny said.

Erlich said, "You wouldn't be here if that were true, and neither would I."

"I just need to ride this out."

"You've been trying to ride it out," Erlich said. "How's that working for you so far? The world is starting to think of you as the oldest Kardashian girl when what you really need is for it to see you as a smart, competent *female* CEO who's getting constantly attacked by men."

Thomas said, "It's like they say in AA, Sis. First step toward recovery is admitting you have a problem."

"I don't have a problem! I have older brothers. Big difference."

Erlich looked at my younger brother and said, "And therein lies the problem."

"What Bobby is trying to say," Thomas said, "what we're *both* trying to say, is that you need to stop being Front Page Jenny Wolf."

"Do either of you think that's what I *want* to be?"

Erlich smiled and sipped the Dragonwell green tea he said he had delivered from China. He'd offered some to both Thomas and me. We'd settled for coffee.

"Your brother didn't punch himself into San Francisco Bay," Erlich said, "whether he deserved it or not."

Erlich leaned forward and tented his fingers under his chin.

"I can help you get out of this, Jenny," he said, "but not if you don't stop acting like you're on a sugar high."

"In my defense, may I point out that the Wolves are actually winning these days?"

"Well, enjoy that while you can," Erlich said, "because the way things are going, you're not going to be running the team for much longer. Which is another reason why you have to change the narrative."

"And how do you propose I do that?"

I hadn't wanted to come and was already tired of being there, despite the fact that Erlich was just trying to help. I knew it wasn't his intention, but he was talking to me as if I'd been a very bad girl and needed to be punished. With just a touch of mansplaining thrown in.

He came around his desk and sat on it, legs dangling over the side.

"First you need to apologize," he said.

"To Jack? I'm more likely to walk over to Ghirardelli Square and set myself on fire."

"You're already doing that," Erlich said. "I'm here trying to take the matches away."

Then he asked if I'd please just hear him out. I told him I owed him the courtesy of doing that. Then Bobby Erlich told me how he would craft a statement, making it funny and contrite at the same time, saying that Jenny Wolf now realized she wasn't twelve any longer and couldn't smack her brother every time he hurt her feelings.

After that, he said, anticipation was the key—trying to stay a step ahead, being prepared no matter what Jack or Danny threw at me next, then making a plan and staying with it.

"The big one," he said finally, "is communication, communication, communication. You need to connect with your fan base apart from, and maybe even above, continuing to win football games."

"The team doing that might actually be the easy part," Thomas said.

"For the time being," Erlich said, "the three people in this room are your most important team, the one that's going to put in place what we call a super-injunction in my business."

"You make the media sound like the Supreme Court," I said.

"Actually," Erlich said, "social media is way more powerful than that."

We sat in silence while we let it all settle.

Finally, I said, "I won't do anything that I think makes me look stupid."

"All due respect, Sis? You mean more stupid than slugging Jack in front of a reporter?"

Bobby Erlich took me through the rest of his game plan then, saving the best for last.

"Wait. You think I need that?"

He nodded solemnly.

"And you can make it happen?"

"It's already in the chute," he said. "Time to even up the sides here."

"She'd really do it?"

"She's already agreed," Erlich said. "All we need is for you to say yes."

I hesitated slightly, but only for dramatic effect.

"Hell, yes."

FIFTY-FIVE

THE WOLVES CAME BACK to beat the Broncos in Denver.

I watched the game from home, happy to be alone, feeling the way I did when I'd sit by myself in the stands and wear headphones so I didn't have to talk to anybody and could just enjoy watching the action on the field without a lot of noise around me.

Ted was cleared to start but proceeded to play worse—a lot worse—than he had all year. Ryan had no choice but to pull him in the middle of the third quarter, with the Broncos leading 38–21, and replace him with Billy McGee.

At that point, Billy promptly forgot what year it was, what his rap sheet looked like, the fact that a few weeks ago he was out of football and largely forgotten by most fans. And proceeded to give everybody an all-around performance to remember, finally winning the game for us in the last minute when he scrambled away from a rush and ran the ball into the end zone.

It was all pretty thrilling to watch, especially if you were rooting for the Wolves, as I sure was, occasionally yelling my head off when Money McGee would make another play. There were even times during the last drive when I walked out of the room because I couldn't bear to watch what might happen next.

Ryan called from the bus about ninety minutes after it ended.

"We've got ourselves one of those quarterback controversies that the media and the fans live for."

"I noticed," I said. "But can we wait until you're back to talk about it? I've had enough controversy for one week. Or maybe one lifetime."

"Money's a better quarterback than Ted. By a lot. By, like, so much it's not close."

"You'll figure it out," I said. "Why I pay you the big bucks."

"I thought we were a team."

"Not when it comes to my ex-husband we're not," I said, and told him I'd see him in the morning.

I got ready to watch the Sunday night game then, happy to have no rooting interest whatsoever. It was only five thirty, but after what had just happened in Denver, I decided it was the time of day that Joe Wolf used to call alcohol o'clock and built myself the first martini I'd had in a long time.

I sat down in the living room, put up my feet, and toasted myself.

You really are a celebrity now, I told myself. *You've got your very own high-priced crisis manager.*

I muted the sound, plucked an olive from the cocktail pick, and ate it. Then I asked myself a question I kept trying to shove to the side.

Does winning make everything I'm going through worthwhile?

I followed it up with what I thought was a very solid question:

Am I happier now than I was before the reading of the will, when the only wins and losses I had to worry about involved the Hunters Point Bears?

At least I hadn't had to worry about my high school players this weekend, because we'd had an open Saturday in our schedule. I was glad to have the day off, as much of a safe place as the team and the school and the kids continued to be. And I was secretly relieved that I didn't have to face the kids and answer their questions about slugging my brother until practice on Monday. I constantly stressed to them that they had to keep themselves under control on the field, no matter what the situation, and now I had hauled off and done what I did to my brother because I was the one who'd lost her head.

No matter how hard I tried to clear the image—not just my fist connecting with his face but also turning around and seeing Dowd pointing his phone at me like a gun—I kept going back there. Tomorrow I would hold my nose and formally apologize in public for hitting Jack, as I had promised Bobby Erlich and Thomas I would.

Like a good girl.

It just wouldn't change how good hitting him had felt. No. It had been even better than that. It had felt *awesome* when I'd connected. Why not? He'd been throwing punches at me for weeks.

Only now I was being forced to apologize, as if I were the bad guy in this story. I still wasn't happy about that, even though I knew Bobby Erlich was right.

Screw Jack, I thought now.

Screw him and the little rowboat he rode in on.

Probably the vodka starting to speak up.

It was near halftime of the Sunday night game when Thomas called. I could hear what sounded like a party going on in the background, laughter and loud voices and the occasional shout. I knew he'd invited a bunch of people to his suite at the stadium to watch our game. Maybe he'd decided to keep the party going and have everybody stay around and watch the Sunday night game with him. One more thing that hadn't changed: the more people Thomas had around him, the better he liked it.

"I'm still at the suite," he said.

"I can tell," I said, then told him he had to speak up because I could barely hear him over the fun in the background.

Thomas said he would step outside. Even after he did, he kept his voice low, as if afraid somebody might be listening to him.

"Where are you?"

"Home celebrating," I said. "Was that a win or was that a win?"

"It was all that," Thomas said. "But that's not why I'm calling."

I could hear him tell somebody he'd be right back in.

"I need to see you tonight," he said. Still keeping his voice conspiratorial. "I may have found out why they're so desperate to get rid of us and what's really going on here."

His voice faded out: "...need to talk to somebody."

I knew what cell service could be like at Wolves Stadium.

"Who's *they*, little brother?"

"All of them," he said, his voice not much more than a whisper now. "I'll tell you the rest when I see you."

He still hadn't arrived when the game was over, but that wasn't even slightly unusual with Thomas Wolf. He'd gotten a lot more reliable since rehab. It was why I trusted him enough to make him general manager. But he was still Thomas. Punctuality still wasn't his strong suit. You invited him to dinner at a restaurant at your own peril.

I called and got the same voice mail message as always: "This is Thomas. You called my phone. You know what to do."

Then I promptly lay down on the couch, thinking I would watch some of the highlight shows from a horizontal position, and proceeded to close my eyes and go right to sleep, as if the past few days—or the past month—had finally caught up with me.

It was the doorbell that awakened me. I reached over and found my phone on the coffee table and saw that it was past eleven. *Nice going, Thomas,* I thought. I pulled myself up off the couch and rubbed the sleep out of my eyes, prepared to tell my brother that this was a new record for being late, even for him.

But when I looked through the peephole, it wasn't my kid brother.

It was Ben Cantor standing on my front porch, about to reach for the doorbell again. And even though the image was distorted, I somehow knew, maybe instinctively knew, that this wasn't Cantor the cute guy.

This was Cantor the cop.

When I opened the door he said, "It's about Thomas."

FIFTY-SIX

"THOMAS WOULDN'T KILL HIMSELF," I kept saying to Cantor, when I could get the words out.

We were on my couch. I had collapsed into Cantor's arms when he told me where Thomas's body had been discovered at Wolves Stadium: in the stands below his suite. Back up in the suite, they'd found the syringe and the baggie filled with what they were sure was heroin and an empty bottle of Grey Goose vodka.

The crying was starting and stopping by now; there was no way for me to control it. Cantor had found the whiskey in the kitchen and poured me a glass, and I managed to choke it down. I told him I wanted him to drive me over to the stadium. Cantor said not yet, not when I was like this.

"Like *what*?"

He quietly said, "When you get yourself together enough, I'll take you there. But not until then. Okay?"

"Okay."

I kept shaking my head.

"You're telling me that I'm supposed to believe that he got drunk and shot up and then jumped from up there..."

Now I started to cry again.

"I'm telling you what the scene looks like," Cantor said. Then he said he made it a practice to not jump to conclusions, immediately apologizing for his choice of words.

"Where's his body right now?"

"Where one of the security guys found it," Cantor said. "Field-level box. You know as well as anybody how much of a drop that is."

I drank some whiskey and ran a distracted hand through my hair. I'd gone into the bathroom and stayed there awhile, not caring what a wreck I looked like when I saw myself in the mirror.

Thomas.

My kid brother.

Dead.

At Wolves Stadium.

I started gulping in air again, and Cantor put a hand on my shoulder.

"He was deathly afraid of needles, from the time he was a kid," I said. "If he had to get some kind of shot, he'd make me go to the doctor with him and squeeze his hand, and even then I thought he might pass out."

"I saw the needle marks in his arm myself," Cantor said.

"I don't care if his arm looked like a goddamn pincushion! Are you listening to me? There is no way he would stick a needle in his arm himself!"

"Maybe he had a slip," Cantor said. "Happens. And people can't deal with it afterward."

I let out some air. I didn't want to fight with him. I knew he was trying to help. I was glad he was there.

"He didn't slip. And he didn't fall."

I could feel the tears coming down my cheeks again.

"No," I said, rocking back and forth. "No...no...*no*."

Thomas.

Cantor said, "Had he ever used heroin?"

"Right before he went to rehab," I said. "But he snorted it, the way he used to snort everything else. I always thought it was the heroin that finally got him to go."

I turned to look at Cantor. "He said he was killing himself one party at a time," I said.

"There were no signs that he might go back to using," Cantor said.

"No," I said. "He was *happy*. He was working here. We were working together." I was once again trying to get my breathing under control. I drank more whiskey.

"No," I said again.

"Tell me again what he said when you talked to him."

"He said he'd found out something," I said. "That he needed to talk to somebody before he came over here."

"But not who?"

I shook my head. "Just that he might know why they were coming at us so hard and what was really going on. Something like that."

"But not who 'they' might be."

I shook my head again.

"I checked his phone," Cantor said. "It was in his pocket. The last call he made was to you."

I stood up.

"Give me a minute to clean myself up. Then let's go."

It was like I was the one in some kind of drug-induced state, trying to do what Thomas said he did when he was out of rehab. Put one foot in front of the other. Not a day at a time. One minute at a time.

"What happens to his share of the team now that he's gone,

if you don't mind my asking?" Cantor said. "No chance he would have left it to either of your older brothers, right?"

"Not in ten thousand years."

"I have to ask," Cantor said.

"It goes to me," I said. "If Thomas had outlived me, I was going to do the same for him."

I felt so tired all of a sudden.

"Is it out yet?"

"You know what the goddamn world is like," Cantor said. "Before long everybody will know."

Cantor put a flasher on the dashboard of his car and we drove, fast, through the streets of San Francisco in the night, blowing through one light after another. I was afraid to close my eyes because every time I did there was the image of my brother's body where Cantor said they'd found him. I remembered all the times when he stood in the front row of his suite and talked about how much he loved the view.

From way up here, he'd always say.

We drove through the Port of San Francisco, still going fast. My father had been trying for as long as I could remember, without success, to get a new stadium for the Wolves built in South Bay.

"Tell me what he said again," Cantor said.

I did, trying to remain patient in the retelling, driving a fingernail into the palm of my hand so I wouldn't start crying all over again.

Cantor got a call. I saw him nodding until he finally said, "And Chuck? If anything is disturbed when I get back there, if anybody is around who shouldn't be, it will be your ass."

"First my father . . . ," I said, not even finishing the thought.

There was nothing for Cantor to say to that, so he didn't.

We pulled into the lot, past Thomas's car. Once I'd made

Thomas the general manager, he'd told me he needed a better parking space. Now if he'd parked any closer to the field, he would have been on the fifty yard line.

"When Thomas was a little boy," I said to Cantor, "he thought he could fly."

It just came out of me.

I turned so I was facing Cantor.

"I know I'm his sister. But I'm telling you for the last time that Thomas would never do something like this."

Cantor said, "He didn't."

FIFTY-SEVEN

FOR THE SECOND TIME in a little over a month, there was a funeral at the Cathedral of Saint Mary of the Assumption. It was the Thursday after Thomas died.

The coverage of Thomas's death over the past few days hadn't been as lurid as I'd expected it to be. Somehow Cantor, who had fast-tracked the toxicology report, had managed to keep it out of the media that there had been both alcohol and heroin in Thomas's system when he died. But the world knew about the needle and all about Thomas's drug-filled past, chapter and verse. At least neither Wolf.com nor the *Tribune* had published the pictures of Thomas's broken body draped across two seats in section 115 of Wolves Stadium, which ghouls could easily find on the internet.

I still hadn't said a public word about Thomas, letting the PR department issue a release about how the entire Wolf family and the entire Wolves organization were grieving the tragic loss of Thomas Wolf. I knew people were going to think what they wanted to think, and there wasn't a thing I could do about it. I knew by now that there was nothing better than an easy story, and they thought they had one now.

Former addict goes back to using and kills himself.

One of Thomas's grade-school friends had also told Seth Dowd that Thomas as a boy had thought he could fly, and Dowd, along with everybody else, ran with that for a couple of days.

My mother had said that it would be impossible for her to get through a eulogy for Thomas. She had, she told me, always stayed out of the spotlight even when my father was alive, and that wasn't going to change now. Danny said he didn't want to speak. So there would be two eulogies in addition to the monsignor's. First Jack's, then mine.

I sat next to my mother in the front pew. This week had presented the first opportunity to spend any time with her since Dad died—initially at the house on Jones Street, then at the wake. Now here. Before that, the only time I'd laid eyes on my mother had been when I'd seen John Gallo walking out her front door. It had seemed tremendously important at the time, seeing my father's sworn enemy kissing her hand like some gentleman caller when I knew Gallo was the opposite of that.

She'd asked at the wake why I hadn't been around to see her more.

"I've been busy," I said.

"Too busy for your own mother?" she'd said, fixing me with the same icy glare that she'd always used on all of us, one I was certain she practiced.

"As a matter of fact, yes."

"Have I done something to offend you?"

It almost, but not quite, got a smile out of me.

How much time do you have?

At one point during the mass, she reached over and tried to take my hand. I casually shifted position and moved it away from her.

The church wasn't as packed at it had been for my father. Still, there were only a few empty rows at the very back. Some of the people, I knew, were there out of curiosity, because Thomas was a Wolf and because the family had recently suffered two mysterious deaths. And because of the death-plunge coverage about the boy who thought he could fly.

I looked up as Jack got out of his seat at the end of our row and walked up to the pulpit.

When he got there, he started off by saying, "Brothers fight. You can look it up. It's right there on the first page of the manual. Brothers start to fight when they're kids, and they keep fighting until they're a lot older." He paused and put his head down and looked up.

"They still act like kids no matter how old they are," he continued.

He took a deep breath. I saw that he had no notes with him. But if this was nothing more than an act, if Jack were just playing the part of an older brother in mourning, he was doing a good job of it—at least so far—sounding human for once in his life.

"So Thomas and I fought," he said. "Anyone who knows either one of us, or both of us, knows that's hardly breaking news. But he was my kid brother, and nothing was ever going to change that. In my mind, he was still twelve years old."

He seemed to be staring out to the back of the church, not at any of the faces in front of him.

"Oh, we kept fighting, all right." Jack smiled. "I'm sure you've all been reading about that. But we're Wolfs. It's what you do in our family. Sometimes we'd go at each other as soon as one of our parents finished saying grace."

Another deep breath.

"I went at him, and I went at our father even harder," he

said. "And what kills *me* is that the last thing I remember when they were still here was fighting with both of them."

He stopped then, for what felt like a long time. Then he shook his head and held up his hands as if surrendering to the moment and started to cry before he walked down from the podium, taking his seat and staring straight ahead.

If it *had* been an act, I thought, it was some acting job, even for him.

My turn then.

I thought about starting with a joke as I made my way past Jack, saying that I wanted to apologize to Monsignor Galardi in advance, but that seeing my brother Jack cry had to mean that hell had likely just frozen over.

But then I read the room and stopped myself.

I took my own deep breath and looked out at the congregation, fixing my eyes on the place in the middle of the cathedral where the Hunters Point Bears all sat. For some reason I started to think of the trip to the cemetery the family would be making once the mass was over. Thomas would be buried next to our father.

It would be the closest the two of them had been in years.

I saw Cantor standing in the back of the church. When I caught his eye, he nodded at me. In front of him, in the last row, I saw John Gallo, that sonofabitch, sitting alone.

"My brother Thomas was the best of us," I said. "He was the best of all of us, and the toughest person I've ever known."

Don't stop.

Just keep going.

"I loved his heart," I continued. "I loved his sense of humor, and his charm, and all the fun he had in him."

And don't you cry.

"And I loved his loyalty. Nobody knows better than I do that Thomas Wolf was foxhole loyal until the night he died."

I stared down at my hands.

"But the best thing about Thomas, at least for me, was that he always told the truth—about himself and everybody else. So the only way I can properly honor him and his memory today is by telling the absolute God's honest truth about him."

I looked all the way down to Ben Cantor, who nodded at me again.

"My brother didn't kill himself," I said.

FIFTY-EIGHT

I'D ALWAYS HEARD PEOPLE in sports saying that when their own lives seemed to have gone completely off the rails, it really was the games that kept them sane. I wasn't so sure about the sane part right now, at least for me. But being back on the field with the kids, against a St. Francis team that was far and away the best these players had faced all season, made the world feel at least a little bit like the one I desperately wanted it to be.

The one that had Thomas still in it just a few days ago.

The game came down to the last minute, St. Francis ahead 13–12. But we had the ball and were driving down the field with enough time left to win.

Finally, it was fourth down at St. Francis's twenty yard line. Thirty seconds left. Chris Tinelli, our quarterback, called our last time-out and came walking toward me.

I was deeply into the game by now, nearly lost in it, coaching as hard as I'd ever coached these kids. I wanted them to win so badly. But in this moment, I wanted *me* to win just as much.

Maybe more.

"Hey," I heard from behind me.

I turned and saw Ryan Morrissey standing behind our bench, Wolves hat pulled down tight over his head.

"Shouldn't you be coaching your own team?"

He pointed past me, and I saw that Chris had finally gotten to the sideline.

"Shouldn't you be coaching yours?" he said.

"Got a play for me?"

"Nah," he said. "You'll figure something out."

"Thanks a bunch."

We needed eight yards. If we didn't get them and keep the drive going, this would be our first loss of the season. Even if we did get the first down, we still might have only a couple of plays after that to try to win the game.

"What are we doing, Coach?" Chris said.

And then I smiled, hearing a familiar voice inside my head.

Thomas's.

When we'd watch a game together, and there would be a moment like this, he'd always say the same thing:

Throw the damn money on the table.

"Something funny?" Chris said.

I said, "Just to me," and then told him the play I wanted him to run.

"Seriously?"

I told him I was serious but not too serious—it was just football. Not life and death.

He smiled at me and put his helmet back on and ran to the huddle and told his teammates the play they were about to run. Then he took the snap and rolled to his right, blockers in front of him, a lot of them, and made the defense think he might run for the first down.

But at the last second, he stopped and threw the ball all the way across to the other side of the field, to where Davontae Lillis was wide open in the left corner of the end zone.

And when Davontae caught the ball, it meant that the Bears had won again.

While the kids were still on the field, I went and sat by myself on our bench until I felt a tap on my shoulder and saw Ryan grinning down at me.

I looked up to the sky then and said, "Thanks."

"I didn't do anything," he said.

"Wasn't talking to you."

FIFTY-NINE

JOHN GALLO WAS IN another private room, this one at Original Joe's, an old-school San Francisco steak house on Union Street. The room was quite narrow, with a long table stretching the length of it, ending with JOE'S written in script behind the place where Gallo sat.

Jack knew this was where Gallo came to eat most Saturday nights, sometimes with guests. Jack had been one of the invited guests a few times. Sometimes Gallo came here alone and ate at this same long table.

"I am not one of those people," Gallo had told Jack once, "who thinks that having a good steak is a criminal offense."

When he looked up and saw the manager escorting Jack in, Gallo did not seem surprised or upset.

"Should I have another place set?" he said.

In front of him were a small bowl of olives and a basket that Jack knew was filled with fresh bread made just for Gallo. He also knew that the glass of Chianti in front of John Gallo came from a bottle that cost two hundred dollars—at least.

Gallo motioned for Jack to sit next to him.

"Would you care for a glass of wine?" Gallo said.

"I won't be staying long," Jack said.

"You'll drink."

"As you wish."

"How's my friend Danny taking all this?" Gallo said. "He seems so fragile sometimes."

"I was just with him," Jack said. "He's doing about as well as any of us are."

"Brotherly love," Gallo said. "Such a beautiful thing to behold."

A waiter appeared with another wineglass, set it down in front of Jack, and poured. When the waiter was gone, Gallo raised a glass.

"To Thomas," Gallo said. "Gone far too soon."

He drank. Jack reluctantly drank along with him.

"You heard what my sister said at the church the other day," Jack said to him. "She believes he was murdered."

"She is a stubborn and headstrong woman," Gallo said, "allowed to believe what she wants to believe."

Jack looked at him.

"Did you have anything to do with his death?" he said to Gallo.

Gallo didn't hesitate.

"Did *you*?" he asked Jack.

"That's a bullshit question, and you know it."

"I'm not sure I appreciate your tone," Gallo said.

"I don't appreciate the idea that somebody might have thrown my kid brother out a goddamn window."

"*If* somebody threw him out a window," Gallo said, "I can swear on my own children that I had nothing to do with it."

They stared at each other.

"None of this was ever supposed to go this far," Jack said.

Gallo smiled, sipped more wine, then picked up his napkin and dabbed at the corners of his mouth. When he put his glass down, he leaned across the table so that his face was only a foot or so from Jack's.

His voice was suddenly harsh, as if made of razor blades.

"As if you worried about what might or might not happen to your youngest brother when he was alive, you pretentious shit," Gallo said. "As if you expect me to believe those crocodile tears you shed at the church."

"You were the one who told me to run the story about Thomas and the dead player and the drugs," Jack said.

"And what's worse, Jack, if you don't mind me asking?" Gallo said. "My wanting that, or your running a story that made your own brother look like some kind of pusher?"

"As if I had a choice."

"There are always choices," Gallo said. "You made a stupid one when you began an affair with your father's second wife."

Jack looked at him.

"You know about that?"

"A better question," Gallo said, "is what *don't* I know about you." Gallo shook his head, an almost pitying look on his face. "I don't care why you started up with her in the first place. But you need to end it."

"I thought I might be able to use her somehow," Jack said. "I think she looked at me the same way."

"The scandals are supposed to be about your sister, not you," Gallo said. "Don't give her something she might use against you by acting like a horny adolescent."

He leaned back.

"I understand," Jack said. "This is all supposed to be about Jenny. It was never supposed to be about Thomas."

"Keep it that way," Gallo said.

The waiter poked his head in at the other end of the room. Gallo shook his head. The door closed.

"Perhaps," Gallo said, "and I'm only speaking theoretically, of course, Thomas ended up getting in the way of something much bigger than he was. And interfering with business that was not his own."

Gallo made a helpless gesture with his hands, a slight shrug of his shoulders. Jack didn't feel as if he were seeing him for the first time as he really was. Jack had always known who, and what, Gallo really was, the way he had always known those same things about himself. And about his father before him.

But the difference between him and his father, Jack knew, was that his father would never have gotten into bed with John Gallo, no matter what the stakes or possible rewards.

So Jack wasn't seeing Gallo for the first time. Just more in focus than ever before. As if the real alpha wolf was sitting across the table from him.

"*Do* you know anything about how Thomas died?"

"You really came here to ask me *that*?" Gallo said.

"Do you?"

Gallo paused.

"I'm no good and can prove it," he said. "And I have done many things of which I am not proud. But I am not a murderer."

Jack started to say something. Gallo put up a hand to stop him.

"I probably should be insulted by your accusation," he said. "But I am not. Most likely it is your grief about your brother talking. But what I will tell you now is that I want you to leave this room before you insult me further and say something that will only get you into much deeper trouble with me than you already are."

The waiter appeared with Gallo's food now, a huge fillet with mashed potatoes and green beans. He set it down in front of

Gallo. Gallo cut off a small piece of steak, washed it down with wine, then made a kissing motion with his fingers before the waiter once again left.

He's not just playing the part of an old boss, Jack thought. *He is an old boss.*

Capable of anything.

Including murder.

"What do we do now?" Jack said.

"We proceed as if nothing has changed," Gallo said, and smiled again.

Jack stood. He knew he had been dismissed without Gallo saying he had.

"You know, Jack," Gallo said, "we have discovered recently what a random place the world can be. Imagine what an unspeakable tragedy it would be for your beautiful mother if something else happened to one of her other children with all of us this close to getting what we want."

Another small shrug.

"Or even if something happened to her," Gallo said.

"Even you're not capable of that," Jack said.

"Perhaps so," Gallo said. "But that doesn't mean I don't have associates who are."

Now he stood, and it was as if his voice rose up along with him, filling the small room, as he pointed a finger at Jack.

"Now find a way to finish your sister once and for all."

SIXTY

AFTER THE HUNTERS POINT game against St. Francis, Ryan Morrissey had walked me to my car—and then asked me to dinner. It was the first time he'd asked since I'd given him the job.

I'd thanked him but told him no, that I'd already made other plans.

"Am I allowed to ask with whom?" he'd said.

"As a matter of fact, you're not."

"He actually asked you that?" Detective Ben Cantor said to me now.

"He did."

"And here I thought the two of you were practically a couple," Cantor said.

"Don't believe everything you read."

"I still can't believe you said yes to me when I asked," Cantor said.

"To tell you the truth, Detective, I can't believe you *did* ask."

He had picked the place, Fogata, a few blocks from his house, in Potrero Hill. It was a bit of a dive, Cantor said, but had great food, and it wasn't the kind of place where we had to worry about the paparazzi staking us out.

Right before I left my own house, Cantor called and said there was still time for me to change my mind. If I wanted to be alone tonight, he'd totally understand.

I told him I wanted a margarita and wanted it now and don't try to get out of it.

"Are you still happy with the way I delivered my bombshell at the church about Thomas not killing himself?" I said at our table, in the back.

"You did it like a pro," Cantor said. "It produced a headline I think helps you for a change."

"Helps us, you mean."

"Either way," Cantor said. "Let people worry about what you might know."

"What *we* might know."

He grinned. "Either way," he said again, and drank some margarita as I did the same.

"You changed the narrative," Cantor said, "from why did Thomas do it to who might have done it to him."

Nothing he found at the suite that night had changed his mind. Cantor told me that he had the ability to lift finger-prints at a crime scene and even have them run through the system. Only there were no fingerprints on the railing from which Thomas would have had to jump. No fingerprints and no prints from the bottom of his shoes, if he'd stood on the railing.

"Unless he really did think he could fly," Cantor told her again, "someone drugged him and then threw him *over* the railing. On top of all that, there were no prints on the vodka bottle, which meant that somebody wiped it clean."

"But you said those were Thomas's prints on the syringe."

"Yeah. Like I told you that night, those did belong to your brother. But I am still of the opinion that he was unconscious before he went over the railing. I still believe that they stuck him and poured vodka down his throat."

I suddenly thought I might need more than one margarita tonight.

"If you're right..."

"I am right."

"...somebody did that to the nicest one of all of us."

"And went to a lot of trouble to make it look like a suicide," Cantor said. "Maybe they didn't want it to look like another potential murder in the family this close to your father getting tossed."

"You're convinced my father *did* get tossed?"

"Aren't you?"

"All over a football team," I said. "And a failing newspaper. But mostly the football team."

"Not even three dozen of them in existence," Cantor said.

"But it's got to be about more than just the team, for somebody to do this to my brother."

"Somebody who doesn't give a rip if there's a run of Wolfs dying these days."

He licked some salt around the rim of his glass, tasted it, smacked his lips. Then he was staring at me with those big, deep, dark eyes. I finally took a bit of rice and beans just to have a reason to look away.

Is he hitting on me?

Or am I hitting on him?

Good questions both.

I wondered if he thought something happening between the two of us was as bad an idea as I did, and not just because it was a couple of days after Thomas's funeral. What kind of circle of life was that?

I knew the answer to that. It had hardly anything to do with the circle of life and practically everything to do with my not wanting to spend one more night alone in the house. And if Ben Cantor hadn't asked me out, I would have been having dinner somewhere else with Ryan Morrissey.

"I'm sorry," I said. "What were you saying?"

"Was once again wondering out loud if one of your brothers or both of them might have had something to do with it."

"We've gone over this. Is Jack capable of it? I think he's capable of a lot, but maybe not that. And I think Danny is too much of a coward. But *could* one of them have been involved? We'd both have to be nuts to rule out the possibility."

I was trying to pace myself with my drink. I was driving. Thomas had joked before he died about getting another DUI. This would be a lousy time for me to get my first.

"Let's talk about something else," I said to Cantor.

"What shall we talk about? The crash of the crypto market?"

He smiled then. The smile, which continued to be a pretty impressive smile, went quite nicely with his eyes.

Like some kind of matched set.

"Holy shit!" I said, slapping my forehead. "Crypto went south? Now I'm really screwed."

Cantor laughed. Somehow, after one of the worst days of recorded worst days, I laughed along with him. I kept telling myself this wasn't a real date. But it suddenly felt like one.

"I didn't even trust you when I first met you."

"I tend to bring that out in people," Cantor said. "But now you're stuck with me, because other than your coach, I seem to be all the backup you've got these days." He smiled again. "Other than an undefeated high school football team."

"And my very own crisis manager."

"Forgot about him," Cantor said.

He ate some burrito, then reached over and forked some of

my enchilada. The food was every bit as good as he'd said it was going to be.

"I've been meaning to ask you and keep forgetting, just because of everything going on," he said. "But why are you still coaching?"

"Because I don't quit."

"This has to be about more than football with you," he said.

"No shit, Sherlock."

SIXTY-ONE

BEN CANTOR DIDN'T FEEL like any kind of ace detective at the moment.

No shit, Sherlock, she'd joked from her side of the small table.

It was like he told her: he *couldn't* believe she'd agreed to go out with him, especially after she said she'd turned down an invitation from her coach.

Maybe she was just blowing smoke at him. But he didn't think she was the type. Cantor had known a lot of women in his life, been *with* a lot of women. Been married, divorced, and nearly married again. Jenny Wolf was the most right-there, up-front woman he'd ever met. Sometimes he'd forget, but only for a couple of minutes at a time, that she owned the football team in town. And one of the newspapers.

For the life of him he couldn't come up with a good reason why the two of them being here like this was a good idea, and not just because he felt out of his league. And that didn't mean the National Football League.

He still couldn't escape how attracted he was to her, how attracted to her he'd been from the start, even when he was treating her like a suspect, talking about what a star swimmer she'd been. She'd asked him, before the margaritas were delivered tonight, why he had *stopped* looking at her as a suspect.

"Unless your phone went to Sausalito for dinner that night, like you said you did, and you went to the boat without it, you couldn't have been in two places at once."

"You went in and checked my *phone* records?"

He gave her a little salute. "Just doing my job, ma'am."

"Don't 'ma'am' me."

He hoped now that she couldn't tell he kept searching for reasons to look away when she was staring at him across the table.

"I wasn't expecting to have this good a time," Jenny said.

"Stop," Cantor said, "before you make me blush."

"You know what I'm trying to say."

"Yeah, actually, I do."

They were walking back to his old Victorian house on 18th Street by now, where she'd left her car. Before dinner, he'd asked her if she wanted to come in for a drink, but she'd said she was saving herself for her first margarita.

Jenny asked now why so many of the cross streets in the area were named after states. Texas. Missouri. Mississippi. Like that. Cantor said he happened to know the answer: it had all started before California became a state and a guy named Dr. John Townsend was mayor of San Francisco.

"Townsend saw this as an intersection of Mexican California and the United States," he said. "So naming the streets after states was another way of kissing up to the government."

"Why in the world do you know that?"

"Just a naturally curious guy."

They made the turn off Mississippi, and there was his house. And her car parked in the driveway.

"I'm glad we did this," Jenny Wolf said.

"Same."

"Please find out who did this to my brother."

"What about your father?"

"Thomas first."

Cantor said, "You're good at what you do. I'm good at what I do."

Somehow they were close to each other.

"You want to come in?" Cantor said.

SIXTY-TWO

I SAT BY MYSELF in the stands on Sunday to watch the Rams game.

I'd asked Cantor to join me, but he said he had work of his own to do, as he kept trying to compile as complete a list as he could of Thomas's guests and the waitstaff who were in the suite one week ago and interview them one by one.

Even after a week, Thomas's suite was still considered a crime scene. My brother. The general manager of the Wolves. His suite. Crime scene.

"He had a lot of friends," Cantor had said to me the night before.

"Nobody had more friends than Thomas did," I'd said. "Some of them were even real friends."

There was a moment of silence for Thomas before the game. I saw his smiling face on the giant screens above the end zones and started to cry all over again. All of a sudden, the Wolves were leading the league in moments of silence.

After that the Wolves proceeded to play their worst game of the season, as our winning streak—and mine—came to an end. Against what he said was his own better judgment, Ryan had decided to start Ted Skyler at quarterback. It took one quarter for that decision to turn into a complete disaster. Ted fumbled once. In our next series, he threw an interception that was returned for a touchdown. Then he threw another inter-ception. By the end of the quarter, we were losing 21–0.

Even Money McGee couldn't bring us all the way back this time. At halftime, I'd left my seat and taken the elevator up-stairs and sat in my office alone and watched the rest of the game on television.

At least for a few hours today, I wasn't a grieving sister. I turned my brain back on and went back to being a boss. At that moment an extremely pissed-off boss. But even that was a relief, a way to not continue to obsess about Thomas.

I was still in my office forty-five minutes after the game had ended when my ex-husband came storming in.

"Do you and your boyfriend think I'm going to continue to let you humiliate me this way after everything I've done for this franchise?"

"Lower your voice," I said.

"Or what?"

"And you know he's not my boyfriend, Ted."

"Just your hero. The Mike Tyson of football coaches."

"You want to sit down and calm down?" I said. "Or just keep shouting at me?"

"This won't take long."

At least there's some good news today.

"Have you spoken to Ryan about this?" I said.

"I've got nothing to say to him."

"He's your coach."

"No, honey," Ted said. "He's *your* coach."

Honey.

The last person to call me that had been our former coach, downstairs in what was now Ryan Morrissey's office, right before I fired him.

"Our coach."

"You two have been setting me up for a fall since you signed that junkie," Ted said. "Or maybe it was your brother—he always had a soft spot for junkies."

"For your own good, Ted, don't say another word about Thomas. Not another goddamn word. And by the way? Are you under the impression that those interceptions threw themselves today?"

"They weren't my fault."

"In your mind, they never are."

"Nobody blocks on this team."

I didn't want to be in my office now. I didn't want to be having this conversation. I didn't want to be at the stadium any longer, not today. Mostly I didn't want to be just down the hall from Thomas's suite.

"They seem to block well enough for Billy McGee," I said quietly.

"You rotten bitch."

And there it was.

"What happened to 'honey'?"

He walked over and put his bruised hands on my desk and leaned as far across it as he could.

At least he finally lowered his voice.

"I know a lot about you, Jen. Stuff that you wouldn't want the people voting for you to know in a million years."

"Are you threatening me, Ted?"

"Think of this as more of a warning."

"Are we done here? Because I'm so hoping we're done here."

"Just for now."

He slammed the door behind him when he left. I sat where I was for a few moments before I called down to Ryan's office and told him what had just happened in mine.

"What are we going to do?" he said.

"Cut him."

SIXTY-THREE

IT HAD TAKEN ONE DECISION, the Wolves releasing my ex-husband, to turn me back into Front Page Jenny—as Bobby Erlich had referred to me—all over again. Even as I couldn't help wishing that the end of my marriage to Ted Skyler had been as easy.

The next day Wolf.com led with:

WHO'S AFRAID OF JENNY WOLF?
(Spoiler Alert: Her Ex-Hubby)

I wasn't treated all that much better in the *Tribune,* where they went with BIG BAD WOLF above an old photograph of Ted and me, from better times, made to look as if it had been torn in two.

The Wolves won the next Sunday, but the story was swallowed up, all over the country, by the story about my releasing the greatest quarterback in Wolves history, the one my father used to say was his all-time favorite player even after he allowed him to marry his only daughter.

Ted had been on a nonstop media tour since he'd gotten the word from Ryan. His boilerplate response to what had happened was this: "She finally got even with me for dumping her." He knew it was the other way around, and I knew it was the other way around—I was the one who'd decided to end our marriage—but it didn't seem to matter.

Now it was Sunday night. I had used some of Joe Wolf's money to hire a private plane to fly me down to Montecito after our game and was now seated in the living room of Bobby Erlich's lavish second home there. The league meetings would begin in LA on Monday. I'd get to address the owners on Tuesday, after my brother Danny did. I hadn't invited him. The other owners had.

The vote would be on Wednesday.

It meant that by Wednesday night I'd be either still running the Wolves or out of business. The only football team I would be running at that point would be the Hunters Point Bears.

Bobby Erlich had been doing most of the talking, but then he always did, continuing to express his extreme displeasure about what I'd done to Ted without consulting him first.

His theme, all week long, had been consistent: after Thomas's death I had public sentiment firmly on my side and was riding a wave of sympathy, and then I proceeded to throw it away with both hands.

"You just wouldn't let me do my job," he said now, "because you were too interested in doing him. Or undoing him." He sighed. "What*ever.*"

"He would have ripped our team apart once Ryan benched him for good," I said, trying to remain patient, because I knew he genuinely wanted to help, even as he was charging me what he was charging me. "Forget that I was married to that idiot. I've seen it happen to other teams, and I wasn't going to let it happen to ours."

"So that's your story, and you're sticking to it," Erlich said. "It was strictly a football decision."

"Mostly. I'd be lying if I didn't factor in the fact that he *is* a raging, self-absorbed, over-the-hill moron."

"Yeah," Bobby Erlich said. "He must be the only one of those in all of professional sports."

Erlich was even more a bundle of nervous energy than usual tonight because of what was about to happen in half an hour, because of where we were about to go. The person we were about to meet.

"To borrow an expression from football," he said, "and from your faith, it's Hail Mary time."

"It probably was from the start."

His housekeeper brought us more herbal tea. Erlich said he drank this particular brand because of its calming effect on him. I told him it wasn't working tonight.

"Jokes," he said. "You're killing me and my reputation, and it's jokes I get."

He came and sat next to me on the couch.

"You don't have the votes—you're aware of that, right?"

"More like something I intuited."

"We need to turn this thing around."

"Why I'm here," I said. Then I sighed. "But maybe even this won't be enough. Maybe nothing was going to be once I started getting jumped in the media every other day."

"I don't like to lose," he said.

"It's my experience that hardly anybody does."

"It's why you need to kill it in this interview. Kill. It. You've got to come across as a competent woman that powerful men won't allow to succeed. Then let her do the rest."

"Gonna try to be a team player." I grinned. "Finally."

"We have to regroup now and go back and build on the

231

eulogy," Bobby Erlich said. "I was just getting ready to use that big-time when you looked at your ex and did the *Apprentice* thing and told him he was fired."

"I'm glad you find my brother dying useful, Bobby. It would have been tragic if his death had gone to waste."

"That didn't come out right," he said. "But you knew who I was when you and Thomas hired me."

He smiled helplessly.

"I am who I am."

He stood up then.

"You ready to do this?"

"As ready as I ever could be. Not like it was something I studied at Stanford."

We got into his Porsche and made the short ride across town to the studio.

She was waiting for us outside.

"Hi," she said, smiling and extending her hand to me. "I'm Oprah."

SIXTY-FOUR

CANTOR COULDN'T BELIEVE IT when Jenny called to tell him where she was and who she was with and what she was about to do in Montecito.

"You never felt the urge to give me a heads-up that this might happen?" Cantor said.

By now they were talking on the phone most nights. Even though the closest they'd come to being a real couple was when they'd kissed in front of his house the night they'd had dinner at Fogata, before she got into her car and drove off.

"I didn't believe this was going to happen until it was actually happening," Jenny said.

"Now the Wolfs have really turned into a royal family," Cantor said.

"Except ours is even more messed up than theirs is," she said, and told him she would call when the interview was, mercifully, over.

He went back to his notes then, and his notebooks, spread out in front of him on the kitchen table. Two murders. Father and son. Looking for common denominators *other* than the two of them being related. One man, he was certain, had been thrown over the side of a boat. The other man, Cantor was even more certain, had been thrown out the open window of a suite, his own, at Wolves Stadium as part of a staged event.

Ben Cantor did not believe in coincidence. No good detective did. Two members of the family, what he'd just called the royal family of football in San Francisco, dying like this, this close together—well, what were the odds of *that*, Detective Cantor?

He'd told Jenny he'd find out what happened to her brother. But Cantor never lost sight of the fact that he'd come into this because of her father, who, he knew, had plenty of enemies. All guys like Joe Wolf made enemies. Cantor was still trying to figure out if the most dangerous enemies of all were in Wolf's own family.

He opened the notebook closest to him. Found his notes on a conversation—a bombshell one at that—he'd had just that afternoon with a guy named Patrick Tate, one of Thomas Wolf's childhood friends, who'd been with him in the suite the night Thomas died. An old drinking and drugging buddy who told Cantor that he was another one who'd finally taken what he called "the cure."

Tate had talked about how geeked up Thomas had been that night, more antic than he'd been since rehab, but Tate had just written it off to the Wolves coming back and winning the game the way they had.

Before they'd finished the interview, Tate had said he wanted to ask Cantor a question.

"You find out who offed Joe yet?"

Cantor told him he was still working on it.

"Thomas hated him *so* much," Tate said. "You know that, right? It doesn't make any difference to either one of them now, obviously, but he told me one time, back when we were in high school, that he fantasized about throwing his father off the Golden Gate Bridge."

"The father must have treated him pretty badly," Cantor said.

"The way he treated everybody, far as I could ever tell," Tate said. "I figured Thomas just let all that anger go finally. Part of his getting the cure. The 'let go and let God' thing from the program. But he always used to say that he wished the world knew what a criminal his father was."

"Kindly old Joe Wolf?" Cantor said.

"Thomas even told me one night when we were partying pretty hard that he thought his father was the one capable of murder if it meant finally getting full control of the team," Tate said. "You know, getting the other half from the original Tommy Wolf. Thomas's uncle."

"He died in a car accident," Cantor said.

"Thomas never mentioned it again," Tate said. "Hey, it was probably the vodka talking that night. But he sure didn't seem convinced it had been an accident."

SIXTY-FIVE

THE NFL OWNERS AND Commissioner Joel Abrams and most of his New York staff had taken up residence in the Beverly Wilshire Hotel, just off Rodeo Drive, for the league meetings.

Jenny Wolf was staying there. So was Danny Wolf, simply because in the eyes of the league he still had as much standing with the other owners as his sister did, if not more.

John Gallo had taken a suite at the Four Seasons. His plane had landed at Burbank Airport an hour ago, and he had called Danny from his limousine and told him to be waiting for him at the Four Seasons when he got there—he had already checked in.

Now he and Gallo were in the living area of his suite. Danny felt as if he'd been called to the principal's office, as if he'd gotten caught smoking in the boys' room.

"How could you possibly not have known about the Oprah interview?" Gallo said.

"No one knew about it until they released a few clips from it this morning," Danny said. "They kept the whole thing buttoned up."

He had seen Gallo angry plenty of times before, at him and

at Jack, especially when the subject was Jenny. Danny thought Gallo liked going at him the most, maybe because he knew Danny would take it. It was different with Jack. Jack would at least make a show of standing up to Gallo, pushing back, if not for very long, just to reaffirm that he didn't take shit from anybody, even though both Jack and Danny knew they were basically both making a career out of doing just that with John Gallo now.

"You and your brother assured me you were on top of this," Gallo said. "The last thing I said to your brother was that it was time to finish her."

Danny started to speak.

"Shut up and listen," Gallo said. "I'd like for you to ask your brother the next time the two of you speak if he's under the impression that a prime-time interview with Oprah Winfrey is his idea of finishing her. I'd very much like to know the answer to that question."

Danny wanted to tell Gallo to ask Jack himself. But he didn't.

By now he knew that Gallo prided himself on not raising his voice, as if doing that would be a show of weakness. But he was raising it now.

"You know how this is going to play out!" Gallo snapped at him. "Oprah will make your sister seem more sympathetic than that actress the prince married!"

"May I speak?" Danny said.

"By all means."

"I have been talking to the other owners since I got here," he said. "I spoke to at least a dozen today. I'm telling you that she doesn't have the votes. She may think Oprah can drag her across the goal line. But I'm telling you, it can't happen. This is all about the numbers now."

Gallo offered a thin smile. It was a gesture that always made Danny feel as if he were being knifed.

"You're *telling* me," he said, clearly mimicking Danny.

He makes my father, Danny thought, *seem more lovable than Oprah.*

"Are you suggesting that this interview isn't going to change any minds?" Gallo said. "Or any votes?"

"It's a goddamn television interview," Danny said, "not a presidential address!"

Suddenly he was shouting, too.

Gallo stared at him.

"Conducted by a powerful and influential woman who most people probably like *more* than the president," Gallo said.

"You don't even know what she's going to say."

Danny knew it sounded as if he were whining, probably because he was.

"You occasionally come across as a bright boy, Daniel. So see if you can figure out how your fellow owners might react if they get the idea that Oprah might begin to think badly of them—and that she might tell all the people who hang on her every word that she thinks badly of them."

"This vote is just business," Danny said.

"Precisely," Gallo said. "And they may very well make the determination that it's bad for business if a group largely comprising wealthy and powerful men comes across as bullying poor Jenny Wolf."

There was something else going on here today with John Gallo besides his obvious anger and frustration about the interview. Danny found himself wondering what it took to make Gallo afraid.

But of what?

Or of whom?

"She doesn't have the votes. I'll be back running the team by next Sunday's game."

The house phone next to Gallo rang. He picked it up, listened, said, "Tell him to come up," then put the phone back down.

"I have another appointment," he said to Danny. "Now, you get back over to *your* hotel and get your ass back to work."

Talking to Danny like he wanted him to go pick up his shirts.

Danny was in the elevator, the doors about to close, when he saw someone he thought he recognized step out of the next elevator bank.

Danny waited until the little guy passed by him, then he poked his head out and watched him walk down the hall and knock on Gallo's door.

"Mr. Gallo," the guy said.

"Well, well, well," Danny heard John Gallo say. "The famous Bobby Erlich."

SIXTY-SIX

THE INTERVIEW WITH OPRAH was scheduled for eight Eastern time and would run three hours later on the West Coast.

I was scheduled to have a drink in the bar downstairs with Bobby Erlich around six o'clock, right before the owners' reception, but he had called to say he was running late and might not show up at all.

"It's Hollywood, baby!" he said, as if that were all the explanation he needed. "It's when I turn into Bobby Erlich on steroids!"

The Oprah people had just sent me the link to the interview, which I was about to watch on my laptop. I remembered the one she'd done with Prince Harry and Meghan Markle a couple of years ago, remembered watching along with everybody else in America that night. Only now I was the one sitting across from her in a huge house overlooking the ocean that her people had rented for the occasion, the backyard behind us seeming bigger than the field at Wolves Stadium.

"Go big or go home," Oprah had said when we'd arrived and I'd been properly blown away by the house and the view.

Oprah got me to open up about my difficult relationship with my father and how I'd walked away from him and the family. She asked me about Jack and Danny, and I told her that my relationship with them now hadn't changed much since our growing-up years. I managed to hold it together, barely, when she asked about Thomas.

Fun shots of me coaching the Hunters Point Bears lifted the mood.

"You can take the girl out of football," I said, shrugging. "But I discovered that you can't take football out of the girl."

Oprah didn't pull any punches or go easy on me. She'd let me know going in that no subject was off-limits. She asked about Ted and the decision to release him from the Wolves, joking that since I was the one who'd filed for divorce, it was technically the second time I'd fired him. She wanted to know if I was motivated by business or vindictiveness.

I asked her if she'd ask a man that question. She smiled an Oprah smile and let out a shriek and said, "You got me!"

Then she focused on my trying to punch Jack Wolf's lights out.

"Gotta ask. Did it feel good?"

"Soooo good."

"But wasn't it a dumb thing to do?" she said.

"Soooo dumb."

She asked all the right questions, but then I knew she would. She asked why I thought my brothers had turned on me the way they did.

"It wasn't really a turn. They're right where they always were when I had something they wanted."

Near the end, she wanted to know why I'd put myself through this for a team I'd previously wanted no part of and from which I had walked away, planning never to return.

"Because it was essentially my father's dying wish that I run it."

"And he must have thought you could handle the job," she said.

I smiled.

"Maybe there's another way of looking at it, just in light of everything that's happened since I *took* the job," I said. "Maybe this was Dad's way of punishing me for walking away from him the way I did."

One of the last shots was of Oprah and me walking and talking down on the beach, standard stuff for a show like this. We were both miked up, the ocean behind us.

"What's your message to people who have read and heard about you before this," Oprah said, "but are only getting to know you tonight?"

"I'd ask them to evaluate how I've done the job since I started calling the shots," I said. "That's all that should matter in the end. How have I done my job, and how have the coaches and players done theirs? Everything else is just noise."

"How many games have the Wolves lost since you truly took over?" Oprah said, fully aware of the answer.

"One."

"Wasn't it Bill Parcells who said that you are what your record says you are?" Oprah said.

"Pretty sure it was."

"One last question. Do you think you'd be getting this kind of coverage and this kind of pushback if you were a man?"

I smiled again.

"Let me turn this around and ask Oprah Winfrey a question. What do you think?"

The ending was Oprah alone, staring into the camera.

"Jenny Wolf is every talented woman who has found herself

getting tackled from behind," she said. "But look at how she's turned the Wolves around. Look at the way her team *has* responded to her."

Dramatic pause then.

"So if she does get voted down this week in Los Angeles, I guess we all need to ask ourselves what the other owners are afraid of," Oprah said. "Besides a strong woman."

I closed the laptop and poured myself a small glass of white wine, the bottle having been sent up by the hotel when I checked in. It was five thirty by now, which meant that the first half of the Oprah interview had already aired back East. I had no interest in checking the internet to see how people were reacting.

I knew I might win over a big chunk of viewers tonight. Maybe even a majority of the viewers. But they weren't voting on Wednesday. My target audience was the thirty-one other NFL owners, the same audience I'd be addressing in one of the Wilshire ballrooms tomorrow morning. But most of them, I was afraid, because of everything I'd been hearing for weeks, had already made up their minds about me.

I was about to head for the shower, get myself dressed and ready for the owners' reception, when I heard the knock on the door and opened it to see a bellman standing there, almost hidden by the huge bouquet of flowers in his arms.

I showed him in and went looking for my purse to find some tipping money.

The bellman set the flowers down on the coffee table in the living area of the suite and said, "The general manager wants you to know he apologizes. These were supposed to be waiting for you when you checked in. That was clearly specified when they were ordered some time ago."

I told him to tell the general manager not to worry and gave him a big tip. He left. The flowers had to be from Cantor. If they weren't from Cantor, they had to be from Ryan Morrissey.

Or maybe Bobby Erlich had ordered them, celebrating the Oprah interview before it had even occurred, without any worry about jinxing it or spiking the ball too soon.

I opened the card.

> Hey, you.
> Figured I better get this arrangement sent before I forgot.
> You're gonna kill it tomorrow.
> Hey, nothing can stop us now.

It was signed:

> Thomas

SIXTY-SEVEN

I HAD ONE MORE good cry about my brother Thomas.

In that time, I gave up waiting to hear from Bobby Erlich. I took a quick shower, repaired my face as best I could, got into the same dress I'd worn the day I'd been introduced as the managing owner of the Wolves.

At THEBlvd Privé, an extension of the Wilshire's garden restaurant, there were two bar setups and white-jacketed waiters serving appetizers. By the time I got to the reception, it seemed like most of the other owners were already in attendance.

"It's just a meet and greet," Bobby Erlich had said. "Just make nice with the other boys and girls, and please don't punch anybody."

I told him I would be on my best behavior, and he said, "Low bar."

I got myself a white wine and sat down at a table alone, seeing heads turn in my direction as I did. I pretended to wave at someone. Then I smiled and waved in the other direction, also at nobody. I saw Joel Abrams, the commissioner, in deep conversation with a man I knew was Lew Wyatt, the owner of the Rams. Cissy Meriweather, who had inherited the Seahawks after her husband died, was with them.

I saw Kevin Penders, the league's only Black owner, having bought the Arizona Cardinals two years ago. I even managed a totally fake smile as I gave another wave to A. J. Frost, the owner of the Patriots, when I saw him staring at me. Frost, I knew, was pushing eighty. But he looked pretty good for his age—white hair worn long, somehow carrying off a skinny dark suit and black sneakers. A.J. was the chairman of the ownership committee and had been the one who'd led the charge against me after the pictures of my naked butt ended up in the *Tribune*. Bobby Erlich said I'd be fine with him as long as I didn't make any sudden moves.

I got up and walked straight across the courtyard while he was still standing by himself and stuck out my hand. He shook it reluctantly, as if afraid one of the photographers wandering around might turn us into a photo op.

"Jenny Wolf," I said.

"I feel as if I know all about you, even if we've never met," he said before quickly adding, "Sorry about your brother."

"So am I."

He had a martini in his left hand, I noticed. My father had once told me that if you wanted to get any business done with A. J. Frost it was best to get it done early in the day, before he got into the gin.

"I'm not going to stand here and lie to you, young lady. You're not going to have a very good week."

"I've had worse," I said. "But thanks for calling me young, Mr. Frost."

"It's not too late for you to call this off. Just withdraw your formal application and hand the team back to your brother and we can all move on."

"I keep telling people," I said. "I actually said this to Oprah Winfrey tonight. Joe Wolf didn't raise me to be a quitter."

"I'm asking you to stop because it will be for the good of the league."

"And you know something?" I said, smiling at him. "I honestly believe that *you* believe that."

Then I said, "You ought to check out the interview. It's not half bad."

"I'll be out to dinner."

"Same."

We moved away from each other, like boxers retreating to neutral corners. I said hello to Sam Zorn of the Dolphins, who'd been one of my father's best friends among the owners. I said hello to Karen Hooper, who owned the biggest real estate company in Los Angeles and had used part of her personal fortune to buy the Denver Broncos.

"If you ask me, we could use another girl in the old boys' club," she said.

"I keep thinking of a line my father liked to use. I feel like the whole world's a tuxedo and I'm a pair of brown shoes."

"Tell me about it."

"But you volunteered. I was drafted."

"I just thought it was about time a woman used her own damn money to get one of these teams," Karen Hooper said.

I smiled. "Your truth is a little different from mine."

"But you've managed to piss them off, and in a very short time, more than I have in five years," she said. "I think you broke several league records in the process."

Then she squeezed my hand and said, "Oprah. *Damn*, girl."

I was about to leave on that note. I had texted Bobby Erlich to see if he might still be coming but hadn't heard back. I didn't take it personally. I knew enough about him by now to know that being this close to TV and movie people was like porn for him.

I was heading for the exit, and the elevators, when a tall, good-looking guy, one who appeared to be about half the median age in the room, wearing a sharp-looking blazer and an open-necked shirt and jeans and with a lot of wavy hair piled on top of his head, stepped out in front of me.

"I'm Clay Rosen. May I have your autograph?"

I laughed as we shook hands.

"I know who you are."

He was the owner of the Los Angeles Chargers, is who he was. He'd inherited them from his father, Jerry Rosen, who'd owned most of the oceanfront property from San Diego down to Mexico. Clay Rosen reminded me of an actor, but for the life of me I couldn't remember which one. It was happening to me more and more.

"You want to get a drink?" he said.

"More than you could possibly know."

"You ever been to the Polo Lounge at the Beverly Hills Hotel?"

I told him that sadly, I had to admit that I had not.

"The valet already has my car waiting."

"I was supposed to meet somebody but got stood up."

"A date?" Clay Rosen said.

"My crisis manager."

He laughed loudly enough to turn heads. "I have mine on speed dial." Then he said, "Come on, let's blow this place. What else are you going to do, watch yourself on Oprah and drink alone?"

I told him that would pass for a big night with me.

"Before I give you my final answer," I added, "answer this, Mr. Clay Rosen. Are you going to vote for me?"

"I'd vote for you twice if I could. It would give me more backup with the crypt keepers, so I wouldn't have to keep feeling as if it's me against the world."

His car, a Tesla, was right where he said it was.

When he was pulling out of the drive between the two wings of the hotel, I said to Clay Rosen, "This may sound crazy, but I'm starting to think that maybe I might have a chance of getting approved after all."

"You don't."

SIXTY-EIGHT

DETECTIVE BEN CANTOR TRIED to call Jenny when the Oprah interview was over just to tell her that even though he was hardly an impartial observer, he thought any open-minded person who'd watched her had to be on her side now.

And it wasn't just his opinion. He did something he hardly ever did—checked Twitter and found that the majority of the people weighing in seemed to agree with him about what they'd seen tonight from Jenny Wolf.

Would it help her with the other owners? He had no way of knowing that, and neither did she. She had told him before she got to Los Angeles that she felt like she was down two touchdowns and running out of time.

The call went straight to voice mail. He left a message telling her that he thought she did great, that she should call him when she got the chance, and that there was nothing new to report on Thomas.

Cantor went back to his notes then, spread out once again on his kitchen table. He was still going through the grunt-work process of trying to get as complete a list as he could of the people who'd been in Thomas Wolf's suite that night. It felt like he was assembling one of those thousand-piece puzzles.

He'd talk to people who were there, and they'd give him as many names as they could remember. Working horizontally. Then those people would give him more names. It kept going like that.

Jenny was right. Her brother had had a lot of friends. Cantor was starting to think most of them had been there long after they'd all watched the Wolves game together. And he kept trying to see one or two of them as being capable of staging a drug overdose and then throwing Thomas to his death.

As he did, he was trying to process what the death of Tommy Wolf might have to do with Joe Wolf's death, if anything at all. He knew he had to push that piece of the story, if it even was a piece, to the side. He would get to it at some point. Just not right now. He kept plodding along on Thomas Wolf. Ben Cantor was nothing if not a patient man.

Maybe not with Jenny Wolf. But in general.

"There it is," he said, looking at his list. The guest list for the last party of a former party animal named Thomas Wolf. Next to it was as much of a timeline as Cantor could establish, from when the party seemed to have ended and the custodial staff had cleaned up the suite to the time of death. Two hours at least. Maybe a little more. The head of the custodial staff had told him that Thomas was no longer present when they started the clean-up job.

Did it mean that Thomas could have been somewhere else in the stadium? Or that he had gone to have a face-to-face with the person he told Jenny he needed to talk to?

Who'd you talk to, Thomas?

And about what?

As was standard when the Wolves were playing out of town, a skeleton crew had worked Wolves Stadium that Sunday. By now, Cantor had talked to every one of them on the list provided by the head of stadium operations. Cantor had asked the guy, Gabe Martinez, if somebody could have hidden somewhere and then headed upstairs to Thomas's suite without being seen.

"It's a seventy-six-thousand-seat stadium," Martinez, a former cop, had said. "Figure it out for yourself. And know that Mr. Wolf senior wasn't ever a bear for security cameras."

Cantor already knew that.

He opened his laptop. He was still waiting for Thomas Wolf's cell-phone records, for which he'd needed a subpoena, not just to see who he'd called on the day of his death but also to see who he'd called in the days leading up to it. But even that was complicated, because Jenny had told Cantor that Thomas had more than one phone, a habit from his life drinking and drugging.

Once Cantor had the records, he could check the phone from which Thomas had called Jenny and, more important, track his whereabouts on the night he died.

Cantor's contact at Thomas's service provider, an old friend, had told him that he was working late and that there was a chance the records could come in tonight. And when Cantor went to his email, there were the records he'd been seeking. The PDF documents his friend had attached contained the numbers for the handful of other calls Thomas Wolf had made that day.

For now, Cantor was more interested in where he'd gone in the hours after he'd called Jenny and the party had ended— the GPS tracing of his phone, point to point. One document had the addresses. The other tracked him by longitude and latitude.

Cantor placed them next to each other. Usually he was old-school and preferred longitude and latitude.

This time, though, it was the addresses that caught his eye.

He grabbed one of the notebooks on the table just to make sure he was right.

He was.

"Sonofabitch."

Cantor used the Waze app on his phone to determine how easy it would have been for Thomas Wolf to make the Sunday night round trip between Wolves Stadium and that part of town. Then he grabbed his car keys and drove over to Pacific Heights.

He parked his car at a hydrant on Broadway, walked up to the town house, gave a good loud rap with the door knocker, then another even harder rap, until he heard the voice from inside, "Relax, for chrissakes. I'm coming."

When Jack Wolf finally opened the door, Cantor said, "How come you forgot to tell me that your brother paid you a visit the night somebody threw him out a window?"

Then Cantor was pushing past Jack and saying, "May I come in?"

SIXTY-NINE

"I'M CURRENTLY SINGLE, in case you were wondering," Clay Rosen said to me.

"I wasn't," I said. "We're having a drink together, not thinking of eloping."

He toasted me with his glass in approval. "I'm getting a sense of how you could have fired your ex-husband."

I sipped my wine. "I briefly considered calling him back an hour later and firing him again, if you must know."

It was obvious that Clay Rosen was a regular at the Polo Lounge. Walk in like you belong, Joe Wolf had always taught us. Rosen had done just that. The place was crowded, but I immediately got the feeling that the maître d' would have thrown people out into the lobby to get Rosen his usual banquette in the corner.

He'd explained by now that there was no need for him to watch the Oprah interview.

"I'm sure you were great. But I've been following your reality series from down here and had already come to the conclusion that you *are* pretty great."

He told me then how sorry he was about Thomas; he should have told me that right away. I told him Thomas was the one who was great and would have become a great general manager if he'd gotten the chance.

We sat in silence for a moment. I could already tell that any kind of silence was the only thing that seemed to make Clay Rosen uneasy. I discreetly pointed across the room now and asked if that was the actress who'd been in that thing. I was in LA. I couldn't help myself. I thought everybody was in the movies.

"No," he said. "If it's the thing I think you mean, that's not her. The actress you're thinking of is an old girlfriend of mine. Though not really all that old, to tell you the truth."

"Okay, enough small talk. Back to my reality series. You really think I have no shot?"

He used his fingers to move the ice cubes in his vodka around.

"I don't. You might have a couple more votes than you think, just based on my unofficial canvassing. But with that bloc of hard-liners, all of them between sixty and dead, I think you are royally screwed."

"Because they don't want another woman in the club?"

"Not a woman who scares the shit out of them the way you do," he said. "I like Cissy and Karen, by the way. I do. They are smart, nice, competent women. But at the end of the day, they're just happy to be *in* the club. They just go along to get along. You're different."

"Do I really want to know in what way?"

"Sure," he said. "Because you don't treat this sport like church. Because you don't take any prisoners, the way your father didn't—or at least he didn't before he got old enough to be a crypt keeper himself." He drank some vodka and smacked his lips. "Jeanie Buss is a friend of mine, and she's done really well running the Lakers. But you've dialed it up to a whole nother level. There's never been a woman owner like you in sports that I know about."

"I'm just running my team the way I think it should be run."

"But they can see you're never going to be a team player with *them*," Clay Rosen said. "This group is big on team players. My father was just like them."

I liked Clay. I knew he was flirting with me; I just assumed it was his natural state. But he wasn't being overt about it, or pushy, or weird. He seemed as completely comfortable in his own skin as he was being in this room.

"So you're telling me I can't change minds when I get my face-to-face with them tomorrow?"

"Maybe," he said. "Just not enough of them, in my opinion. The commissioner knows he's got the hard-liners, so he's been lobbying hard against you with everybody else, almost like he's got an agenda here that I sure as hell don't know about. But at the end of the day, I don't see how you can move New England, Chicago, Houston, Indy, Tennessee. The hardest of the hard-liners. They're the ones pushing all the She Wolf stuff. If you could turn them around, you might be able to thread the needle and get to twenty-four votes. But at this point, it would be like turning around a battleship."

"I still have to try. Have you heard anything about my brother Danny wanting to sell the team?"

"Yeah. We all pretty much have. But he denies it."

"He denies it with me, too," I said.

"He could be lying."

"He does that."

"It may have something to do with the new stadium your dad could never seem to get built," Clay Rosen said.

"The city fought him for years, even though the other sports teams in town somehow managed to get theirs."

"It's weird," Rosen said. "Because new stadiums mean Super Bowls, which is like winning the jackpot for the host cities."

"And the host team."

"Tell me about it. We just had one here."

He ordered another vodka. I ordered another wine. I wasn't driving. And the night was going to be long enough once I got back to the suite.

For now I was having a good time with an owner who didn't have a long knife out for me. The waiter brought our drinks. Clay Rosen raised his glass. I raised mine.

"What are we drinking to?"

"Beats the hell out of me."

We both laughed and drank. I was facing the entrance. As I was putting my glass down, I saw the commissioner come walking into the Polo Lounge; followed by A. J. Frost, the Patriots' owner.

The third member of the party was my ex-husband.

SEVENTY

TED SKYLER SPOTTED ME at almost the same moment as I spotted him and led his party directly to our table. Happily, from the look on his face.

"Fancy meeting you here," Ted said.

"*Fancy* is one word beginning with *f* I can think of. But not the one I would have chosen."

"You know the commissioner," he said. "Have you met A.J.?"

"At the reception."

We all looked as if we wanted to be somewhere else, with the exception of Clay Rosen, who suddenly looked as if he were at his own birthday party. He'd stood up as soon as they got to the table and shaken their hands. I'd stayed seated, wishing a trapdoor would open up underneath me.

"You and Clay know each other?" I said to Ted.

"We Zoomed after you cut me," Ted Skyler said. "He said the Chargers might be looking for another quarterback before the season is over."

Clay grinned at me. "Did I forget to mention that?"

"Are you *still* job-hunting?" I said to Ted. "Is that why you're here?"

"Not anymore."

A. J. Frost slapped Ted on the back and said, "The Patriots just signed the big guy, as a matter of fact. And are damn happy to have him."

"Mr. Frost is flying me back to Boston in his plane tonight," Ted said. "I get my physical tomorrow and plan to be at practice on Wednesday."

"Ted never should have been out of work in the first place," Commissioner Joel Abrams said.

Ted smiled at me.

"Is Boston far enough away to suit you?"

"Only until the commissioner puts a franchise on the moon."

The maître d' came over and told them their table was ready. But before Joel Abrams left, he said to me, "It's still not too late for you to change your mind."

"Funny. A.J. told me the same thing at the reception."

"We're just both looking out for the shield," A. J. Frost said solemnly.

It was what they called the NFL logo, without any sense of irony. The shield. Like it was the family coat of arms. Or something that gave them all superpowers.

"This whole thing has become too much of a circus," Frost said. "Now we've got Oprah up in our business. How does that help anybody?"

Clay Rosen, smiling, said, "I mean, good Lord, man, imagine what she did to the fourth-quarter ratings for *Monday Night Football*!"

"Let's go sit down," Ted Skyler said to Abrams and Frost. "We've got a lot to talk about before I head for the airport."

"Like what?" I asked.

"Like your big week, of course," Ted said.

He turned and started to follow the commissioner and A. J. Frost to their table. I stood and put a hand on his arm to stop him. He looked down at it and said, "You're not going to slug me, too, are you?"

"Of course not. I just want to give you a hug and wish you luck with the Patriots. I really don't hate you, you know."

It was too late for him to do anything but let me put my arms around him.

As I did, I whispered something in his ear.

SEVENTY-ONE

MY FIRST CALL WHEN I got back to the suite was from Bobby Erlich.

"You never showed."

"Just ran into a potential client," he said.

"Anybody interesting?"

"When they're willing to pay, they're *all* interesting."

Then he told me that the response to my sit-down with Oprah was positive across the board and on all platforms, even better than he had expected. He said he hoped as many of the other owners as possible had watched.

I told him I doubted it, because the general vibe I'd gotten was that if it was good for me, it was bad for them.

"Trust me," Bobby Erlich said. "By the time they go to bed, they're going to feel as if they saw it whether they did or not."

Then he said we should meet downstairs for breakfast before I addressed the owners, and he promised not to stand me up this time.

"Who loves you?" he said before telling me he had another call coming in.

I had taken a long bath and was about to go to bed when Ben Cantor called and told me about his visit with Jack.

"So he lied to you," I said.

"By omission. But still a lie."

"One he managed to leave out of his tearful eulogy, when he was so regretful about all the fighting he and Thomas had done."

I paused then, looking at the flowers next to where my feet were perched on the coffee table.

"*Did* the two of them have one more fight that night?" I said to Cantor.

"He says no. He says that Thomas only went there to ask Jack and Danny to back off. And that he even took one more shot at the family maybe working together."

"That wasn't the feeling I got from Thomas. Did you believe Jack?"

"I did not. Because if the whole thing was so innocent, why did he hide it from me in the first place?"

"Did you ask him that?"

"I did, being a trained detective. He said he just thought it would look bad even though Thomas's visit was completely innocent and so was he."

I pulled a rose out of the bouquet, drank in the smell of it.

"Thanks for telling me. And now I am going to try, most likely in vain, to get some sleep."

Cantor said, "Not before I finish telling you about my night."

"There's more?"

"There is."

I waited.

"It turns out Thomas made one other stop that night."

SEVENTY-TWO

I WAITED OUTSIDE THE Bordeaux Room while Danny addressed the owners first.

"Sorry it had to come to this," he'd said, passing me on the way into the conference room.

"I'm glad it's going to be over soon, one way or another."

"I never wanted this," Danny had said. "Not that I expect you to believe me."

"Do what you have to do."

It was becoming my default position with my two older brothers.

Danny was in there about twenty minutes. At no point did I have any urge to crack open the door and sneak a listen. Danny, for his whole life, had been full of what our father called palaver. It was Joe Wolf's polite way of saying "BS"— on the rare occasions when he made the effort to clean up his language at the dinner table.

When Danny came out, he walked right past me, this time without even looking at me. I knew there would be a fifteen-minute break before it was my turn to basically defend my life.

Or, in the words of Thomas Wolf, to throw the damn money on the table.

I smiled to myself, thinking, *Where's Oprah when I really need her?*

As the doors opened and the owners headed for the coffee setup or the restrooms, Clay Rosen saw me and came walking over.

"Public speaking really isn't your brother's thing, is it?"

"The English language isn't his thing."

All in all, I was surprisingly calm. Maybe it was because of lack of sleep after my conversation with Ben Cantor. I ended up pacing the suite before I finally did go to bed, practicing what I wanted to say, then did the same thing after I'd awakened.

At ten o'clock sharp, the appointed hour, one of the league PR guys poked his head out of the Bordeaux Room and said, "It's time, Ms. Wolf."

I managed not to ask for a blindfold and cigarette.

The commissioner gave me a brief introduction, his remarks about as welcoming as those I would have gotten from a clerk at the Department of Motor Vehicles. I thanked him when I stepped to the podium and thanked the men and women in front of me for allowing me the opportunity to speak to them this morning.

I offered them what I hoped was my most winning smile.

"Though by now," I said, "you probably all think you've not only *heard* enough from me, you've also *seen* enough."

The women laughed. So did Clay Rosen, if a bit too enthusiastically.

"But I want to tell you myself that I'm not the person you have been reading about and hearing about, the one who felt she needed to defend herself with Oprah Winfrey last night," I said. "I'm who I've always been: Joe Wolf's daughter. And I'm here because he wanted me to be here."

I told them that I was like every other owner in the room. I was a caretaker of a public trust. And I wanted to win, pointing out that my team *had* been winning since I took over and had gotten a new coach and a new quarterback.

"My dad always said that one thing had never changed in pro football and would never change. In the end, this is a results business. And I've been getting results."

There was more I had planned to say. But I decided to get to it now, my big finish, pulling the envelope out of the side pocket of my blazer, then carefully removing the single piece of paper within it.

"I haven't shown this to anybody or told anybody about it until today," I said. "But this is a letter I received from my father a couple of weeks after he died. Most of you know he was never much for email. But he still wrote letters, and the only reason this one took as long to get to me as it did is because my father, *being* my father, sent it to the wrong street address."

I made a show of smoothing out the paper and cleared my throat.

"By now," I read, "you know the team is yours. It's yours because I finally realized you're the one to run it, mostly because you're the one most like me. Nobody could ever take the Wolves away from me. Don't let anybody ever take them away from you."

I paused, then looked down one last time.

"Love, Dad," I said.

SEVENTY-THREE

I WALKED DOWN THE middle aisle then, not looking left or right or making eye contact with any of them, walked through the double doors, walked past the elevators and down a long stairway to the street level.

I was done talking for now. I just wanted to take a walk up Rodeo Drive and look at ridiculously overpriced clothes and maybe even buy some of them on what might be my last official day running the Wolves.

I was out on the street when Clay Rosen caught up with me.

"Want some company?"

"Do I have a choice?"

He smiled. "I'm going to take that as a rhetorical question."

We headed up Beverly Drive first, past Nate 'n Al's, which had been my father's favorite breakfast place whenever he came to Los Angeles. Clay asked if I wanted to stop in. I said I couldn't eat right now if I tried.

"It might have been a little too late," he said, "but I honestly think you might have changed a few minds in there."

"Just not enough of them."

"I don't see how. But I gotta say, you got their attention with that letter from your dad."

"Did I?"

"It sure blew me away."

We stopped at the corner of Canon and Beverly. I took the envelope back out of my pocket, took out the piece of paper, handed it to Clay Rosen.

He looked at it, then at me, then said, "Well, I'll be damned." He wasn't just looking at me now. He was staring.

"You trust me not to tell?"

"You want to have another drink sometime?"

"I do."

"I know," I said.

What I showed him was the letter from the general manager of the Beverly Wilshire, welcoming me to the hotel and telling me not to hesitate to call him if I needed anything during my stay.

"I told you whose daughter I am," I said to Clay Rosen.

SEVENTY-FOUR

JOHN GALLO WAS BACK in his office in San Francisco in the late morning when Danny Wolf called him.

"Where are we?" Gallo said.

"Still five to seven votes short."

"By whose count?"

"Mine," Danny said, "and the commissioner's."

Gallo didn't say anything right away. Never a good sign, Danny knew.

"Do not screw with me on this," Gallo said. "I've waited a long time to put this thing in motion."

If there's life on Mars, Danny thought, *they know how long you've waited to get what you want.*

"I'm aware," was all Danny said.

"What time is the vote tomorrow?" Gallo said.

"Ten o'clock."

"Secret ballot?"

"Show of hands."

"Then who will deliver the news to your sister?"

"The commissioner."

Danny heard Gallo chuckle now.

"If only it could be me," he said.

SEVENTY-FIVE

THE NEXT MORNING, I didn't want to wait outside the Bordeaux Room. The owners had other business once they'd voted and might be in there awhile.

Clay Rosen had said he'd let me know how the vote had gone as soon as he could get outside and make a call.

"How long will it take?" I said.

"No way of knowing with these things," he said. "Anybody who wants to say something before the vote is allowed to. The commish will probably weigh in, too. And A.J., because he runs the ownership committee, will probably ramble on awhile."

"Are you going to say something on my behalf?"

"Bet your ass," he said. "I got you on this."

"Thank you."

"You prepared for whatever's going to happen?"

"I am."

Then I said, "So the hard-liners are the ones who are going to do me in."

"They're so dug in it's like they're calcified."

He asked where I'd be. I told him I was going to take another walk around Beverly Hills, maybe up to Santa Monica

Boulevard and back. Or maybe all the way to Malibu and back. But I would try to return to my room before it was over.

He asked if I was taking my phone with me.

I said no.

He asked why.

"Not sure," I said.

Bobby Erlich called then.

"It might be closer than we thought. But you just don't have the votes, from what I heard last night."

"Thanks for sharing."

"But I'm already thinking, like, six moves ahead," he said. "A book deal, definitely. Maybe a talk show. Maybe a reality series about you and the high school kids. Even if you lose, you win, because you're going to be more famous than ever."

"Just without my pro football team."

"Who knows? Maybe you'll be better off in the long run."

I told him to take a long walk off the Santa Monica Pier and ended the call.

I walked up to Nate 'n Al's, ordered a coffee to go, and sipped it as I started wandering aimlessly around Beverly Hills.

Maybe I never had a chance.

Maybe Bobby is right, and I will be better off.

But I knew that was a lie—a big fat lie—because I had found out something about myself by now: I was good at this. Damn good. *I wanted this.*

I didn't know if there was anything I could have done differently with all the sharks circling me in the water— the water, I thought, where everything really started—but I couldn't come up with a thing I could have done to change the outcome. Other than perhaps not punching my brother Jack's lights out.

There was no appeals court for me after the decision I fully expected was coming. The vote would be final. The *verdict* would be final.

Money on the table.

I always thought Thomas was referring to a let-it-ride bid in poker. But today this felt more like throwing dice to me.

One roll for everything.

When I was back in my room, still an hour to go before the vote, the phone rang.

It was A. J. Frost, the Patriots owner.

"I'm in the penthouse suite," he said. "I'd appreciate it if you'd come up here as soon as you can."

SEVENTY-SIX

A FEW MINUTES LATER I was sitting in the penthouse suite of the Beverly Wilshire with a group of men I thought of by then as the Hard-liners, like they were a rock band—one even older than the Beach Boys.

A. J. Frost. Carl Paulson, the eighty-two-year-old owner of the Chicago Bears. Rex Cardwell of the Texans. Ed McGrath of the Tennessee Titans. Amos Lester of the Colts.

I had made up my mind that I wasn't going to beg them for their votes, especially since they'd all made it abundantly clear that they'd pretty much made up their minds about me before I'd even left San Francisco.

The living room of the suite made mine downstairs look like a closet in comparison. When I'd taken my seat in one of the antique chairs, A. J. Frost said, "Thank you for coming."

They had placed my chair so I could face all of them.

I smiled now.

"Wouldn't have missed it for the world."

"You don't take any shit, do you, young lady?" Rex Cardwell said in his booming cowboy voice.

"Not that you'd ever notice."

"Neither did her father," Amos Lester said.

"Before we head downstairs to vote," Frost said, "we need to make clear to you where we're all coming from, especially in light of all the history we had with your father. And, I might add, in light of where we're going."

I kept my smile fixed firmly in place. Not only wasn't I going to beg to keep my team, I also wasn't going to lose my temper.

"With all due respect, for all of you to be any more clear, you'd have had to hire a skywriter."

I thought I might have heard some throat clearing from a couple of members of the firing squad. I just couldn't tell which ones.

"Before A.J. says what he wants to say," Ed McGrath said, "I just want you to know that as a parent and a grandparent, that letter Joe sent you really got to me."

"Yes. It was pretty amazing, wasn't it?"

"He was an amazing man, your father," Frost said. "It's one of the reasons why you're here with us right now and not downstairs with the others."

"I'm not sure I understand. I thought everything that needed to be said *had* been said. Which is why I have sort of an existential question for you gentlemen. *Why are we here?*"

"We just didn't want you to leave thinking that we're just a bunch of stubborn old fools," Rex Cardwell said.

"As if I'd ever," I said, unable to stop myself.

At least Rex Cardwell laughed.

"There's that attitude."

"A chronic condition, I'm afraid."

"What did I tell you boys last night when we were sitting here in this same damned room and talking about what's best for the damned league?" Cardwell said. "We need some fresh blood."

"I frankly thought I was only here to shed some," I said to Cardwell.

Cardwell barked out another laugh.

"Nope."

Nope?

"See, as it turns out we're not as stubborn as you think we are," A. J. Frost said.

And smiled himself now.

And stood.

"The reason we called you up here," he said, "is to tell you to your face that you've got our votes."

I wasn't sure at first if I had heard him correctly.

"Wait . . . *what*?"

"You're going to pass," he said.

SEVENTY-SEVEN

CLAY ROSEN HAD ASKED me to have a drink with him before I checked out. I told him I had a plane to catch, not to mention two football teams with which I had to catch up.

"You haven't seen the last of me," he said.

I asked if that was a threat or a promise.

"Little bit of both."

Then he asked me what I'd said after Frost told me that the Hard-liners were suddenly behind me.

"I looked at him as solemnly as I could, summoned up all my personal grace, and said, 'You have *got* to be shitting me.'"

I was just about to finish my packing when I heard the knock at the door. When I opened it, there was a bellman standing there, holding a single red rose.

He handed me the rose and the card that came with it. I tipped him a twenty, feeling flush today.

I went back into the bedroom and laid the rose on the bed next to my suitcase. Then I sat down and opened the card.

This flower wasn't from my brother Thomas.

The card said only: *"You're welcome."*

SEVENTY-EIGHT

DETECTIVE BEN CANTOR SAT across from Elise Wolf in a living room that brought the word *regal* to mind, as if he'd somehow been granted an audience with a woman Jenny often referred to as the queen.

"I must say," Elise Wolf said to him, "you were rather vague about the need to see me this evening."

He let that one go for the moment.

"Have you heard from Jenny?" Cantor said. "You must be happy for her that she got to hold on to the team."

"I *suppose* happy is one way to look at it," she said. "It was at her brother Daniel's expense, of course. So there's that."

"But your late husband clearly wanted her to take over the running of the team," Cantor said, "or he wouldn't have left the team to her."

"My late husband wanted many things, usually *when* he wanted them," she said with a dismissive wave of her hand. "And he often didn't consider the consequences of what he wanted at any given time."

She was dressed as if about to leave for some kind of formal reception. Black dress. A strand of pearls around her neck. A diamond ring on her left hand that looked big enough and even strong enough to light the rest of the house if there were some kind of power failure—even bigger than the rock Rachel Wolf had been wearing when he'd met her for drinks. Elise Wolf's attitude, just in the few minutes Cantor had been here, was a combination of haughtiness and impatience, as if she were talking to the help.

She was exactly the way Jenny described her: a piece of work.

"Do you often conduct your interviews at this time of night?" she said to him. "And your business?"

She was sipping sherry. She'd offered him something to drink, but he said he was working.

"My business is rather transactional, Mrs. Wolf," he said, "and often involves the exchange of information."

"I'm quite sure I'm not following you. Are you being intentionally opaque?"

"I'm trying to quit."

"You really are impertinent, aren't you?"

He couldn't help himself. He felt himself grinning. "You have no idea."

"I might remind you that I don't have all night."

Jenny must have been raised by real wolves, Cantor thought, not for the first time.

Or maybe the real kill-or-be-killed Wolf was seated across from him in her high-backed antique chair.

"I'm really only here to ask you one question, which happens to be the same one I've already asked another member of your family."

"I'm waiting."

"How come when I spoke to you last week you didn't think your son Thomas showing up here about an hour before he died was worth sharing with me?" Cantor said.

SEVENTY-NINE

JOHN GALLO HAD PLACED no calls to either Jack or Danny Wolf, nor had he taken calls from them, since their sister had gotten the votes she needed in Los Angeles, having somehow defied gravity on a day when she was supposed to crash and burn.

The brothers had both been so sure. So had the commissioner, now fully in the pocket of Gallo and his associates. So, too, had her crisis manager, that grasping little twerp. But John Gallo had made the mistake of convincing himself it was a sure thing. That wasn't his nature. He never trusted that a job was done until it was impossible for it to be *undone*.

Gallo heard a single rap on his door and called out "Enter" as Erik Mason came into his office, immediately apologizing for being late, saying he had run into a series of closed roads this afternoon.

"No need to explain," Gallo said. "On the rare occasions when you are a few minutes late, you always have a very good reason."

Erik Mason was the person in his organization John Gallo trusted the most. And the one who was most fiercely loyal to him. He was a former LAPD cop, tall and lean, all hard angles and edges and an almost military bearing that Gallo thought was part of his DNA. From the time he had hired him away from his job overseeing security for Joe Wolf, Gallo had never seen Mason in anything other than a black suit, white shirt, and black tie, despite the frequent changes in the San Francisco weather.

Mason was head of Gallo's security now, his body man, as the expression went, even his occasional driver. But perhaps more than anything else, Erik Mason was a fixer. What was the name of the character in that TV show Gallo used to watch? Ray Donovan? Erik Mason was *that* kind of fixer for John Gallo. And more, when more was necessary.

"Have you given any further thought to our conversation this morning about Ms. Wolf?" Gallo said as Mason took a seat in front of him.

Mason's black shoes, as always, gleamed.

"I have, sir."

"And have you come up with any ideas about how I should deal with the current situation?"

"As a matter of fact, sir, I do have some thoughts on this matter."

"As I expected you would," Gallo said.

"As you *knew* I would."

Gallo liked to refer to Mason as his top cop. And with Gallo, Mason had found the kind of structure he'd missed since he'd been fired from Robbery-Homicide in Los Angeles after a career-long habit of making up rules as he went along and after what Gallo considered a rather impressive history of excessive force.

On the way to work this morning, Mason driving him today, Gallo had told him that he didn't just want Jenny Wolf out of the National Football League. He wanted her out of San Francisco when they were finished with her.

"I'm all ears," Gallo said now.

He saw a small smile on Mason's face. *I should have had him handle the situation with this woman from the start,* Gallo thought. The brothers, in the end, ultimately didn't have the stomach for this kind of fight. They would never go far enough. In Gallo's eyes, it just made them weak. John Gallo despised weakness.

The antithesis of that was seated across his desk, a person every bit as ruthless and cold-blooded as he was, as ruthless as the only man from whom John Gallo took orders. And feared.

"The key, sir, is to continue to attack the enemy at their weakest point. Or hers, in this case."

"You mean the people she cares about the most," Gallo said.

Mason nodded.

"It's a very small circle with her. We've discussed this previously."

"All due respect," Mason said, "she does oversee two football teams."

Now Gallo smiled fully. He had only been focused on the Wolves.

"Obviously you're including the players on her high school team?"

"Yes, sir, absolutely."

"You'd go after them?" John Gallo said.

"Why not?"

EIGHTY

BEN CANTOR AND I were having burgers at Causwells, on Chestnut Street, the first time we'd been together since I'd returned from Los Angeles. He said he couldn't think of a better way to celebrate than with the best burger in town and a pitcher of beer.

"I'm a man of simple tastes," he said.

"Sure. Go with that."

"You still haven't fully explained to me why those owners ended up doing a one-eighty," Cantor said.

"It was obviously my heartfelt appeal to their better angels."

"Sure," he said, smiling at me with those eyes. "Go with *that*."

He drank some of his beer and smacked his lips contentedly after he did.

"You really don't know why they flipped, or you're not telling me?"

"Hey, you're the detective."

We were waiting for our cheeseburgers. He'd picked the place, but once he did, I told him Causwells had always been, and would always be, my go-to when I was in need of a burger fix. Like the Urgent Care of burger joints, at least for me. The front room was crowded for a Thursday night, televisions tuned to the Thursday night game between the Panthers and Falcons. I had come here straight from practice at Hunters Point. We had the biggest game of the year coming up on Saturday afternoon, at home, against St. Joseph's.

And the day after that the Wolves had a home game against my new buddy Rex Cardwell's Texans. A win would put us in a division-leading tie with the Rams.

"I went to see your mother," Cantor said.

"Without being coerced?"

He told me all about it.

I asked why he'd waited to tell me.

He said he figured I had enough on my plate, but he also wanted to give me this piece in person.

When he finished his replay of their conversation, I said, "So the Queen Mum lied to you."

"Another one of omission. Can't keep track of the liars in your family without a scorecard."

"I know how Jack tried to explain away Thomas's visit to him that night. What about my mother?"

Cantor drank more beer.

"It's almost as if she and Jack got their stories lined up," Cantor said. "She said Thomas came to the house to plead with her, as the head of the family, to broker a peace with Danny and Jack. Bring all the sibs together for practically a kumbaya moment."

The waiter brought our burgers. We paused until he was gone.

"Well, that certainly doesn't line up with what Thomas told me on the phone," I said. "He said he needed to talk to somebody who could tell him why they were so desperate to get rid of us. Meaning Thomas and me."

"I remember."

"So they're both lying their asses off."

"Seems so."

"And to you, an officer of the law," I said.

"What's the world coming to?"

He reached over and took one of my fries.

I pointed out that he had some of his own.

He said he couldn't explain it, but they simply tasted better off my plate.

I said, "No other stops after he left the house and got back to the stadium?"

Cantor shook his head.

We ate in silence for a few minutes after that. I was just about to finish my burger when my phone rang from inside my purse.

I took it out and checked the screen.

Ryan.

"My coach. Gotta take it."

"Go ahead," Cantor said, winking at me. "*I* can take it."

"Hey, Coach."

"We can't find Billy McGee," he said.

EIGHTY-ONE

RYAN GAVE ME AN address in Chinatown, on Jackson Street, and said he was on his way there himself.

I asked him why Chinatown.

He said he'd called Amanda, Billy's wife, and she said her husband had gone off to get dinner at the Z & Y Bistro with an old teammate from Arizona State, and she hadn't heard from him since.

She said she kept tracking his phone, but it was still in the same place on Jackson Street, even though she'd called the restaurant and Billy had left a couple of hours ago.

Cantor paid the check and said he'd drive me and worry about coming back for my car later.

"Not sure this is a police matter. At least not yet."

"Think of me as a concerned Wolves fan," Cantor said, "one who might be able to help out a little more than most in a situation like this."

I called Ryan back when we were in Cantor's car and put him on speaker.

"We had a deal, Billy and me," Ryan said, "one I didn't tell you about. He had to call me every night at nine o'clock, and then at eleven, whether he was at home with Amanda or not.

If he was out, he had to tell me where he was and who he was with."

"Makes you sound like a parole officer," Cantor said.

"Wait," Ryan said. "Who's with you, Jenny?"

"Detective Ben Cantor. San Francisco Police Department."

"Oh, right," Ryan said over the speaker. "You're the cop."

I saw Cantor grin.

"Well, I'm *a* cop."

"So Billy didn't call tonight when he was supposed to," I said.

"Nope. I gave myself half an hour or so, hoping he just forgot, before I called Amanda."

Ryan sighed audibly.

"I called the restaurant myself. They told me what they told Amanda—that he was long gone and that nobody had found a phone he might have left behind."

"If he got lucky and found a parking space out front," Cantor said, "maybe he left the phone in the car."

"Had Billy ever missed one of his nightly calls?" I said to Ryan.

"Not one time since we signed him."

"When was the last time you spoke to the wife?" Cantor said.

"Right after I called Jenny."

I told Ryan we'd see him when we got there. About a minute later, my phone rang again. I didn't even look at the screen this time, just assumed it was Ryan calling back.

"This is Jenny," I said.

There was silence at the other end, until I finally heard a muffled voice say, "This is Money."

I immediately put the call on speaker.

"Billy, are you all right?"

"No," he said before the line went dead.

EIGHTY-TWO

CANTOR DROVE VERY FAST.

He said driving this way through the streets of San Francisco was one of the perks of his job, along with being able to badge his way into Wolves games any time he wanted to.

"Wait—you did that even before you met me?"

"Only if it was a particularly big game."

Ryan was waiting for us in front of the restaurant. Cantor parked next to a hydrant.

"Billy just called me," I said.

"Where is he?" Ryan said.

"He didn't say."

"How did he sound?"

"Not good."

Ryan said, "We've got a game in thirty-six hours."

"I'm aware."

Cantor said, "Let's find him first and then worry about that."

"I'm a coach," Ryan said.

"*I'm* aware," Cantor said.

"Maybe the whole thing was too good to be true," Ryan said.

Another incoming call.

"Billy?" I said.

His voice sounded weaker than before.

"Sorry . . . I got a little sick while I was talking to you."

"Try to figure out where you are, and Coach and I will come get you."

"Still Chinatown . . . pretty sure."

"*Where* in Chinatown? Can you get to a window and look outside and give us some kind of landmark?"

Another silence. I was afraid the phone had gone dead again.

"'Kay," he said.

He'd put my number in his phone the day I met him. I'd done the same with his. I never thought he'd need it like this. Or maybe I did.

I had him on speaker. We all stood there staring at my phone.

"*Money,*" Ryan yelled. "*Where the hell are you?*"

We all waited.

"Across from where I ate," Billy McGee said finally.

Ryan said, "Are you at a window right now?"

"Yeah . . . but feel like I might be sick again."

I said, "When you look outside, what do you see?"

A long pause. I thought he had gone off to be sick again.

"You guys," he said.

We finally spotted him in a third-floor window across the street, waving feebly at us with one hand, the other to his face, shirtless, his chest and arms covered with all his tattoos, before he disappeared.

The three of us ran across Jackson and through an open door into an ancient brownstone, up the stairs to the third floor, yelling Billy's name when we got up there.

Nothing at first.

Then: "Here."

His voice was coming from 3F, a few feet up the hallway on our right.

I went in first, Ryan and Cantor right behind me. We all stopped when we had eyes on Billy McGee.

"Oh, no," I said.

EIGHTY-THREE

IT WAS ONE DINGY ROOM, a small bathroom attached to it. Billy McGee was on the bed, on his back.

His face was a bloody mess.

There was a bucket next to the bed, with empty vials and what I assumed was a crack pipe next to them on the small bedside table. A half-full bottle of tequila was at the other end of the bed, next to his bare feet. There was blood on the front of his jeans and even smeared across the tats on his chest and arms.

Cantor quietly said, "He cannot stay here. And you, Jenny, and you, Ryan, cannot be here."

Billy McGee opened his eyes and raised his head a few inches with what looked to be all the strength he had in him and said, "Somebody...somebody did this."

He grimaced and said, "Beat me up."

I looked at Ryan Morrissey, who did look as if he wanted to be anywhere on the planet except here.

"Coach..." Billy said through swollen lips, "...gotta believe me."

His head fell back down. He tried to lift it again but couldn't, as if doing it once had already exhausted him. For a moment I thought he had passed out.

Then his lips were moving, barely.

"...set me up..." he said.

There was a back window in the apartment, if you could even call it an apartment. Cantor went to it, stared down. I walked over and stood next to him and saw that we were both looking down into an alley.

"If somebody could set up Thomas," Cantor said, "they could certainly set up this jamoke."

"Indeed," I said.

"We can't take him out the front," Cantor said. "Once he's on the street it will be like begging people to take pictures with their phones."

"What are we going to do?" Ryan said.

"Jenny," Cantor said, taking charge, "you bring my car around. Ryan, you and I will get him down the back stairs."

Ben Cantor handed me his keys.

"The Wolves cap you gave me is in the back seat," Cantor told me. "Have it ready to slap on his head when you pull around."

I ran back down the front stairs to the car, eased it away from the hydrant, and made a left into a narrow opening, just wide enough for the car. Then I made another left and saw that no one was in the alley, at least for the moment.

I pulled up and opened the door to the back seat. Cantor and Ryan half carried and half dragged the quarterback of the Wolves to Cantor's car. Ryan got into the back seat with him. I went around to the front passenger seat. Cantor got behind the wheel.

"Where to?" he said.

"The stadium," I said. "I'll call our team doctor and tell him to meet us there."

As Cantor drove even more quickly than he had on the way

over here, I turned around and looked at Billy McGee, head resting against the window. Ryan had somehow found a way to clean the blood off Billy's face, so I could see the cut over Billy's left eye, which was swollen to nothing more than a slit.

"Call my wife," Billy said. He winced as he started to cough. "Tell her I didn't let her down."

"When we get to the stadium," I said, "you can tell her yourself."

As we pulled into the players' lot at Wolves Stadium, I saw Dr. Ron Barnes waiting for us near the entrance.

Cantor and Ryan got Billy out of the car, placing his arms around their shoulders.

"You need help?" Ron Barnes said to them.

I said, "We all do."

I walked behind Cantor and Ryan as they helped Billy toward the Wolves' locker room.

Once we had him inside, my phone made the little jingle noise it makes when there's a news alert.

EIGHTY-FOUR

THE IMAGES OF BILLY on that bed, exactly as we'd found him, blood all over him, the drug paraphernalia next to him and the tequila bottle at his feet, were already splashed across the home page of Wolf.com under the headline:

CRACKED AND SACKED

Amanda McGee arrived about fifteen minutes later. Barnes had Billy stretched out on one of the training tables while he stitched the cut over his eye. He had bandaged the wound on top of his right hand and said that he'd only given Billy a cursory exam but that there seemed to be no broken bones.

Amanda, a beautiful redhead, turned to the rest of us and said, "May my husband and I have the room, please?"

The rest of us walked back out into the locker room. Ryan was thinking out loud by then, almost stream of consciousness, saying that the way he understood the collective bargaining agreement, the league had the right to suspend Billy if it wanted to, but it wouldn't happen before Sunday's game once Billy appealed any suspension through the players' union.

"It means that if he's healthy enough," Ryan said, "he can still play on Sunday."

"That's where we're going with this right now?" I said.

He shrugged. "I'm a coach," he said again.

Cantor said, "I don't know how drug testing works in the league. But if they don't test him until Sunday morning, there's a chance that whatever drugs he took, or somebody made him take, will be out of his system."

By then I'd shown them all the home page of Wolf.com.

"He didn't use," we all heard now, and we saw Amanda McGee, hands on hips, like she was ready to fight all of us, standing in the doorway to the trainer's room. "I believe my husband. I believe somebody did this to him and set him up."

Billy McGee had told her the same version of things he had told us when he'd finally sat up in the car. He'd gone to dinner at Z & Y Bistro with Matt Daley, his old college tight end. He'd had nothing stronger to drink than seltzer water. They both ordered coffee when they finished dinner. Billy went to the men's room, came back, finished his coffee, paid the check.

He said when they got outside and into the air, he felt the world start to spin. Matt Daley, he said, tried to catch him, but Billy said he hit the sidewalk hard, just managing to break his fall with his right hand.

He didn't know who'd beaten him up. Said he had no idea what happened to Matt Daley.

As we drove to the stadium, Billy had reached into his pocket and found that somehow his car keys were still in there.

"What about my car?"

Ryan had taken the keys from him and said he'd take care of it.

I was sitting on one of the long couches in the middle of our locker room. Amanda came over and sat down next to me.

"Do you believe him?" she said. "I need to know if you believe him. Billy and I both do."

"I do believe him," I said.

"You're not just saying that."

"You don't know her well enough yet," Cantor said. "She doesn't just say stuff to say it."

"Billy says that the only thing that makes sense is that somebody paid Matt to set him up," she said. "But who would do something like that to my husband?"

"Somebody who wanted to get at me," I said. "It's a big club, growing all the time."

Dr. Barnes went back in to check on Billy.

"You need to go somewhere tonight," Ryan Morrissey said. "Somewhere out of town where the league and the media can't find Billy and you. If you need clothes, buy them tomorrow. Drive all the way to Oregon if you want to; I don't care. Check in under your maiden name and somehow smuggle Billy into the room even if you have to throw a bag over his head while you're getting him in there."

I told Amanda that Ryan was right. I gave her the name of an inn near Napa that had cottages instead of rooms, a place I'd stayed once with Ted Skyler. She could leave Billy in the car while she checked in, then get him into one of the cottages. I told her I would make the reservation.

Billy came out of the trainer's room then, walking slowly, hunched over, helped to his locker by Ron Barnes, who reached down and got him one of the pairs of sneakers in there as well as a Warriors sweatshirt hanging on a hook.

Then Billy walked on his own over to Ryan and me. Cantor stood off to the side.

"You gotta know, I wouldn't do this to either one of you," Billy McGee said. "Not after what you did for me."

"I can't describe to you how much I want that to be true," Ryan said.

Amanda stood. Billy put his arm around his wife's shoulders. Cantor looked out into the hallway and said there was no one in sight.

Amanda and Billy left. Ryan said he'd Uber back to Jackson Street and get Billy's car and drive it to the stadium tomorrow. Cantor drove me back to Causwells to pick up mine. I thanked him for everything he'd done. He said he really hadn't done very much except drive.

"You did a lot," I said.

"Then you're welcome."

"I think you've pretty much locked up Wolves Fan of the Week," I said, then kissed him quickly on the cheek and drove home.

When I was finally back inside the house, I saw the note somebody had slid underneath the front door.

THIS IS ONLY THE BEGINNING

EIGHTY-FIVE

BY SATURDAY MORNING, Billy and Amanda McGee were still hiding out at the inn in Napa. It was the quarterback for my Hunters Point team who didn't show up for our game against St. Joseph's.

Chris Tinelli's mom, Barbara, had called to give me the news, telling me that Chris had been mugged the night before as he walked home from All Good Pizza.

"My son didn't even have twenty dollars in his wallet!" she said.

"Did they hurt him?"

"Not *they*," she said, spitting the words out in anger. "One man. He punched Chris in the ribs and then in the face and took his money and tossed his wallet on top of him and ran off."

Barbara Tinelli paused and said, *"Who would do such a thing?"*

I didn't tell Chris Tinelli's mom about the note that had been slid under my door. I hadn't told anybody about the note yet, not even Ben Cantor or Ryan Morrissey. I was more concerned, in the moment, with riding out the fever-dream, day-after coverage on Billy McGee, especially now that no one could locate him. It all made the various feeding frenzies I'd encountered since I'd taken over the team look like speed bumps by comparison.

The fact that he *was* in hiding, and that both Ryan and I had made ourselves spectacularly unavailable to the media, only dialed everything up—exponentially.

Wolf.com broke their morning end-of-the-world headline:

SHOW US (THE) MONEY

Right before I'd gotten into my car for the short ride to school, Megan Callahan had called from her office at the *Tribune*.

"I'm assuming you know where your quarterback is," she said.

"On or off the record?"

"I work for you, remember?" she said.

"I do know where he is. And I know somebody worked awfully hard to set him up the other night. And couldn't wait to get that picture over to my brother Jack, pretty much at record speed."

"Can you guys prove he was set up?" she said.

"Not yet. It turns out that the guy we think drugged him has made a sudden unplanned trip to Europe."

"I don't suppose you'd like to shoot a girl the guy's name," she said.

"Rather shoot *him*, if you want to know the truth."

"Are you of the opinion that Billy McGee is going to play on Sunday?" Megan said.

"To be determined."

"May I at least quote you on that?"

"Knock yourself out."

By noon I was getting ready to coach my high school team. It was just one more day in what felt like an endless number of them by now. But it was a day when I was happy to have the kids around me, almost like a force field, even though we were missing our starting quarterback.

St. Joseph's was undefeated, same as we were. Now we'd be trying to hand them their first loss of the season and avoid one of our own with our backup quarterback, a sophomore named Noah Glynn, who happened to be one of my favorite players on the team.

Noah wasn't even as tall as I was. But the little guy could scramble like a champion and had a much bigger arm than it looked like he should have at five feet six inches. And even with as much talent as he had, and even knowing he was a lock to be next year's starter once Chris Tinelli graduated, I loved Noah's heart most of all. And I knew he was going to need the whole package—scrambling, arm, heart—to give us a chance in the game we were about to play.

Before he took the field for our first offensive series, I put my hands on his shoulders, smiling as I realized I was looking down at him.

"You trust me?"

He smiled. "Is that a trick question, Coach?" he said before quickly adding, "You know I do."

"Then trust me when I tell you that you're going to do something today you'll remember for the rest of your life."

It was exactly what he did.

The defense did more than he did to win us this game and keep us undefeated. But my quarterback was great every time he needed to be, especially in the last couple of minutes, when he took us down the field with the game tied at 12–12, finally scrambling his way into the end zone with forty seconds left and giving us the six-point lead that held up until it was over.

I gave Noah one of the game balls. On my way over to Wolves Stadium to meet with Ryan and talk about our strategy when Billy got to the stadium tomorrow, I stopped at Chris Tinelli's house and gave him a game ball of his own.

When I got to my office an hour later, having stopped on the way to grab a sandwich, my brother Danny was waiting for me.

"I want to come back," he said.

EIGHTY-SIX

ON THE FIELD BELOW ME, the Wolves were finishing up the noncontact drills Ryan always put them through the day before a game.

Danny had taken a seat across from my desk. When I turned away from the window to face him, I said, "You don't have any guts, brother. But you sure didn't get cheated on having a lot of nerve."

"I can help you," he said.

"You want to *help* me?" I said, laughing. "You're like the guy who tries to burn down the house and then runs around trying to find a hose."

I walked over and made myself a cup of coffee from my Keurig machine. I didn't offer Danny one. Ryan and I had a lot to talk about once practice was over. I hadn't come out and said it, but my brother Danny wasn't going to be staying long.

"Did Jack send you?" I said when I sat down. "Slow news day for him now that the poor thing can't seem to locate Billy McGee?"

"I came on my own. You can believe me or not, but I finally got tired of being on the wrong side of this."

"Not to put too fine a point on things," I said, "but you've pretty much been on the wrong side of things with me your whole life."

I sipped some coffee.

"And if you don't mind my asking, what brought about this epiphany?"

He didn't answer right away, as if the question were some kind of brain buster for him.

"It wasn't just one thing. But if it started anywhere, it started with Thomas dying."

"Imagine that."

"I'm being honest."

"And I honestly need to remind you that even after Thomas died, you still went down to LA and tried to torpedo me with the other owners. But now you show up wanting your old job back?"

"You need a general manager," Danny said. "I was always more my own general manager than Mike Sawchuck was."

"Ryan's my acting general manager even though I didn't make an announcement about giving him the title," I said. "You remember Ryan, right? The guy you tried to blackmail into quitting on me?"

Danny shook his head, as if trying to shoo away a fly.

"Things just got out of hand. It's the only way I can explain it. It's time for me to get off the crazy train."

"Gee," I said. "You *think*?"

"I just got crazy trying to get the team back."

"Why? So you could turn around and sell it out of the family at the end of the season? No kidding, Danny, you are some piece of work."

He grinned, as if almost desperate to somehow lighten the mood. "Thanks for saying piece of *work*."

"What's the matter? John Gallo doesn't have the same benefits package you used to have here?"

"He's worse than I thought," Danny said.

"Not sure how something like that is even possible. He really is behind this?"

"I think there might be somebody else in this with him," Danny said. "But before you ask me, I don't know who. Or what. Gallo hasn't told either me or Jack."

"Are you under the impression that he won't come after you as hard as he came after me?"

"I can take it," Danny said.

"No, as a matter of fact, you can't. Let's get real, Danny. If you couldn't take what Dad dished out, you're not going to be able to stand in there against a gangster like Gallo."

"Dad wasn't much better."

"Grading him on a curve? Dad was a lot better than John Gallo."

We sat in silence now, still eyeballing each other. I sipped coffee that had gone cold. I got up and looked back down at the field and saw that practice was ending. When I turned around this time, Danny was already up and out of his chair.

"I had to at least try," he said, and headed for the door.

"Where do you think you're going?" I said.

EIGHTY-SEVEN

I WAS ON THE phone with Billy and Amanda McGee, who were driving back to San Francisco from Napa on Saturday night, having managed to make it through both days up there without being discovered. I told them now not to go to the house they'd rented in the Embarcadero after Billy had signed his Wolves contract. Told them they should go directly to Thomas Wolf's house. I'd text Amanda the address.

She was driving.

"Dude," Billy said to me, "us staying there would creep me out."

"Trust me—it shouldn't," I said. "My brother Thomas lived for drama and intrigue like this."

I told them that if Billy needed to get some exercise in, Thomas had built himself a world-class gym that included one of those Peloton bikes.

"I didn't fall out of shape because of the way they worked me over," Billy said.

He sounded like his old cocky self again, despite everything.

"Funny world, though, right, dude? Now somebody has to knock me unconscious to try to get me to use."

Then I told them both I'd see them in the morning. I also

told them how Ryan and I wanted them to handle things once they arrived at the stadium. Billy swore on his love for his wife that he wouldn't let us down.

"Dude," he said to me one more time. "I'm telling the truth about this; you gotta trust me."

"I explained to Amanda when I talked to her this morning," I said. "You just took a fall for me. Literally. And let's face it, the alternative to not trusting you kind of sucks."

I called Ben Cantor after that and told him what I wanted to do and asked if I had permission to do it.

"Officially or unofficially?"

"Does it make a difference?"

"Go for it," Cantor said.

Then I called Megan Callahan. We talked a long time.

"This is solid?" she said.

"More solid than Alcatraz."

Then I told her there was only one condition—that she hold it off the website and save it for tomorrow morning's print edition, embargoing it until then.

It was exactly what she did.

First thing in the morning I drove over to Pacific Heights, the copy of the Sunday *Tribune* that had been delivered to my house on the seat next to me.

The story splashed across our front page, with Megan Callahan's byline on it, said that the *Tribune* had learned from police department sources that Jack Wolf was now being treated as a person of interest in his brother Thomas's death. And that he might be facing an obstruction charge for withholding information from the police about events in which he was involved the night Thomas died.

Jack Wolf had opened the front door before I made it halfway up the walk.

I handed him the paper. He wouldn't take it, saying he'd already seen it.

"Solid front page, though, don't you think? Almost worthy of Wolf.com."

"You did this," he said. "You and your friend Cantor."

"No idea what you're talking about."

"I'll have his ass," Jack Wolf said.

"Good luck with that."

I dropped the paper at his feet and started back toward my car.

Halfway there, I turned around.

"One more thing, Jack. A message, really. For you and your friend Gallo and whatever other skeevy people you might currently be involved with."

"And what might that be?"

"This is only the beginning," I said.

EIGHTY-EIGHT

BEN CANTOR THOUGHT HE might be the only one who fully appreciated the irony of the *Tribune* "exclusive" naming Jack Wolf as a person of interest in his brother Thomas's death.

They were *all* persons of interest to Cantor by now—the whole family, from the Queen Mother on down.

That included Jenny, as much as Cantor didn't want it to and even though in his mind it really didn't.

For now.

Cantor and Jenny were having their first glass of wine at Harris' steak house, in Russian Hill, both of them in the mood to piss off the red-meat police, when Cantor said to her, "I can't wait to hear the thinking behind your bringing your brother Danny back into the fold."

"It might just be the one about keeping your friends close and your enemies closer," Jenny said. "That doesn't work for you, Detective Cantor?"

"Not with a weasel like Danny."

"Okay, then how about the one about how it's better to have somebody on the inside of the tent pissing out rather than the other way around?" Jenny said, smiling at him.

Cantor grinned. "Okay, I'm begging you to stop."

"I've got more," Jenny said.

"You've clearly talked yourself into believing this is a good idea."

"Are we going to spend our entire date talking about Danny?"

"So these are official dates now?" Cantor said.

"Look at you. No wonder you made detective at such a young age."

"Don't kids post something on Instagram when they're 'official'?" Cantor said, putting air quotes around the word.

"I could post something on the Wolves' Instagram account. We could do a selfie right here. Want to?"

"Did you start drinking before you got here?" he said.

She laughed.

Dinner dates were as far as they'd gotten. But neither one of them had made any kind of move to take things to the next level.

Next level, Cantor?

He felt himself smiling. It even sounded dumb thinking about it that way. Or even joking about their being official. He frankly wasn't sure exactly *what* they were, even as he continually second-guessed himself for having any kind of relationship with her at all. And knowing what his bosses would say if they found out about it.

He had beaten her to the restaurant tonight, knowing he would, because she'd told him that she wanted to go home and change after her practice at Hunters Point. So he was already in the big rounded booth as she came walking briskly through the middle of the room, turning heads as she did. Maybe not everybody at Harris' knew who she was. But a lot of them did.

She was wearing a dress tonight, the first time she'd done that for one of their dinner dates. She apologized for being later than usual. Cantor lied and told her that he'd only beaten her to what billed itself as "the" San Francisco steak house by a couple of minutes.

"You look sensational," Cantor said.

"Thanks. Usually when I get the urge to dress up, I lie down until it passes."

"And you did this for my benefit?"

"Don't push it. Just take the win."

She leaned down before she slid in next to him and kissed him briefly on the lips.

Then they talked for a few minutes about how well Billy McGee, even as banged up as he'd been after Chinatown, had played on Sunday as the Wolves won again.

Cantor asked if McGee still might be facing disciplinary action just on the optics alone.

Jenny said that she and Billy had a Zoom meeting scheduled with the commissioner, but the head of the players' union had told her that since there had been no drugs present in Billy's system when they tested him after Sunday's game, he really couldn't see Billy getting suspended for being set up then beaten up.

That was her story, she said, and she was sticking to it.

"Somebody went to a lot of trouble *to* set him up," Cantor said.

"If it's not my brother Jack, I'd like to know who else it could have been."

"The pictures did go up on Wolf.com at the speed of light," Cantor said.

"Didn't they, though?"

"What about the prodigal brother?"

"Danny? It would have been pretty ballsy to go to all that trouble with Billy and then want to come in from the cold."

"He still could have," Cantor said.

"You're the cop. Who do *you* like for it?"

"Jack," he said without hesitation. "The big bad Wolf. All day long."

Their entrées had arrived when Jenny asked Cantor how his investigations were going. He told her he'd made some progress. She asked on which case, her father's or her brother's, before sighing and shaking her head.

"It's like living in crazy town, asking my date if he's got anything new on the two deaths in my family."

He grinned. "Imagine how I feel."

They were getting to it now—he knew it. There was nothing he could do to stop it, no point in waiting, even if it blew the evening sky-high, as he fully expected it might.

"But you said you *have* made progress?" she said.

"It has to do with your father."

He took one more healthy swallow of red wine, as if he were fortifying himself. Then he put his glass down, took in some air, slowly let it out.

"How come you didn't tell me your father came to see you at your house the night before he died?" Cantor said.

EIGHTY-NINE

I HAD MY GLASS halfway to my lips, but then placed it carefully next to my plate, trying to keep myself calm.

"Excuse me?"

"Pretty simple question," Cantor said. "Your father came to see you. You didn't tell me. I'm just trying to understand why."

"Why what?"

"Why he came to see you," Cantor said. "And why you kept it to yourself."

"So you're still treating me like a suspect," I said. I forced a smile. "Even when I dress up."

"That's not true. And also not an answer."

"Who told you he came to my house?"

"Now you get to ask the questions?" he said.

"Just the one."

"Okay," Cantor said, putting out his hands as if pumping the brakes on the conversation. "Let me explain."

"I can't wait."

Cantor ran a distracted hand through his dark curly hair. Took another deep breath. Leaned slightly forward, lowering his voice.

Cantor said, "I was so fixed on his whereabouts the day and night he died that I didn't think about where he'd been the night before. So I circled back and talked to his driver. That guy Leo. And Leo said that he'd taken Mr. Wolf to your house. Said he was pretty drunk by the time he got there, too. Your dad. Not Leo."

"He was," I said. "From everything I know about the last few months of his life, he was drinking more and more."

"So he *was* there."

"You know he was."

"But you told me you hadn't talked to him during the last few months of his life," Cantor said.

"I barely said anything to him *that* night," she said. "He just wanted to tell me that he was sorry for being a bad father to me. He asked me to forgive him and told me he wanted me back in his life. I told him okay, I was back, just to get rid of him." I paused. "I never liked my father very much. But I *hated* him when he was drunk."

"So why didn't you just tell me all this?"

"Because he died the next day, and a few days later I inherited everything *because* he died," I said. "And I didn't want you to think he'd told me about the will. Because I know how you think by now. And I knew that *would* turn me into some kind of suspect. Or another person of interest in the family."

I reached across the table now, wrists pressed together, and said, "You should probably just go ahead and cuff me right now, Detective."

He managed a smile.

"I didn't know you were into that."

"Not funny."

"I had to ask about this," he said.

"You make it sound as if I've been hiding it."

"Only because you have been hiding it."

"You need to trust me that it had nothing to do with any-thing," I said.

"The way you trusted me?" Cantor said.

"I told him not to come. But he insisted. I told him one of the things I didn't miss was talking to him when he was drunk, and if I was going to let him back into my life, I didn't want him showing up in that condition. He said he wouldn't ever again. He left. End of story."

"I believe you," Cantor said.

"Wow. There's a relief."

I turned and waved at our waiter and made a signing gesture to let him know I wanted a check.

"You're leaving?" Cantor said.

"What was your first clue?"

"I haven't done anything wrong," Cantor said.

"Neither have I."

The waiter brought the check. Cantor took out his wallet, but I had already handed the waiter my credit card. When he got back to the table, I signed and stood up.

"Do you honestly still think that I might have had something to do with my father's death?"

Cantor said, "We could have cleared this up a long time ago if you'd been honest then and told me everything you just told me now."

"Now you're the one not answering the question."

"No," he said, "I don't think you had anything to do with your father's death."

Cantor stood. I noticed people in the room staring at us, and I didn't care.

"Is there anything else I need to know about the weekend your father died?" Cantor asked.

"No."

Lying to him again.

I was on a roll.

NINETY

DANNY HEARD HIS DOORBELL ring a few minutes before eight. His brother Jack was shouldering his way inside almost before Danny had the door all the way open.

"You chump," Jack said in the form of greeting.

Danny had been expecting a visit like this since he'd gone back to the Wolves.

"You stupid chump," Jack said.

When Danny turned around, Jack was standing just a few feet away from him, and when he took half a step forward, Danny flinched, unable to stop himself. But then he'd been in a defensive crouch with Jack pretty much his whole life, more afraid of him than he was of their father, just because he knew the kind of violence his brother had always carried around inside him.

"You didn't even have the guts to tell me yourself," Jack said. "But then you never did have any guts, did you, Danny boy?"

Danny boy.

It's what Joe Wolf had called him as a way of belittling him, even when he was still a boy.

"I'm not staying long," Jack said, clenching and unclenching his fists as he paced in front of Danny. "I just want you to explain to me what the holy hell you were thinking."

"There's no point," Danny said. "I knew you'd react this way. And Gallo, too. I decided this on my own."

"You don't decide shit on your own!" Jack screamed at him, sounding exactly like John Gallo as he did.

He faked a punch now. Danny jerked back, staggering into the door. Remembering another time when he'd seen his brother this full of rage, not even trying to contain himself that time.

It was when they were teenagers. He and Jack had come back from a pickup basketball game in the park. There had been a beef with the other team over a foul call. Jack had ended up on the ground. When he got up to complain, the biggest kid on the other team had broken his nose with one punch. When Danny tried to step in, he'd caught an even worse beating.

When they told their father what had happened, he called them little girls for walking away. Telling them again—the same old song—that he kept forgetting he had three other daughters.

But it turned out to be the day when Jack decided he'd had enough and proceeded to give his father so much of a beating that Elise Wolf finally called the police because she was afraid Jack might beat Joe Wolf to death.

"I put this team together," Danny said. "I have a right to see things through."

"Do you know how pathetic you sound? You're willing to throw everything away to win a few goddamn football games?"

Jack shook his head. "Maybe our father," he said, "maybe he did have more than one daughter. Except that even she's got more balls than you do."

The words just came out of Danny then.

"Maybe you should just kill us, too. Jenny and me both."

Jack stopped pacing now.

"What is that supposed to mean?"

"What it means is that you hated Dad more than the rest of us put together," Danny said. "You hated Thomas for taking Jenny's side after she got the team and the paper." He paused. "And you were the one who nearly killed Dad when we were kids."

"You accusing me of something?"

"I'm just tired of Gallo telling me what to do," Danny said. "I'm tired of you telling me what to do."

Jack laughed at him.

"So what—you're going to let our sister tell you what to do instead?"

"I have to get to the office," Danny said. "Do what you have to do, Jack."

No holding back now.

"Even if it means acting like John Gallo's bitch."

Jack hit him then, threw a punch with his right hand that just exploded into Danny's face, catching him under his left eye and knocking him hard into the front door.

Then he was on him, hitting him again, harder this time, squarely on the nose, and putting Danny down.

When Danny put a hand to his face, he saw it was covered in blood. Jack just stared down at him, eyes still full of rage.

In that moment, Danny felt as if he were looking up at his father.

Or their father's killer.

NINETY-ONE

"YOU CAN'T RUN THESE pictures on the front page of the paper," I said to Megan Callahan in her office at the *Tribune*. "Or on our home page."

We had been going at each other, her door closed, since she'd called and asked me to come over, telling me there was a situation we needed to address immediately. I said that didn't sound good. She said it wasn't even close to being good and that she'd explain when I got there.

The situation involved a series of photographs of Ben Cantor and me at Harris' steak house. One had me leaning down to kiss him on the lips. Another had the two of us leaning across the table, my hand covering his. There were similar pictures from the night we'd eaten at Fogata, where Cantor had said the paparazzi wouldn't find us.

So somebody has been following me all along.

"If we don't run them," Megan said, "you can explain to the next managing editor of the *Tribune* why we didn't run pictures that everybody except *Stars and Stripes* is going to have within the next hour or so."

I heard a ping from her phone. She was on the other side of

her desk. She hit some keys on her huge laptop screen, then swiveled it so I could see the home page of Wolf.com.

"Annnnnnnd," she said, "we're off."

They'd gone with the one of me kissing Cantor when I'd arrived that night, headlined:

UNDERCOVER(S) COP

Plus the secondary headline:

Suspect Behavior from Wolves Owner with Cop "Investigating" Her

I slumped back into my chair.

"It's not what it looks like."

"Are you sleeping with him?" Megan said.

"None of your goddamn business. But no."

"Jenny," Megan said, "there's no way for you to spin this. Or for us to ignore this. What the whole world is about to see is you and the detective investigating two murders in your family gazing longingly into each other's eyes."

"Would it matter to you if I told you how badly that particular dinner date ended?"

"Not even a little bit."

Her phone pinged again. She nodded.

"Okay. *TMZ* is running with it."

"You make it sound as if that's the paper of record."

"With stuff like this, it pretty much is."

"*We* aren't obligated to run with the crowd on this," I said.

"There is no *we* right now," Megan said. "There's just the paper. And so you know? We *are* going to run with the crowd on this, fast as we can. When you gave me this job you told me to edit the paper my way. So let me do that now. If you'd like to give me a quote, we can throw it into the news story. If not, we need to get this up now."

I leaned forward and looked at the photographs she'd spread out on her desk. My eyes had originally passed right over the one of Ben and me standing on his front porch the night he'd invited me in.

I pointed to that one now.

"I didn't even go inside that night. But that doesn't matter, either, does it?"

"You've been in the crosshairs for weeks," Megan said. "You ought to know the rules of engagement by now."

I leaned back in my chair, feeling very tired at the moment. Tired of just about everybody and everything.

"Is it even worth asking where these pictures came from?"

"Sure," Megan said. "It was Bert Patricia."

"Private detective to the stars? I don't even know why he calls himself private. He's in the papers almost as much as I am." I held up a hand. "Wait—didn't Bert Patricia go to jail?"

"On the phone hacking thing," Megan said. "Somehow he beat the rap."

"So he doesn't care that people know he's the one who's been following me?"

"One of the people following you," she said. "Are you kidding? He *wants* people to know it was him, even if he can't come right out and say that himself. It puts him right where he wants to be: in the middle of a big story."

"My brother Jack must have hired him. When Jack wasn't having one of his reporters following me from time to time."

"Nope," Megan said. "If he had, the only place where you'd be able to see these pictures would be at Wolf.com."

"So if he didn't, who do you think did?"

"I was getting to that," Megan said. "I don't think. I know who did."

"I thought private detectives didn't reveal who their clients are."

"The ethical ones usually don't," Megan said. "But Bert couldn't resist telling one of our reporters, who's been covering him for years. On background, of course."

"So who *did* hire him?"

"The commissioner of the National Football League," Megan Callahan said.

NINETY-TWO

WHEN I CALLED JOEL ABRAMS, he denied ever having heard of Bert Patricia and tried to act offended that I would accuse him of stooping to such a thing.

"Our league is better than that," Abrams said.

"Really? Since when?"

"And this isn't about my behavior, anyway," Abrams said. "It's about yours."

"I just hope you're as intrepid the next time one of your other owners gets caught with his pants down."

"I'm not the one having an inappropriate relationship."

"Neither am I," I said, and hung up on him.

I had chosen not to give a quote to my own paper or anybody else about what the whole world was calling an affair, even if both Ben Cantor and I knew it wasn't an affair, never had been, and never *would* be, the way things were going.

What I did instead was leave town.

I made my first road trip of the season with the Wolves, for our Sunday game in Seattle against the Seahawks, even leaving a couple of days early. While I was away, my principal at Hunters Point, Joey Rubino, coached the Bears on Saturday to a tie. It wasn't a win, but it wasn't a loss, either, and the team held first place in our league with the playoffs not far off.

Then the Wolves won big against the Seahawks on Sunday, in perhaps Billy McGee's best performance since he'd returned to the league. With a month left in the regular season, the team was closing in on its first playoff spot in years.

I took one call over the weekend, from Ben Cantor, while waiting for our team plane to take off for the flight back to San Francisco. He said he wanted me to know that he wasn't being taken off either case—my father's or Thomas's.

"Good to know."

"That's it?" he said.

Then I told him what I was always telling my high school players.

"Do your job."

We got back late on Sunday night from Seattle, having been fogged in for a few hours. The next morning, I drove over to the Flood Building, on Market Street, where my brother Jack had rented office space for Wolf.com.

His website had spent the past few days running with the story about Cantor and me, even circling back to Ryan Morrissey's sleepover at my house, doing everything possible to make me sound like either a woman of extremely easy virtue or perhaps a bigger menace to society than the late John Gotti.

The Flood Building was a twelve-story high-rise that despite having undergone several makeovers had stood for more than a hundred years at the corner of Market and Powell. Now the San Francisco landmark housed what I considered a modern form of media whorehouse: Wolf.com.

I took the elevator up to the tenth floor and entered a loftlike space that was big enough to hold a dozen desks. I spotted Seth Dowd in a corner, phone to his ear, typing away.

He nodded at me in greeting. I offered him my most dazzling smile and gave him the finger.

Jack had a glassed-in office that faced Market. His door was closed. I could see that he was talking on the phone but walked right in anyway without knocking.

He put the phone down when he saw me, stood up, and said, "If you take a swing at me this time, Sis, I want to warn you, I'm swinging back."

"At least it won't be the kind of sucker punch you threw at Danny."

"He had it coming. You might forgive and forget. I'm not that guy."

He sat back down, almost impatiently, and said, "What do you want?"

I sat down across from him.

"I want to tell you a story."

"We're always on the lookout for good stories at Wolf.com. What's this one about?"

"About my going to see Dad on his boat the night he died," I said.

I saw genuine surprise on his face.

"You were there?"

"Right before you were," I said.

NINETY-THREE

"I ASSUME THIS IS an off-the-record conversation," Jack said.

"Said a brother to his sister."

"Is it off the record or not?"

"Shouldn't *I* be the one asking *you* that?"

"I've got a better question," he said. "Did your boyfriend ask you to wear a wire?"

"He's not my boyfriend."

"That's not an answer."

"You're right."

"And you know what?" he said. "I frankly don't care if you're recording this or not. I didn't kill him." There was a familiar smug look on his face. "Should I speak louder?"

He leaned back and folded his arms, put his feet up on his desk.

"And, by the way, why are we even having this conversation this much after the fact?"

"Because I'm sick of you and everybody else in this office treating me like a criminal," I said. "That's why."

"Get over it."

"You were there after I was there, even though the only two people who know that are sitting in this room."

"*Did* Cantor send you?" he said.

"He doesn't know that either one of us was at the boat. And

he doesn't know that I came here to see you. All he knows is that Dad came to my house the night before."

I could see that I had surprised my brother again.

"You told anybody who'd listen after he died that you hadn't seen him since you walked away," Jack said.

"I lied. Family trait. Like blue eyes."

He shook his head, almost sadly, from side to side.

"You've never been any better than the rest of us. The only one who thought so was the great Joe Wolf."

There was a knock on the door. Seth Dowd poked his head in.

"Not now," Jack said.

Dowd closed the door and walked away.

"I *am* curious about one thing. What are you hoping to accomplish by coming here?"

"To get you off my back once and for all," I said.

"Not happening. And why would I? Because you think you have some kind of leverage with me now? You don't. The only person who can put me on that boat is you. If it ever came to it, it would be your word against mine."

"Cantor likes me better," I said.

"Obviously."

I grinned.

"What's so funny?"

"We've got something on each other," I said. "Just like when we were kids."

"I didn't kill him," Jack said again. "I hated him. But not enough to kill him and risk going down for it no matter how much better my life would get with him out of the way."

"You nearly killed him once."

"He deserved it that time," Jack said. "And if you ask me, he deserved somebody finishing the job this time."

I stared at him. The older he got, the more he reminded me

of our father. A lot of it was in the eyes. It occurred to me, not for the first time, that Joe Wolf had gotten his way in the end after a lifetime of trying to toughen up his children. Jack had turned out to be as mean as he was.

"Why were you at the boat?" Jack said.

I told him. Told him the drunken things Joe Wolf had said to me before he told me that he loved me.

"You're shitting me!" Jack said. "He told you he loved you and you *believed* him? *Him*?"

"I'm telling you what happened, and why it happened. I felt bad that I hadn't said anything back to him."

"Why would you have?"

His phone buzzed. He ignored it.

"I think back now, and it was almost like he'd had some premonition that he was going to die soon."

"He didn't tell you that he was leaving the team and the paper to you?"

"No."

"And that was it," Jack said.

"That was it. I left. I was sitting in my car when I saw you nearly running up the dock."

He didn't respond right away.

"Did he tell you I'd just left?"

Jack shook his head.

I said, "So what were *you* doing there that night?"

He blew out some air.

"You want to know the truth?"

"Not one of your strong suits. But give it a shot."

"You still don't get it, do you?" he said.

"Help me out."

"I didn't go there to kill him that night," Jack Wolf said to me. "I went there to try to save him."

NINETY-FOUR

AN HOUR AFTER LEAVING Wolf.com, I was back in my own office at Wolves Stadium.

John Gallo was seated across my desk from me.

I had asked him to the stadium for a conversation, just the two of us, about the possible sale of the Wolves. I didn't tell him what Jack had told me, his version of why he'd gone to the boat that night—to bring him John Gallo's final, take-it-or-leave-it offer to buy the Wolves. It turned out they had been negotiating for months. Not only had Gallo's patience finally run out, he had also indicated to Jack that he was under pressure to close the deal sooner rather than later.

"What did Dad say?" I asked Jack.

"He said he'd give Gallo his answer in the morning."

Thomas had always talked about throwing the money on the table. We were about to do that now. Maybe just not the way John Gallo thought.

"I have to admit I was quite surprised to get your call, Ms. Wolf," he said.

"It seemed like a practical matter to me. And I know what a practical man you are."

He wore a light gray suit that matched the color of his

hair, a white shirt, and a blood-red tie. And a smug look on his face.

"Even my brothers tell me they don't fully understand why you seem to want my football team as badly as you do," I said. "They also don't understand the methods you've used to try to get it."

"Your brothers know as much about my business as they need to know," Gallo said. "And considering how useless your brother Danny turned out to be, it's probably for the best that he came running back to you like a little boy running to his mommy."

I smiled.

"Considering what I know about Danny Wolf, I thought he exhibited surprisingly good taste in making this particular choice."

I got up then and went to stand at the window and look down at the Wolves' practice. Kept my back to him for over a minute before turning around.

"So why *do* you want my team so badly? The Denver Broncos were for sale last year, and you didn't go anywhere near them."

"The Wolves were supposed to be mine about ten years ago, but your father reneged on a deal we'd agreed to, one that I thought was overly generous at the time," Gallo said. "The details of his screwing me over the way he did and acting as dishonorably as he did no longer matter. He's gone now. And here the two of us are, and it's time for me to put an offer on the table."

"What *are* you willing to offer?" I said.

"Just like that?"

"Just like that."

"Three billion dollars," he said.

The Carolina Panthers, I knew, had been sold a few years ago for $2.3 billion. The Broncos had gone for $2.5 billion, the highest sale price in league history at that point. He was now willing to top that by half a billion dollars.

"That's serious money."

"When I want something, Ms. Wolf," he said, "I'm not just willing to pay. I'm also willing to overpay. And frankly? I feel as if I have waited long enough to conclude business with your family that should have been concluded long ago."

"No."

Gallo looked confused, as if I'd suddenly spoken to him in French.

"No? Meaning no, you don't think my business with your father should have been concluded years ago?"

From down below, I could hear the sound of a whistle being blown on the field.

"What I meant was no, I am not going to sell my team to you for three billion dollars."

"Three point five," he said, almost before the words were out of my mouth.

Gallo smiled then, looking almost happy even though I'd just turned him down again. He was on familiar ground here. He was John Gallo, the dealmaker. John Gallo the closer. Negotiating for something he really did want was probably like a narcotic with him.

"No." (

"I trust you're quite clear on the fact that I am offering you a billion dollars more than anybody has ever offered for an NFL franchise," he said.

"Crystal."

"Four billion dollars."

I shook my head. Gallo shifted slightly in his chair. He

didn't look rattled, shaken, uncertain, or even perturbed. Maybe he had convinced himself that he could simply roll me when the time came after throwing everything he had at me for months. In his mind, there would reach a tipping point where I would give up and walk away and he would get what he wanted.

"Why don't we try this another way?" he said. "Why don't you name a price?"

"There isn't one. The Wolves aren't for sale, at least not to you. Not for sale today. Not tomorrow. Not ever. Is that clear enough for *you*, John?"

I smiled at him again.

"You stupid bitch."

He didn't seem to say it in anger. It was more like he was verbalizing the obvious, for my own benefit as well as his.

"Now, there's the John Gallo my father knew and hated."

"You stupid, stupid bitch," he said. "Do you know how much worse things can get for you going forward?"

"As another practical matter? Yeah, I probably do."

"You asked me over here to discuss the sale of the team," Gallo said.

"And that's exactly the discussion we've had. Just not the one you anticipated. But that's on you, frankly, and not me."

Gallo stared at me as if somehow really seeing me for the first time.

"May I ask you a question?"

"Of course."

He smiled again and lowered his voice almost to a whisper.

"Do you ever worry that something might happen to you the way it did to your father and your youngest brother?"

"Is that a threat, John?"

"More like a promise."

"And that's an overused cliché," I said. "Or maybe, now that I really think about it, you're the cliché."

I got up then and walked around my desk and went over to my door and opened it.

"Now get out of my office," I said.

NINETY-FIVE

WHEN JOHN GALLO WAS back in the car, Erik Mason said, "He called when you were inside. He wants to see you."

From the back seat, Gallo said, "Now?"

"Yes, sir," Mason said. "Mr. Barr indicated that he wanted me to drive you to his house as soon as you were in the car."

Michael Barr lived in a mansion on Scott Street that was more like a fortress, one that Barr had originally purchased for thirty million dollars back in the 1990s.

If Michael Barr wasn't the wealthiest person in San Francisco, he was close enough. He had made his fortune in construction and real estate, from downtown San Francisco all the way to the Monterey Peninsula, before expanding his interests to casinos in Las Vegas and London and as far away as Macao. Barr, more than any other big casino owner, took the lead in online gambling in the United States when other casino owners were running away from it.

And over time he had become a prominent and respected member of San Francisco society, backing an endless series of good causes in the city, creating foundations for the homeless and abused women.

It meant that somehow Michael Barr had managed, despite being a public figure, to largely keep hidden the fact that he was one of the most powerful and ruthless private arms dealers in the world. John Gallo knew that Barr did enough business with the United States involving legal weapons for the federal government to conveniently overlook the vast illegal business he did internationally, in a world he helped control as well and as formidably as any Saudi Arabian or Syrian or Russian.

In addition, Michael Barr had controlled Gallo, and Gallo's own businesses, for years, ever since Gallo had nearly gone under during the housing crash from the second Bush presidency. The extremely well-kept secret, for both Barr and Gallo, was that it wasn't John Gallo who had become obsessed with owning the Wolves. It was Michael Barr.

It was Barr who first imagined completely altering the map of San Francisco with a new stadium and what would be the biggest municipal real estate development around it in US history. He had watched from across the country the way the Barclays Center had helped transform Brooklyn, in New York City. He had seen this happen with other stadiums and other arenas around the country.

Michael Barr didn't need a team or a football stadium to enhance his arms dealing around the world. Nor did he need it for his various other enterprises, both inside and outside the law. But he saw a world where the two went hand in hand, and the possibilities for money laundering and leveraging other parts of his empire could be limitless.

It almost made Barr laugh sometimes, seeing sports-team owners in the United States act like they were the real gangsters. But they were amateurs. He was not. Maybe there would be a baseball team for him down the line. Or a basketball team. Or both.

Compared to everything else in Michael Barr's life, sports was going to be easy.

But first he needed a football team to complete his vision for San Francisco.

The Wolves.

They sat now in Barr's upstairs den. Barr was a small, trim man with close-cropped white hair, partial to black suits and black shirts. His eyes, Gallo had always thought, matched the color of those outfits.

"*She* told *you* to leave her office?" Barr said now. "As if she were the one giving the orders?"

"There was no point in the two of us continuing the conversation," Gallo said. "But I assure you, it's a temporary setback."

"There seem to have been a series of those," Barr said, "ones that have frequently turned out to be permanent rather than temporary."

"They won't matter in the end when we get what we want," Gallo said.

"Ah, yes. Another assurance about what you continue to tell me is an inevitable conclusion to all this. But you also assured me that her brothers would have her under control by now. Only now you don't even have both of them on your side, do you, John?"

"But we still have *time* on our side," Gallo said. "We knew from the beginning that nothing would happen with the team until after the season, even if the other owners had voted her out of their little club."

Barr tilted his head slightly, his mouth nearly, but not quite, curling into a grin, as if Gallo had said something amusing.

"Essentially, you've failed me again, haven't you, John?" Barr said. "Remember when you told me how if we backed Jack Wolf with Wolf.com, he would weaponize the site even more than he ever did with the newspaper?" Barr leaned back, briefly closed his eyes, then focused them once again on Gallo. "Please show me how *that* has worked out for us, John."

"There's more that I can do," Gallo said. "That *we* can do. We can still play the long game here and still get what you and I both want in the end."

"No more games," Barr said, shaking his head. "You were the one who convinced me that modern warfare was fought through the media, that we would destroy her there. You were the one who convinced me that because of your history with her father, as contentious as it was, you were the perfect lead man on this. That no one would question your aggressively going after the team with him out of the way. And yet? And yet she is still here, isn't she, John? And she just threw you out of her office."

Every time he used Gallo's first name, it felt as if he were being slapped.

"Her brother is thrown out a window, and she is still here," Barr said. "She goes to Los Angeles for a vote you tell me she cannot win."

He smiled now.

"And yet she is still here," Barr said again.

Gallo started to speak. Barr shook his head.

"You understand better than I do what the stakes are here," Barr said. "You understand that I have a chance to control a city in a way that no private citizen ever has in all the city's history. It is all right there for me. And now you let this cow continue to stand in my way."

"Tell me how I can make this right," Gallo said.

"Get rid of her," Barr said.

NINETY-SIX

JOHN GALLO HAD LIVED in the Belvedere section of San Francisco—just over the Golden Gate Bridge, in the big house overlooking the bay—since before his wife died.

It was a spectacular property, with a view that seemed to take in the entire bay at once and an expanse of yard in back that was the size of a football field and stretched to the edge of the cliffs overlooking the beach and the water below. Gallo had loved this place from the time he bought it, imagining it as his own personal version of Lands End Lookout.

But the house was too much for him now with his wife gone. He had decided that when he had concluded his business with Michael Barr, when Barr ended up with the football team, as Gallo knew he inevitably would, he would move back to the city, or even out of it—perhaps finally build a smaller house for himself on property not unlike this that he owned in Monterey.

Perhaps Elise Wolf would be willing to visit him there. She had never hated him the way her husband had, hated him the way her daughter now did. Gallo still held out hope that there was a chance for something to happen between them.

Erik Mason drove him back to Belvedere now. Gallo sat in

the back of the Mercedes and poured himself a glass of Irish whiskey.

He told Mason about the last thing Barr said to him.

"There's always one more loose end, isn't there?" Gallo said.

"This time it will need to look like an accident," Mason said. "But there are ways."

"There are always ways," Gallo said. He put his head back and closed his eyes. "You just have to be willing."

"We should probably start talking about possible options right now," Mason said. "It sounds as if Mr. Barr's patience has run out."

They went inside the house, and Gallo poured them both whiskeys. Then he took off his jacket and put on a sweater, and the two of them walked outside, across the back lawn toward the water, lit brilliantly tonight by the moon and stars on a rare cloudless night in San Francisco. Gallo once thought he might transform the city the way Michael Barr would when he got the Wolves.

"It was supposed to be simple once the father was out of the way," Gallo said. "Then he gave the team to her."

"No one could have seen that coming," Mason said. "Certainly not you, sir."

"She's even more stubborn than her father was," Gallo said, "as impossible as that is for me to believe."

"Look what it got him," Mason said. "His stubbornness, I mean. And look what it got her younger brother when he wouldn't stop pushing until he found out things that only you and Mr. Barr were supposed to know."

"And you, Erik."

"Of course, sir."

"Another loose end," Gallo said. "Thomas Wolf, I mean. But it's not as if he gave anybody a choice."

"He wasn't just another loose end," Erik Mason said. "More like a loose cannon."

Gallo drank, staring out at the sky and the water. It had struck him again tonight how well he continued to fool most of the people he encountered, how they still feared him the way they always had. How they still thought he possessed the kind of power that Michael Barr had.

"We'll do what we need to do," Gallo said to Erik Mason.

"As always," Mason said. "When the situation on the ground changes, adjustments have to be made."

"Do you think the girl will be the last loose end?" Gallo said.

"One of them," Mason said.

"You'll handle it," Gallo said.

"Of course."

Gallo turned to Erik Mason, extending his glass, saying they should drink to that. But Mason was no longer standing next to him.

Mason was behind John Gallo now, his arms around him, effortlessly lifting him into the air before Gallo realized what was happening, carrying him the few steps to the edge of the bluff before letting him go.

NINETY-SEVEN

A WOMAN WALKING HER dog found John Gallo's body trapped by the rocks below his property in the late morning, before the current could carry him away. By the middle of the afternoon, Ben Cantor was in my office at Wolves Stadium, wanting to know what John Gallo and I had talked about when he had been with me here the previous afternoon.

"How'd you know he was here?" I said.

"Knowing stuff is kind of a hobby with me," Cantor said.

I told him as much of the conversation as I could recall and what I'd said to him before he left.

"And that's it?" Cantor said.

"Yes, Detective. That's it."

It was the first time I'd seen him since I walked out of the restaurant that night, right before Cantor and I had been turned into San Francisco's fun couple by the media.

"You're not leaving anything out this time?"

"I've learned that only opens me up to heartbreak. Or opens you up to heartbreak. Or both of us."

"He act like somebody who might go home and jump?" Cantor said.

"Because of a football team?"

"Somebody threw your father into the water over a football team," Cantor said, "and someone threw your brother out a window. Maybe the same person threw Gallo off a cliff."

"Let me know when you figure it out."

"Is this the way it's going to be with us from now on?"

"I'm not really sure, Detective. But if you don't have any further questions for me, I have a team meeting to attend."

"With the Wolves?"

"The Hunters Point Bears, as a matter of fact."

Cantor went down the hall to talk to Danny Wolf about the death of John Gallo. I drove over to the high school. Chris Tinelli, my quarterback, was the one who'd emailed me earlier and said he and the other players wanted to meet with me in the gym before practice.

The Bears' first playoff game was scheduled for Saturday, against Archbishop Riordan. If we won, the championship game would be in two weeks. I'd already arranged that it would be played at Wolves Stadium, whether the Bears were in it or not.

The players were waiting for me when I got there, already suited up for practice. They were seated in bleachers that had been pulled down off the gym walls, as if this were some kind of assembly. When I walked in, it occurred to me how good it was to see them. I'd missed three consecutive practices last week and then been in Seattle when we'd nearly suffered our first loss of the season.

I looked up at them and grinned and said, "Why don't I make a few opening comments and then throw it open to questions?"

Nobody laughed.

Crickets.

Chris Tinelli had been sitting in the bottom row of the

338

bleachers. He got up now and walked up to me, his face serious, his rubber cleats sounding loud on the gym floor.

"What's going on, Chris?" I said to him.

He took a deep breath, looked up at his teammates, and then said, "We don't want you to coach us anymore."

I looked at him as if I hadn't heard him correctly.

"I'm sorry. What did you just say?"

"We feel bad about it, Coach. We really do. But we're kind of firing you."

NINETY-EIGHT

"YOU CAN'T BE SERIOUS, CHRIS," I said. "You know how important you are to me. How important you all are."

But everything about him, everything in the air we were all breathing, told me he wasn't joking at all. And neither were his teammates.

"Well, you sure don't act like we're all that important lately. We don't know when you're going to be around and when you're not going to be around. And we nearly lost the other day because you *weren't* around."

Carlos Quintera stood now, halfway up the bleachers.

"You're always talking about choices. It seems to us like you've made yours. And it's not us."

"But you guys really *do* know I've had a lot going on, right?" I said, and I knew how lame that sounded almost before the words were out of my mouth.

"We've got a lot going on, too," Chris Tinelli said quietly. "And our stuff matters just as much to us as your stuff does to you. Maybe more."

And I knew he was right.

I knew they were *all* right to call me out like this. I kept telling myself how special they were and how special it was for me to coach them and how, no matter how much craziness I was experiencing in my other football life, this team really was my safe place. When I was with them, I still felt like the person I used to be before I became Front Page Jenny Wolf.

Only now I wasn't there for them.

You got me.

"So we've basically asked Mr. Rubino to keep coaching us the rest of the way," Chris Tinelli said. "And my dad has offered to help him out."

"And Mr. Rubino is okay with this?"

"He basically said it was up to us," Chris said. "He said it wasn't his team or even your team. It was ours."

"Mr. Rubino pretty much said what we're saying to you," Carlos said. "You're probably going to run the Wolves for a long time. But we all just get one chance to be high school players, especially on a team this good."

"Truth is," Chris Tinelli said, "it's like we've been pretty much coaching ourselves lately, which is kind of a bunch of BS with us this close to maybe winning the first football championship our school has ever won."

I looked up into the bleachers again.

"Anybody else care to weigh in?"

Noah Glynn, who'd subbed for Chris after he'd gotten mugged and kept us unbeaten that day, stood up.

"We all like you, Coach. I don't think there's anybody in this gym who doesn't like you. But you're the one always telling us to do our jobs. Except now you're not doing yours, at least not with us, anyway."

I stared hard into the faces staring back at me, thinking about how happy I really had been from the first day, being on the field with them. How pure it all was compared to so much of what I'd encountered with the Wolves and to everything that had happened to me and around me *because* of the Wolves, all the way to the death of John Gallo.

Suddenly I smiled. Couldn't help myself. There it was.

"Something funny, Coach?" Chris said.

"I was thinking how much better I like things here than where I just came from."

How much better I like myself here.

"That's nice to hear," Chris said. "But if that's all you got, we sort of need to get out on the field."

I thought: a guy yesterday offered me four billion dollars for a football team.

But right now this one felt like it was worth more to me.

"There's one last thing I want to say," I said to the Hunters Point Bears.

I hesitated.

"Please give me another chance."

NINETY-NINE

SUDDENLY IT WAS THE morning of the league championship game at Wolves Stadium, the Hunters Point Bears against the Basin Park Patriots.

The Bears had decided that day to keep me on as coach. Had given me a second chance after they held one more team meeting of their own with me out of the gym.

Now I was on the field watching my players warm up, as excited about the big game as they were. Feeling like I was the one back in high school. The Wolves were still winning, were now two victories away from being back in the playoffs. But the Wolves didn't need me. In the end, these kids decided they did.

Just not nearly as much as I needed them.

I had spent the past couple of weeks focused on them, managing to stay out of the media for the first time since I'd taken over the Wolves.

The city was currently more obsessed with the mysterious death of John Gallo, speculating on almost an hourly basis about what might have driven one of the most powerful men in San Francisco to suicide. There had been more than one story written about the blood feud between Joe Wolf and Gallo and how both of them had died the way they had, in different parts of the bay.

When we were all on the field, a few minutes before the kickoff, I walked over to Chris Tinelli.

"Thanks for taking me back. Because I sure would have hated to miss this."

He tipped back his helmet and smiled.

"Thanks for letting us use your football stadium."

"It's not mine today. It's yours."

The Bears just didn't play that way—weren't nearly up to what Ryan Morrissey liked to call the circumstances of the occasion, quickly falling behind by two touchdowns. Chris had fumbled a ball away when he got hit from the blind side, and the Patriots had driven down the field for their first touchdown. Carlos had fallen down in the open field, and Basin Park's star running back, a kid named Mazeeka Brown, had run seventy yards for his team's second store.

Things had gotten very quiet on the Hunters Point side of Wolves Stadium. With two minutes left in the first half, we had the ball at midfield. I always told the kids to be their best selves as players. I felt like I had to do the same now as a coach, somehow change the energy of the game so that we didn't go into the locker room still down two scores.

I called a time-out and waved Chris over.

"You know that play we always mess around with at the end of practice?"

He said he knew which one.

I turned and yelled at Noah Glynn. When he was standing there with us, I told him what we were going to do.

"Cool."

Noah lined up at quarterback. Chris lined up at wide receiver. After Noah took the snap, Chris stepped back so that he was behind Noah. Noah threw him a pass. As soon as Chris caught the ball again, Noah was flying down the left sideline. *He* was a wide receiver now. And wide open. Chris hit him with as long a pass as he'd thrown all season.

I kept Noah in the game. Even though Chris lined up at quarterback, our center direct-snapped the ball to Noah, who ran in for the two-point conversion.

Now we were only losing 14–8.

Yeah, I thought.

Yeah.

The kids were back in the game. So was I. The only drama in my life right now was in front of me on the field. I realized as we walked to the locker room what it would have been like to sit this out—and how close I'd come to doing just that.

"They've already played their best game," I said to them at halftime. "But we haven't."

As I walked back on the field, I saw Ryan and Billy McGee sitting in the stands. Because of the Hunters Point–Basin Park game, the Wolves' normal Saturday morning walk-through of their plays would be held later in the afternoon. Money McGee came down through the stands and leaned over the railing.

"Any words of wisdom?"

"Yeah, dude. Keep both your quarterbacks in the game."

"Really?"

"I like your starter," McGee said. "But the little guy reminds me of me." He winked. "It's a good thing."

"Got any good plays?"

"Just one."

He told me, and I said, "Does that still work?" Billy McGee winked again. "Only, like, since the beginning of time."

The Bears didn't move the ball much in the third quarter. But we didn't fall further behind, either, because the defense just kept getting better and better, not letting the Patriots past midfield. I paced the sideline and couldn't believe how fast the second half was unfolding, my team still down six points.

The kids had told me they'd nearly lost a couple of weeks ago because I wasn't there. Now I had this fourth quarter to prove I was worth having back. That I was as present as I'd been all season.

Ryan had once told me that he felt sorry for people who couldn't experience what he did in close games like this.

Now I understood what he was talking about.

We got the ball back on our thirty yard line with three minutes left and began to move it again, really for the first time in the second half. I did keep both Chris Tinelli and Noah Glynn on the field, just like Money McGee had told me to. They were both getting chances to throw the ball and keeping the Basin Park defense off balance because of it.

Finally, there were twenty seconds left when we had a second down from the Basin Park five yard line. I had to call our last time-out. Both Chris and Noah came running over to me.

I gave them two plays. One that I promised them would get us the touchdown that would tie the game. And another for the two-point conversion that would win it.

"Really?" Chris said.

"Those are the plays?" Noah said. "Like, for real?"

I bumped them both some fist.

"We having any fun yet?"

Chris lined up under center. Noah was behind him. Chris took the snap and rolled to his right and threw a short pass to Noah, who caught the ball but had two defenders in front of him and no daylight.

But almost as soon as he caught the ball, Chris Tinelli was flying out of the backfield, and Noah lateraled the ball to him before he was tackled. Chris ran into the end zone untouched to tie the championship game 14–14.

Chris and Noah knew what to run next. Chris was back under center; Noah was lined up as a wide receiver to his left. Chris dropped back to pass. Now it was Noah flying around from his left, grabbing the ball out of Chris's hand.

What had always been known as the Statue of Liberty play. The one Money McGee said really was still money.

Nobody caught Noah before he got to the end zone, the little guy a streak of light one last time this season as he got us the two points that won the Bears the championship game.

Bears 16, Patriots 14.

Final.

There would be a picture the next day in the *Tribune* of me jumping higher than I ever could before that moment. Looking happier than I had been in a long time.

The kids tried to hand me the championship trophy during the presentation ceremony, but I handed it right back to Chris and Noah. I looked into the stands and saw Money McGee grinning at me, arms out, palms facing the sky, as if to say, *Told you.*

We all went back to have a party at All Good Pizza, the place where Chris had eaten before he'd gotten mugged that night. Mugged, I was still certain, because of me. I'd always thought it was somebody John Gallo or my brother Jack had sent, even though I might not ever know for sure.

I had paid All Good to close the place down for us, both the front and back rooms. Before I left, I took one last look at the Hunters Point Bears and tried to remember if there was a single time that I'd had a day like this when I was in high school, when I was growing up in the house of Wolf.

I went outside and got into my car.

The guy was sitting on my front steps when I got home, as if he'd been waiting for me.

"My name is Erik Mason," he said.

I asked him what he wanted. He told me that Mr. Michael Barr would very much like to meet with me and that he was prepared to drive me to Mr. Barr's residence on Scott Street right now if that was all right with me.

"Not happening."

Mason smiled amiably, as if we were pals.

"It's not really a request."

I told him I had already picked up on that. Then I told Mason that since he had come to my house, he obviously knew who I was.

"Jenny Wolf. That's w-o-l-f."

Mason frowned.

Then I told him that there was probably no way that either he or his boss knew who my father's best friend had been since childhood, the man who had always been like an uncle to me.

The one who had sent the rose to me at the Beverly Wilshire after he had persuaded the hard-line owners to change their votes.

I slowly spelled out my uncle's last name for him.

"Five letters. Three vowels. Easy to remember."

Erik Mason stared at me when I finished, but only briefly, before turning and walking to his car and driving away.

ONE HUNDRED

BY A LITTLE AFTER nine in the morning, Ben Cantor had been sitting in his car for an hour, waiting for the guy to come out of Hit Fit SF, the fancy high-end gym on Harrison Street, thinking, thinking about something an old detective who'd mentored him, Pat Lynch, had once told Cantor about coincidence.

"Just speaking as a good Catholic and former altar boy," Lynch had said, "there's no way that God would leave that much to chance."

Cantor didn't believe in coincidence, either. First Joe Wolf had gone into the water. Now John Gallo had taken a flier a few hours after he had tried to buy the Wolves from Jenny Wolf. In between there had been what Cantor was more certain than ever was the staged suicide of Thomas Wolf.

Joe Wolf had owned the team; Thomas had worked for it; Gallo wanted it. All gone.

What were the odds?

Cantor had been to Gallo's home in Belvedere a few times, hoping to find something, anything, that might prove that Gallo had been shoved, but he had come up with nothing, at least so far. He had hoped there might be security cameras, but it turned out that Gallo had fired one home-security company, something he did routinely, and hired another one the previous week, and the new system wasn't up and running on the day he died.

In the past, when Cantor couldn't decide what his next move should be, he'd look for someone to annoy. So he had decided to make another run at Erik Mason, knowing he came to the gym at the same time every morning. Now here Mason was, still in his exercise clothes, leather bag over his shoulder, holding some kind of green smoothie drink in his hand.

Cantor got out of his car and walked over to Mason as he was about to get into his Mercedes.

"We need to have another talk."

"We already talked," Mason said.

"Got a few more questions."

"I've got someplace I need to be."

"Almost everybody does," Cantor said.

"You can't possibly think I killed Mr. Gallo."

"Well, yeah. But let's face it, Erik. You didn't do very much to keep him alive, either."

ONE HUNDRED ONE

THE WOLVES SHOULD HAVE already clinched a playoff spot, but we had lost our previous two games, suddenly looking like the team we'd been at the start of the season, when Rich Kopka, that jerk, had been the coach and my ex-husband, Ted Skyler, a much bigger jerk, had been the quarterback.

It was mostly happening because Billy McGee, out of nowhere, was acting as if he'd forgotten how to play football, or at least NFL-level football. He was throwing interceptions. He was making bad decisions. On top of everything else, he'd fumbled four times in the two losses.

"What are we going to do?" I said to Ryan Morrissey after the Titans had beaten the Wolves 35–17.

"I don't want to get too technical or take you too deep into the weeds," Ryan said, "but what we're going to do is hope he starts playing better."

Our last game was against the Patriots on *Sunday Night Football*. For the league, it was a dream ending to the regular season, even though nobody could have seen it coming when the schedule was announced.

Ted Skyler's new team, the one for which he was now the

starter, was playing the Wolves, the team run by his ex-wife, who also happened to be the person who fired him.

What made it even better was that in the seventeenth game of the regular season, we needed to win to make the playoffs from our division. And so did the Patriots from theirs.

Loser went home.

I was pondering the magnitude of the game, and the stakes, alone at home on Saturday night. I had been alone a lot lately once I left Wolves Stadium, staying there later and later. Cantor would occasionally call with some question related to his various investigations. I had called him after Erik Mason showed up at the house, telling Cantor that Mason was now working for Michael Barr, whom my father had always referred to as "that gunny."

"So Mason goes from one rich dirtbag to another," Cantor said.

"Like destiny brought them together."

"Or a bunch of murders."

Before the call ended, he asked how I was holding up.

"Just trying to figure out a way to win one more game for the local football team."

By then the stories about the two of us had finally run their course, absent any new information or photos. The public was even starting to lose interest in the death of John Gallo.

There had been a couple of days when the media had revisited the death of DeLavarious Harmon, the narcotics division of the San Francisco Police Department having concluded after a thorough investigation that his death had not been the result of foul play but an accidental overdose and that no member of the Wolves organization had been complicit in it.

Michael Barr hadn't reached out again. Neither had Mason. I'd never heard of Barr having expressed an interest in buying the Wolves. But that didn't mean he didn't want them. I some-times thought every rich guy in America wanted to own his own football team.

And I had found out firsthand how much some of them were willing to do to get one and gain entrance to the club.

How much do I still want to be in the club?

Now, there was a good question, one maybe I wouldn't answer until the season ended.

Maybe as soon as tomorrow night.

I finished my wine. Turned off the Saturday night game be-tween the Dolphins and Jets, which I'd been watching without really watching. There had been a missed call a few minutes ago from Ted. When I saw his name on the screen, I'd let it go straight to voice mail. I had no interest in speaking to the quarterback of the opposing team the night before a big game, whether I'd been married to the bastard or not.

It almost scared me how much I wanted this game. Not because it would mean he lost. Just because it would mean we won.

It's like my father used to say when he told us all to hush and listen, that he had something important to say.

"You never understand how much you want the game until you have skin in it," Joe Wolf said.

It was a little after midnight when I heard the loud pound-ing on my front door, heard somebody yelling for me to open up.

When I did open the door, I saw Billy McGee standing there, grinning at me, weaving from side to side, clearly drunk out of his mind, taking another swig from the Champagne bottle in his hand. He had sworn to me, up and down, that he would stay clean and sober. He had told me one day in my office that it was as if I had thrown him a life preserver.

353

Now this.

But why?

"You have *got* to be shitting me," I said before he stumbled past me and fell face forward on the floor.

As if somebody had just tackled him from behind.

At that moment I felt exactly same way.

ONE HUNDRED TWO

THE ONLY BREAK THAT we caught, if you could call it that, was that it was the Sunday night game, which meant that it didn't start until five thirty San Francisco time, not the usual one o'clock.

I checked in with Ryan Morrissey an hour before kickoff.

Billy McGee had spent the night at my house, after I called his wife to tell her I had him and not to bother coming to pick him up. He was going to sleep it off right where he was. Ryan had come by to collect him in the morning and driven him straight to the stadium, where our medical staff had spent all morning and all afternoon with him, even putting him on an IV drip at one point. Our head trainer told Ryan that it was a good thing Billy hadn't been driving the night before, simply because his blood alcohol level probably would have registered at around a million.

"Is he well enough to start?" I said.

"He's going to start," Ryan said. He sighed. "You know why I never ask players how they're feeling? Because they might tell me."

"But is he well enough to play in an NFL game?"

"It doesn't matter, because he's going to."

Ryan paused.

"This kid has been acting like a punk and letting people down his whole life, starting with himself. We're just the latest."

Then he told me about another McGee—Max McGee, a wide receiver with the Green Bay Packers in the first Super Bowl ever played. According to Ryan, Max stayed out all night in Los Angeles the night before, not arriving back at the team's hotel until eight in the morning. He didn't think he was going to play that day. Then the starting wide receiver got hurt, and Max McGee caught seven passes and scored two touchdowns and the Packers won.

"Some people, when they knew the whole story, called him the greatest Super Bowl hero of them all," Ryan said. "Max said he was fine once he started figuring out which of the three balls he saw coming toward him was the real one."

"And that's supposed to make me feel better?"

"At least Billy's stopped throwing up," the coach of the Wolves said about his starting quarterback. Then he said he had to go; it was time to coach his team.

Then Billy McGee went out and played the first half as if he were *still* drunk.

ONE HUNDRED THREE

WHILE BILLY MCGEE WAS still stumbling around, Ted Skyler was playing as if I had been crazy to ever let him go.

Billy threw interceptions the first two times the Wolves had the ball. Ted threw touchdown passes after both of them. Just like that, it was 14–0.

I was watching the game with Danny in his suite. Just the two of us, no guests tonight. I had called him in the morning to tell him about Billy's condition. He'd asked if there was anything he could do and I told him yeah—he could think about prayer.

"This is on me," I said now, after Billy was nearly intercepted again. "I knew who he was before I signed him."

"Who he was and what he was."

"The thing is, we wouldn't have made it this far without him."

"Now I'm wondering if he was hungover for the last two games, too, as badly as he played," Danny said.

I slid deeper into my chair.

"This isn't the way the story is supposed to end."

With two minutes left before halftime, the Patriots led, 21–3. Billy had just thrown his third interception, but at least it hadn't led to a Patriots score this time. When our offense came off the field and our defense went on, he ran past our bench and straight to the locker room. I just assumed he was going to be sick again.

But he was back on the field by the time our offense got the ball, and somehow he seemed to rouse himself. He completed three passes in a row, finally scrambling away from the Patriots' rush and in for a score with fifty seconds left in the half. So at that point the Wolves were trailing only 21–10.

"I want this game so much it hurts," I said to Danny.

"You sound like Dad."

"Don't be mean."

It was different from the way I felt on the field with my kids from Hunters Point during the championship game. At least I had some control there, just because I could call the plays. I felt as if I were *in* the game, even though I was coaching it and not playing in it. This Wolves game was different and occasionally making me feel a little sick. I felt helpless. After all the fighting I'd had to do since my father had left the team to me, everything was in the hands—literally—of a guy who had been falling-down drunk at my house last night.

When the Patriots went running off the field at the end of the half, I was sure Ted Skyler stopped just long enough to look up at Danny's suite, as if he somehow knew I was in there.

Then he waved.

I thought, *Thirty minutes of football left before I might not just lose my season but also lose it to that guy.*

I didn't leave my seat during halftime. Just sat there and remembered the night when Cantor and Ryan and I had saved Billy McGee's ass in Chinatown.

Last night and tonight were how he'd repaid me. And his coach.

It was still 21–10 for the Patriots when my ex-husband,

being chased around his own end zone, stopped and threw a dumb desperation pass deep down the middle of the field. Andre DeWitt, the defensive back who'd smart-mouthed me in such a funny way the day I'd introduced myself to the team, intercepted the ball.

After ten yards he had broken a couple of tackles and suddenly had all this open field in front of him.

Now I got out of my seat again.

"Let's go!" I yelled in Danny's suite.

The last person between him and the end zone was someone who actually used to refer to himself as Touchdown Ted. Now he was trying to prevent one. He had no chance, even though he clumsily tried to throw himself in front of Andre DeWitt.

Andre ran right over him, knocking Ted's helmet sideways.

Suddenly the Patriots led by only four points with a quarter of football still left to play.

"We're not out of this," Danny said.

"Don't talk."

It was still 21–17 when Billy McGee somehow started to look like a real quarterback and not a total shit. It was on a drive that started at the Wolves' ten yard line, with four minutes left. He completed two straight passes to get us away from our own end zone. Then two more.

Just like that, we were driving.

It was finally third and ten, three minutes to go, at the Patriots' thirty-eight yard line. Billy dropped back and was under pressure again from a Patriots blitz. They'd been blitzing him all game long once they saw he was a couple of steps slow.

Only this time he got loose, heading for the sideline and the first-down marker.

At the last moment, it was a question of whether he would get to the marker before the Patriots' star outside linebacker, a monster of a player named Anfernee McCarron, could get to *him*.

Billy could have run out-of-bounds. He'd still have one more shot at the first down if he didn't make it.

But he didn't run out-of-bounds. Billy McGee was a player now and not a punk, almost laying out as he lunged for the marker.

He didn't make it.

Anfernee McCarron hit him as hard as I'd seen any quarterback—whether standing in the pocket or running in the open field—get hit all season. Somehow Billy, even short of the first down, still had the ball in his right hand when he hit the ground.

I realized I had moved to the front of the suite now to get a better look at what everybody in Wolves Stadium, suddenly very quiet, could see down on the field.

Billy McGee was lying motionless on his back.

He stayed that way for the next several minutes, Dr. Ron Barnes and Ryan Morrissey kneeling next to him.

Finally, I saw the flatbed cart making its way slowly out of the tunnel and heading for the sideline, where Billy McGee still hadn't moved.

Then the trainers were getting Billy onto a stretcher and securing his head and neck, lifting the stretcher onto the injury cart.

The crowd was standing and cheering then. At the last moment, before the cart disappeared back into the tunnel, Billy McGee managed to lift his hand into the air before it dropped back to his side.

Then he was gone.

ONE HUNDRED FOUR

I DROVE AROUND FOR a long time after I finally left the stadium, not listening to any of the sports stations as the hosts recapped the game, not listening to music.

Not listening to anything.

I even stopped by Hunters Point High School, got out and walked on the field, trying to remember what it had been like, trying to recapture the feeling I'd had the day my Bears had beaten Basin Park to win the championship, the kids acting as if they'd won the championship of the whole world.

I didn't decide where I was going when I was back in the car until I was almost all the way there, as if I owned one of those self-driving cars and it had programmed itself.

When I'd finally made my way down to the parking lot after the game, all the traffic gone by then, even my brother Danny long gone, I'd only thought about going home, being alone there just because I was tired of being alone in the suite after Danny left.

Then I wasn't on my way home.

It just happened.

The way a lot of things just happened, starting last night, when I'd opened the door and there Billy McGee had been, drunk out of his mind.

If Detective Ben Cantor was surprised to see me when he opened *his* front door, he hid it pretty well.

"I was just wondering if you're a fan of the local football team."

He smiled.

I thought: *Still a good smile.*

Dammit.

"As a matter of fact, I do check in on them from time to time around my busy work schedule. Especially this late in the season."

"Well," I said to him, holding up the bottle of red wine I'd brought with me from Danny's suite, "it turns out they won a pretty big game tonight."

"Speaking both as a member of the law enforcement community and as a die-hard Wolves fan," Cantor said, "it seems to me that it would be practically criminal for you to even attempt to celebrate something like that alone."

Then he smiled again and said, "Would you like to come in and celebrate with me?"

"I would."

When we were inside Cantor opened the wine and poured. We were sitting on his couch by then. I could hear jazz coming from two speakers in the corners. It occurred to me that this was the first time I had actually made it through the front door. Previously, that was as far as we'd gone.

In all ways.

Cantor raised a glass.

"To the Wolves."

"To the Wolves," I said, before adding a toast I used to hear sometimes from my father.

"Here's to them, and screw everybody else."

I told Cantor then about Billy McGee and the condition

he'd been in when he showed up at my front door the night before and how it was a minor miracle that he'd gotten on the field at all.

"You want to keep talking about football?"

"Not so much, now that I think about it."

"Same."

"I'm glad I came."

"Not nearly as glad as I am," Ben Cantor said.

I curled my legs underneath me and turned so I was facing him on the couch.

"I'm sorry for the way I acted at dinner that night."

"So am I."

"But I was the one acting defensive. And treating you like one of the people coming after me."

"I have been after you," he said, smiling again. "Just not as an intrepid crime fighter."

"I *am* sorry," I said. "I've become so conditioned to acting like a tough guy that I didn't know when to turn it off. And let's just say that in the years since my divorce, I haven't exactly specialized in successful relationships."

I paused and took another sip of wine. "You were just doing your job."

"Not as artfully as I might've wished," Cantor said.

"I wasn't sure you'd invite me in."

"Then you're never going to make detective, Ms. Wolf, are you?"

We both laughed then. It felt good. But then it had been a good night, ever since Chase Charles shocked the world and probably himself most of all by coming off the bench to complete three straight passes after Billy McGee got hurt, the last one a sweet throw to Calvin Robeson in the back of the end zone that put the Wolves back in the playoffs.

"I'm still sort of on probation with my bosses," Cantor said. "They don't like that kind of publicity. Meaning the kind they got because of those pictures of us."

I grinned. "I'm still on probation with the other owners. Who absolutely *hate* the kind of publicity I've been giving them."

"They'll get over it."

"You sure?"

The music had stopped. I noticed that both our glasses were empty. Somehow Cantor had covered the distance between us on the sofa. I might not have been much of a detective in his eyes.

But I had picked up on that.

"You sure about this?" he said now.

"This?"

"Us."

"We have a saying in the Wolf family that I might not have mentioned to you before."

"And what might that be?"

"Kiss or be kissed."

"I'm almost certain it was something else," Ben Cantor said.

"Whatever."

ONE HUNDRED FIVE

I WAS DRESSED ONLY in an oversize SFPD sweatshirt that Ben had given me to wear when I stepped outside the next morning to pick up the copy of the *San Francisco Tribune* that had been delivered to his front door.

As I was reaching down to pick it up, I realized I wasn't alone in front of Ben Cantor's house.

Standing on his front walk were two photographers, a man and a woman, the man telling me to smile the way Seth Dowd had that day after I knocked my brother Jack into the water.

I should have slammed the door and gone right back inside. But I was through being shamed by people like this for living my life.

"Do I even have to ask who you two are with?"

The man didn't answer, just gave a jerk to his head. I looked past him and across the street to the spot where Jack Wolf was leaning out the window of his cherished Aston Martin, the one that made him feel like James Bond.

Jack waved at me.

I surprised everybody then, maybe even myself, by brushing past the photographers, making them get out of my way, and walking straight for my brother's car.

Feeling like a tough guy again. The truth was, sometimes it wasn't so bad.

"Aren't Detective Cantor and I old news by now?"

"Maybe at your publication. Not mine. At our shop, Sis, you remain the gift that just keeps on giving."

"So now you're the one having me followed?"

"Got a tip that you were here."

"My ass."

"Which you might think about doing a better job of covering up," Jack Wolf said.

I raised the paper a bit and was delighted to see him recoil, if only just slightly.

"Still scared I might beat you up, Jack? Wow. Maybe Dad was right. Maybe he really did have more than one daughter."

I made a slight feint at him again. He flinched again. Then he turned the key in the ignition and started the car.

"We're done here. I got what I came for."

I reached in and put a hand on his shoulder to stop him from pulling away.

"You know, it occurred to me when I saw you sitting there how many pricks I've had to deal with since Dad left the team and the paper to me."

He said, "And I'm one of those pricks, right?"

"Just smaller."

ONE HUNDRED SIX

Six weeks later

IT WAS THE FRIDAY of Super Bowl week at the owners' hotel, the Four Seasons Miami. But I suddenly felt as if I'd gone back to the future, having once again been summoned by A. J. Frost to meet with him and the rest of the Hard-liners in Frost's penthouse suite, this one on the other side of the country from the Beverly Wilshire.

The Wolves hadn't made it to the Super Bowl. Billy McGee had recovered enough to play the next week and had gotten us all the way to the conference championship game before we lost, pretty badly, to the Vikings.

I had come to Miami for Super Bowl week anyway. All the owners came to the Super Bowl as far as I could tell, for the parties and the face time and a handful of league meetings, some of which included me.

I was pretty sure why they wanted to see me. It had to be about the second wave of coverage of my relationship with Ben Cantor. The pictures of me in a sweatshirt that barely left anything to the imagination went viral the way the college pictures of me had, as if I had once again become the pinup girl for bad—and slutty—behavior in the NFL.

This time Cantor really had been suspended by the SFPD.

Indefinitely. With no guarantee that he'd ever get his old job back or be any kind of cop ever again.

Now came this call from A. J. Frost, telling me that it wasn't just me he'd invited up to his suite tonight but Commissioner Joel Abrams as well.

"What's this all about, A.J.? Or should I be able to figure it out for myself?"

"You'll understand when you arrive," A. J. Frost said.

I had known since the league meetings in Los Angeles that the rest of the season would essentially be a probationary period for me, even if my team did finally get to within a win of the Super Bowl. Maybe my uncle's influence with them extended only so far. Maybe there had been an understanding with all the other owners that all bets were off if I embarrassed the league again. I wasn't sure. Maybe I was projecting.

But I didn't like any of this. And I wasn't sure whether I was more angry or sad that I might once again face losing the Wolves. Probably a little bit of both. I knew by now how much I had come to love doing this job, running this team, how much I'd wanted the Wolves to make it all the way to Miami. And couldn't lie to myself about one other thing: I didn't exactly hate giving orders.

My brothers hadn't been able to take the team away from me. John Gallo hadn't been able to, either. I was going to make sure that Michael Barr didn't, even though I wasn't entirely sure how or what the rules of engagement were going to be with him going forward.

I just didn't want the Hard-liners to do to me now what I had been sure they were going to do to me in Los Angeles.

I'm good at this, I told myself in the elevator. *That has to count for something.*

With the exception of the commissioner, they were all

waiting for me when I arrived. Carl Paulson of the Bears. Rex Cardwell and Ed McGrath and Amos Lester. The annual commissioner's party would be held later at Zoo Miami, a setting I found completely appropriate. But that wasn't for a few hours. Still plenty of time for me to face a trial by jury.

As I looked around the room, I suddenly remembered a touring musical my mother had taken me to at the old Orpheum Theatre in San Francisco when I was twelve or thirteen years old. It was called *Woman of the Year*. I couldn't even remember who played the lead. But for some reason, the lyrics to her big showstopping number have always stayed with me: "I'm one of the girls who's one of the boys."

But for how much longer?

When the pictures of me at Ben Cantor's house were first published, I had gotten a call from Joel Abrams within the hour. He told me that what he called my *situation* would be addressed during Super Bowl week, the next time all the NFL owners would be together in one place.

Now here we all were. I idly wondered if the machinery that would get me removed from their club once and for all had been slowly grinding back to life without my officially knowing it.

Maybe I wasn't experiencing anger or sadness—those were just ways of sugarcoating things. Maybe it was just fear, plain and simple, that they might really take the Wolves team away from me this time.

A. J. Frost offered me a drink. I said a Grey Goose on the rocks would do me nicely, thank you.

"Your father's drink of choice, as I recall," Frost said.

"I don't suppose you'd like to give me a heads-up about what's about to happen here."

"Let's wait until the commissioner arrives," Frost said as he went to get me my vodka. "Then I'll explain everything."

While we did wait, the men made awkward small talk about Sunday's game, between the hometown Dolphins and the Vikings. Carl Paulson congratulated me on what he called the Wolves' "cracking good season."

"I believe it's the first of many. I don't know if anybody in this room agrees, but I feel as if I know how to do this now."

Rex Cardwell laughed and raised his own glass and said, "And them paparazzi back in your town sure know how to do you, missy!"

There was a knock on the door then, and Joel Abrams walked in. When he saw me, he said, "I was wondering if she would even have the guts to show up."

"It was important that she see, and hear, what's about to happen," Frost said.

"At least we're going to correct the mistake that was made in Los Angeles," Abrams said.

"We think the mistake was made well before that," Amos Lester said.

"Whatever," Abrams said. "I'm glad you gentlemen finally came to your senses."

I raised my glass, as if in a toast. "I'm *here,* guys. I can hear you."

Frost looked around the room.

"Any of my friends want to say anything before I get to it?" he said.

"You go ahead, A.J.," Ed McGrath of the Titans said. "It was really you who got the ball rolling on this thing in the first place."

"Before I do," Frost said, "is there anything you'd like to say, Jenny?"

"Do I have to defend my life again?"

"As a matter of fact, no," Frost said.

"Then why *are* we all here?"

A. J. Frost walked to the window then, the lights of downtown Miami behind him, almost like backlighting, as he turned around. Before he could say anything, Joel Abrams said, "We really do need to get to this, A.J. I mean, we do have my commissioner's party to attend."

"Not you," Frost said.

I was watching Abrams, who looked genuinely confused.

"What does that mean?"

"What it means," Frost said, "is that we called you here to tell you you're fired, Joel."

ONE HUNDRED SEVEN

IT FELT LIKE THE first good news Ben Cantor had received since he'd been suspended.

"They banged the little creep just like that?" he said when Jenny called. "And he had no warning that he was in trouble with them?"

"Somehow they found out he was in it with Michael Barr and Gallo," she said. "I don't know how they did, but they did. And they knew damn well that he'd hired Bert Patricia to follow us instead of using NFL security, which is the protocol. But it was being in business with Barr that took him down."

"Lie down with dogs," Cantor said.

"Frost finally told the commish that if he was going to be this kind of whore to make sure he got his money up front next time," she told Ben Cantor. "And then he laid into him all over again about pimping the league out to somebody like Michael Barr."

"Pimp *and* whore?"

"What can I tell you? The old boy was on a roll at that point."

Cantor said, "I thought commissioners like Abrams make

more money than most players. You're telling me it still wasn't enough?"

"Apparently not. John Gallo didn't think he had enough, either. Nor does Michael Barr. My father was probably the same way."

"How'd he leave it with them?" Cantor said. "The commissioner, I mean?"

"He said they'd given him no choice but to retire, now that they'd betrayed his trust in this manner."

"No shit," Cantor said. "*His* trust? Like they betrayed *him*?"

He laughed.

"I'm almost positive I read somewhere that karma is a bitch."

"I saved the best part for last," Jenny said. "Before Abrams left, he turned and pointed a finger at me, like he was still the most powerful guy in the room, and said that this wasn't over between us."

"Him and you," Cantor said.

"Yes, sir."

"And how did you respond to a terrifying threat like that?"

"I told him that he probably knew league rules a lot better than I did," Jenny said, "but I was pretty sure that when you got your ass kicked the way he just had, they didn't let you play overtime."

They spoke for a few more minutes more about the scene in A. J. Frost's suite after Abrams had left and about Jenny's riding to the commissioner's party with Frost and the rest of them in one of those giant-size party limos.

"Like we were all going to the prom together."

Eventually she got around to asking Cantor how he was doing, the two of them not having spoken since she'd gotten to Miami. He told her that he was not just suspended without pay, he'd also been asked to turn over all his files relating to the deaths of Joe Wolf, Thomas Wolf, and John Gallo and ordered to stay away from the ongoing investigation being conducted by the new detectives assigned to the cases.

"So they've completely shut you down," Jenny Wolf said.

"Well," Cantor said, "they think they have."

Then he asked her to check in with him later—he had another call coming in that he needed to take.

ONE HUNDRED EIGHT

CANTOR HAD BEEN WONDERING when he would call.

He'd been following him off and on for a couple of weeks and doing almost nothing to hide the fact that he was. He'd done the same thing with Danny Wolf and his brother Jack, just not as often. He wanted them all to know that he was still on their asses, maybe for no other reason than that he was going crazy with boredom.

But there was a through line, he knew, from the night Joe Wolf went into the water to the night John Gallo did the same, a line that ran directly through the Wolf brothers and the guy now speaking to him at the other end of the line.

"We need to talk," Erik Mason said.

"Wait—I thought that was my line the last time we were together," Cantor said to him.

"So now it's my turn."

"And what exactly do we need to talk *about*?"

"About how you've got me all wrong," Mason said. "Me and my boss."

"I assume you mean the boss who's still alive."

"When you hear what I have to say, you'll understand why

I'm calling you," Mason said. "You'll also know most of what you want to know."

"I'm listening right now."

"You know where Harris' steak house is, right?" Mason said.

Where Jenny had walked out on him that night.

"I grew up not far from there. Russian Hill."

"So you know there's a lot across the street. I'll meet you there at eleven o'clock. I'll be driving Mr. Barr around before that. He's got a couple of charity events he needs to attend."

"Charity," Cantor said, "always begins at the arms dealer's home."

Mason let that one go.

"Why not just meet at a bar someplace?" Cantor said.

"Because I don't want to be seen with you, and you don't want to be seen with me," Mason said. "We'll do this face-to-face, out in the open. Straight up."

"As a practical matter, why should I trust you?"

"Because it's like I told you that day outside the gym," Mason said. "I didn't kill anybody. And I'm not interested in busting your balls the way you've been busting mine by tailing me."

"To be determined," Cantor said. "On the ball-busting part, I mean."

"Listen," Mason said. "I'm doing us both a solid here. You find out things you want to know. And I get you off my ass in the process."

"Not making any promises on the last part until I hear what you have to say."

"And don't wear a wire. I've got a gadget that'll tell me if you are," Mason said. "If you do wear one, all bets are off. All's you'll have done is waste my time, and yours."

"Got it."

"We're doing this cop to cop," Mason said.

"Don't flatter yourself."

"Come alone. And remember, no wire."

"No wire," Cantor said.

He didn't tell him what else he planned to wear.

Everything except a badge, of course.

ONE HUNDRED NINE

CANTOR WAS TEN MINUTES early. When he pulled past Harris', he saw that it was closed. He couldn't help but think back to the night when he'd been there with Jenny and she left him standing in front of the place before they'd both been busted for a date that turned into a train wreck.

Now he made a U-turn on Van Ness, came back around, and pulled into the lot directly across the street from the restaurant, empty now.

Turned off the car and waited.

He wasn't officially a cop right now. But he hadn't forgotten how to be one. Or how to wait.

He was thinking about Mason again. The former cop who had worked for Joe Wolf and then John Gallo and now Michael Barr once Gallo had either jumped or been pushed. Mason had been sent to Jenny's house by Barr, who was clearly the guy behind the curtain with Gallo's relentless pursuit of the Wolves. But Mason *had* worked for Gallo before that. The Wolf brothers had been working with Gallo. If Jack and Danny had been with Gallo on what had essentially been an attempted hostile take-over of the Wolves, did that mean they were with Barr now, even if Danny had finished the season working for the Wolves?

Pimping themselves out to Barr the way the former commissioner of the National Football League had?

He could see Jack doing it, looking out for himself that way.
And maybe Danny had just been giving Jenny a head fake by
coming back to the team and had been working against her
all along, as if Gallo or Barr or both had embedded him in his
old office.

One thing was certain: if anybody in this group was capable
of murder, it was Mason. All day long, Cantor had been
making calls to LA about him. Learned about the excessive
force tags on his sheet before they finally let him go for good.
And about the shooting of a gang member on which he'd
eventually skated, a shooting that everybody thought looked
like an execution. White cop. Black kid. Shocker.

Cantor checked his watch. Ten after the hour. Now Mason
was ten minutes late. Maybe the last charity event for Barr
had run long. Maybe Mason was bluffing. Or wasn't. And was
coming here tonight to point a finger at either Danny Wolf or
Jack or both of them, because if Mason wasn't the one who'd
gotten the killing done, it could only be one of the two Wolf
brothers still standing.

Or both, as odd a couple as they were.

Cantor still liked Mason for it. Mason: taking orders now
from Michael Barr, the one who wanted the team and everything that came with it and didn't care what he had to do
to get it.

All Cantor knew for sure was that he felt like a cop again
tonight, back to working his case whether his bosses wanted
him to be anywhere near it or not.

With or without his badge.

He saw a Mercedes ease into the lot then. Cantor flashed his
lights, got out of his car. Mason pulled up, shut off his own

lights, got out of the Mercedes. Once the car lights had been turned off, the lot was very dark.

The two cars were maybe thirty yards apart. Maybe a little more. Cantor was standing next to the open door of his, leaning an arm on it.

Then there was just enough light, even in the semidarkness of the lot, for Cantor to see that Mason was wearing a ski mask and walking quickly toward him.

"Face-to-face," Mason barked, "just like I promised."

Before Cantor could react, Mason was raising what looked to be a long handgun, and then there was the sound a gun like that made, like a cork coming out of a bottle, with a suppressor attached.

The first bullet hit Cantor squarely in the chest.

Then the second.

ONE HUNDRED TEN

HE HAD BEEN COMPLETELY honest with Mason when he said he wouldn't wear a wire.

He hadn't said anything about wearing a vest.

But even wearing one, Cantor felt as if he had been hit—twice—in the middle of his chest with a sledgehammer, the pain both fierce and immediate, making him feel as if his chest had been concussed, the bullets taking most of the air out of him as he went down hard.

They were center-mass shots, just as cops were taught to fire, the two shots grouped as if Ben Cantor were nothing more than a target at the range.

Maybe the arrogant bastard hadn't anticipated that Cantor would wear a vest. Maybe he thought he was in complete control of the situation. Maybe he planned to stand over Cantor and finish him if he discovered that Cantor was still alive.

Cantor wasn't waiting to find out. He rolled behind his open car door now and cleared his Glock from the holster on his hip as he did.

Face-to-face, Mason had said.

Cantor didn't hesitate. His chest still hurt like hell, and he was having trouble breathing. But he got to his feet, using the door for cover, aiming the Glock over the top of the car door and firing.

Then he was the one taking a center-mass shot at Erik Mason. And then another.

Putting Mason down.

Cantor waited to see if Mason was moving. If maybe he had worn a vest. He was an ex-cop, after all.

Or maybe he had just underestimated Cantor.

Cantor moved out from behind the door now, moved slowly toward Mason, two hands on his gun, keeping it pointed until he was convinced Erik Mason *wasn't* moving.

"Mason," Cantor said.

No response.

"Talk to me."

Still nothing.

Cantor covered the last ten yards between them, stood over Mason, and recognized what he knew was a Magnum Desert Eagle, one of the most dangerous handguns on the planet, next to Mason's outstretched right hand. He had been wearing a dark windbreaker, but even with that Cantor could see blood soaking the front of it. Only now did Cantor feel his own breathing, and the beat of his own heart, slowly return to normal.

He told himself that he had come here tonight as a cop, albeit one without a badge right now, and that solving this case could save his career. But Cantor knew it wasn't just about him. It was about Jenny Wolf, too. And maybe his belief that they might still have a future together.

Cantor knelt down and pulled the ski mask off Mason's face. Saw that his eyes were open. And that he was still breathing, if faintly and with great effort.

"I need an ambulance or I'm going to bleed out," Mason said to Cantor, choking out the words.

"How about this?" Cantor said. "How about we talk about what I need first?"

ONE HUNDRED ELEVEN

IN THE MORNING, after Ben Cantor had awakened me to tell me what had happened across from Harris' and what he'd learned from Erik Mason—that it was Mason who'd been a strong enough swimmer to make it back to shore the night he threw my father overboard—I decided to drive up to Palm Beach and see my uncle Nick Amato, whom I hadn't seen in years.

The last time we'd been together, at a home on South Ocean Boulevard that was more like a palace, he'd joked to me that he'd financed it the old-fashioned way.

"Ill-gotten gains."

"Oh," I'd said. *"Those."*

"The best kind."

He had reminded me that day, even though I didn't need reminding, that if I ever needed anything, and that meant anything at all, I just had to pick up the phone. And when I didn't think I had the votes to maintain control of the Wolves— when I had convinced myself I didn't have the votes and was about to lose my team—I had done just that.

I tried to call him before I left my hotel in Miami but got no answer, not even voice mail. I tried again when I was in the car. This time he did pick up, and right away I started to tell him about the shoot-out in San Francisco and was about to tell him what happened with the commissioner the previous night when the voice at the other end cut me off.

"This is his son, Vincent."

"You're kidding. You sound just like him."

"So I've been told," Vincent Amato said, and he told me that unfortunately this might not be the best day to see his father.

I promised not to stay long. I said I was probably flying back to San Francisco tonight and was already past Boca Raton and that it was silly for me to turn around.

"Not staying for the Super Bowl?"

"We have televisions in San Francisco."

"But it's the big game," he said.

"Not for me it's not."

It took me another hour to get to South Ocean, slowed by traffic on Florida's Turnpike and then again when I caught a bridge going up over the Intracoastal Waterway. When I finally was making my way up the driveway, I saw Vincent Amato waiting for me outside, smiling as he walked toward the car to greet me.

I hadn't spent much time with him. He and his father had moved permanently from New York City to Florida after Vincent's mother passed away. I was struck again today by how much he reminded me of my brother Thomas, a slightly older version. But handsome in a dark Italian way, same as his father had been as a young man. I'd seen the pictures, sometimes of Nick standing next to a younger version of Joe Wolf.

"It's good to see you again," he said, taking my hand and kissing it the way his father always had.

"It's been too long between visits."

"In more ways than one," Vincent said.

The inside of the house was as spectacular as I remembered. I knew that the ocean views from the upstairs rooms were even better. As he walked me upstairs, I was reminded of an interview I'd read with a comedian talking about his first visit to Johnny Carson's lavish home in Malibu.

"Where's the gift shop?" the man had asked.

"Listen," Vincent said, "I should have prepared you."

"For what?"

"This."

We walked into the spacious den where I'd last sat with my uncle, all dark wood and floor-to-ceiling windows facing the water, and saw him sitting there in his wheelchair, blanket covering his legs, the chair turned away from the Atlantic, staring blankly at a huge flat-screen television showing *Wheel of Fortune*. Pasty skin hung from his face. He looked to have aged a hundred years since I'd last seen him, almost as if he had collapsed within himself.

He didn't turn as Vincent and I walked in, either because he hadn't heard us or didn't know we were there.

"How long has he been like this?"

"About a year," Vincent said.

"But I've spoken to him a few times recently."

"You spoke to me," Vincent Amato said. "A tiny deception, for which I apologize. When he was more lucid than he is now, before the decline really began, he ordered me not to tell anyone about his diminished state. Said it might be bad for business."

"Which you're now running."

He nodded.

"The way I'm running my father's businesses."

"I resisted for a long time," Vincent said.

"We may be more alike than we ever realized."

"Reluctant bosses," he said.

"So it was you who was calling the shots?"

"He was always fond of you," Vincent said. "You know that. I simply honored his wishes to give you whatever support you needed. He hardly speaks anymore. But he made that quite clear."

"I might need your help again, by the way. This man Michael Barr seems to be even more formidable than my father and I thought John Gallo was."

Vincent offered a small smile.

"It's already being taken care of. Or perhaps I should say we have set in motion plans to take care of it."

By then we had walked out of his father's study and were at the top of the stairs when I suddenly turned, went back, and hugged Nicholas Amato, kissed him on top of his head.

"You were a better father to me than he was."

He didn't move, change his expression, or indicate that he'd heard. But I believed he had, perhaps because I wanted to believe it. And I wondered in that moment if my father, his childhood friend, might be better off.

I was at the door when I heard "Wait" from behind me. But barely.

I quickly walked back to him and leaned down close to him one last time.

Then my uncle Nick whispered to me.

ONE HUNDRED TWELVE

VINCENT AND I SAT on the back deck overlooking an expanse of perfectly manicured lawn that looked as if it belonged on a golf course, drinking the delicious iced tea the houseman had brought out to us.

"You were the one who pressured the other owners."

He nodded.

"But you didn't feel as if you could tell me."

"I was honor bound. If I told you, I would have had to tell you what had become of him." He paused. "Your father's word always mattered quite mightily where my father is concerned. So does mine."

"May I ask how you got me the votes I needed?"

"It's not really all that complicated or worth getting too deeply into," he said. "At various times, all those old men have needed favors, and my father has provided them in various ways. Always making clear, of course, that favors such as these do not come free."

"Of course not."

"You had to suspect we had leverage with these men," Vincent said, "or you wouldn't have finally called."

"You were the one who sent the rose, weren't you?"

"It's what my father would have done."

"Thank you," I said. "Thank *both* of you."

"He always told your father that he would watch over you if anything ever happened."

He turned so he was facing me more directly.

"There's something else you need to know. Maybe something you should have been told when Joe died. Or should have been allowed to know all along."

He smiled again. He wasn't family, but it felt like he was in this moment.

"From the beginning, the Wolves have been owned by my father as much as they were owned by your father," Vincent said. "When those men in San Francisco tried to take it away from you, it was as if they were trying to take the Wolves from us at the same time." He paused. "Things have never worked that way in my father's world. Or mine."

I should have been knocked back by the news. Or surprised. Somehow I wasn't. In so many ways, it made perfect sense. There had always been part of me that wondered how my father had come up with the money to buy the Wolves in the first place. I'd only asked him about it one time, when stories were being written several years ago about Joe Wolf being in deep financial trouble. Again.

"You just have to know what banks to use," my father had said.

Now I knew which bank.

Vincent asked if I wanted more iced tea. I told him I had to be going. We talked more about Erik Mason and what he'd told Cantor before Cantor had finally called 911. I said that Cantor was convinced now that Mason, under orders from Michael Barr, really had killed them all.

"It sounds as if Mason is going to live."

"Pity," Vincent said. "It would make things far less complicated if he didn't." He sighed. "But if this is true, there will eventually be a reckoning for Mr. Barr. One that's long overdue. One you can leave to us."

"So this was all about Barr from the beginning?"

"Some of it. Perhaps not all."

I left that alone, still trying to process everything else I had learned today. We walked back through the house. There was no point for me to go back upstairs and see my uncle. I'd already said my goodbye.

"I'm sorry you had to see him this way," Vincent said.

"I'm still glad I came. Because I found out something today."

"About the team, you mean?"

I said, "About how your family is more loyal to me than my own."

I was walking to my rental car when he called out to me.

"One more thing," he said.

I turned.

"Those things the owners discovered about the commissioner and Mr. Barr? The things that gave *them* leverage over him?"

"What about them?"

"You're welcome."

I told him that by tomorrow morning I'd be back behind my desk, that it was never too soon to start getting ready for next season.

"Time for me to get back to my team."

Vincent Amato smiled.

"You mean our team."

"Actually," I said, "I don't."

I moved closer to him, away from the car, so I didn't have to shout.

"Your father let my father run the team. Now you're going to do the same with me."

"And why would I do something like that?"

"Ask your father," I said. "He just told me something upstairs *my* father told me my whole life."

"And what was that?"

I quickly covered the distance between us, seemed to surprise him by hugging him goodbye, then whispered to him what his father had said to me upstairs in a voice so weak I almost couldn't hear him.

"Kill or be killed," I said to Vincent Amato.

Introducing Patterson's best new series
since the Women's Murder Club . . .

12
MONTHS
TO LIVE

She has a year to live.
If they don't kill her first.

OUT NOW!

Read on for an exclusive extract . . .

ONE

"FOR *THE* LAST TIME," my client says to me. "I. Did. Not. Kill. Those. People."

He adds, "You have to believe me. I didn't do it."

The opposing counsel will refer to him as "the defendant." It's a way of putting him in a box, since opposing counsel absolutely believe he *did* kill all those people. The victims. The Gates family. Father. Mother. And teenage daughter. All shot in the head. Sometime in the middle of the last night of their lives. Whoever did it, and the state says my client did, had to have used a suppressor.

"Rob," I say, "I might have mentioned this before: I. Don't. Give. A. Shit."

Rob is Rob Jacobson, heir to a legendary publishing house and also owner of the biggest real estate company in the Hamptons. Life was good for Rob until he ended up in jail, but that's true for pretty much everybody, rich or poor. Guilty or innocent. I've defended both.

Me? I'm Jane. Jane Smith. It's not an assumed name, even though I might be wishing it were by the end of this trial.

There was a time when I would have been trying to keep some-body like Rob Jacobson away from the needle, back when New

York was still a death penalty state. Now it's my job to help him beat a life sentence. Starting tomorrow. Suffolk County Court, Riverhead, New York. Maybe forty-five minutes from where Rob Jacobson stands accused of shooting the Gates family dead.

That's forty-five minutes with no traffic. Good luck with that.

"I've told you this before," he says. "It's important to me that you believe me."

No surprise there. He's been conditioned his entire life to people telling him what he wants to hear. It's another perk that's come with being a Jacobson.

Until now, that is.

We are in one of the attorney rooms down the hall from the courtroom. My client and me. Long window at the other end of the room where the guard can keep an eye on us. Not for my safety, I tell myself. Rob Jacobson's. Maybe the guard can tell from my body language that I occasionally feel the urge to strangle him.

He's wearing his orange jumpsuit. I'm in the same dark-gray skirt and jacket I'll be wearing tomorrow. What I think of as my sincerity suit.

"Important to *you*," I say, "not to me. I need twelve people to believe you. And I'm not one of the twelve."

"You have to know that I'm not capable of doing something like this."

"Sure. Let's go with that."

"You sound sarcastic," he says.

"No. I *am* sarcastic."

This is our last pretrial meeting, one he's asked for and that is a complete waste of time. Mine, not his. He looks for any excuse to get out of his cell at the Riverhead Correctional Facility for even an hour and has insisted on going over once more what he calls "our game plan."

Our—I run into a lot of that.

I've tried to explain to him that any lawyer who allows his or her client to run the show ought to save everybody a lot of time and effort—and a boatload of the state's money—and drive the client straight to Attica or Green Haven Correctional. But Rob Jacobson never listens. Lifelong affliction, as far as I can tell.

"Rob, you don't just want me to believe you. You want me to like you."

"Is there something so wrong with that?" he asks.

"This is a murder trial," I tell him. "Not a dating app."

Looks-wise he reminds me of George Clooney. But all good-looking guys with salt-and-pepper hair remind me of George. If I had met him several years ago and could have gotten him to stay still long enough, I might have married him.

But only if I had been between marriages at the time.

"Stop me if you've heard me say this before, but I was set up."

I sigh. It's louder than I intended. "Okay. Stop."

"I *was*," he says. "Set up. Nothing else makes sense."

"Now, you stop me if you've heard this one from me before. Set up by whom? And with your DNA and fingerprints sprinkled around that house like pixie dust?"

"That's for you to find out," he says. "One of the reasons I hired you is because I was told you're as good a detective as you are a lawyer. You and your guy."

Jimmy Cunniff. Ex-NYPD, the way I'm ex-NYPD, even if I only lasted a grand total of eight months as a street cop, before lasting barely longer than that as a licensed private investigator. It was why I'd served as my own investigator for the first few years after I'd gotten my law degree. Then I'd hired Jimmy, and finally started delegating, almost as a last resort.

"Not to put too fine a point on things," I say to him, "we're not just good. We happen to be the best. Which *is* why you hired both of us."

"And why I'm counting on you to find the real killers eventually. So people will know I'm innocent."

I lean forward and smile at him.

"Rob? Do me a favor and never talk about the real killers ever again."

"I'm not O.J.," he says.

"Well, yeah, he only killed two people."

I see his face change now. See something in his eyes that I don't much like. But then I don't much like him. Something else I run into a lot.

He slowly regains his composure. And the rich-guy certainty that this is all some kind of big mistake. "Sometimes I wonder whose side you're on."

"Yours."

"So despite how much you like giving me a hard time, you do believe I'm telling you the truth."

"Who said anything about the truth?" I ask.

TWO

GREGG McCALL, NASSAU COUNTY district attorney, is waiting for me outside the courthouse.

Rob Jacobson has been taken back to the jail and I'm finally on my way back to my little saltbox house in Amagansett, east of East Hampton, maybe twenty miles from Montauk and land's end.

A tourist one night wandered into the tavern Jimmy Cunniff owns down at the end of Main Street in Sag Harbor, where Jimmy says it's been, in one form or another, practically since the town was a whaling port. The visitor asked what came after Montauk. He was talking to the bartender, but I happened to be on the stool next to his.

"Portugal," I said.

But now the trip home is going to have to wait because of McCall, six foot eight, former Columbia basketball player, divorced, handsome, extremely eligible by all accounts. And an honest-to-God public servant. I've always had kind of a thing for him, even when he was still married, and even though my sport at Boston College was ice hockey. Even with his decided size advantage, I figure we could make a mixed relationship like that work, with counseling.

McCall has made the drive out here from his home in Garden City, which even on a weekday can feel like a trip to Kansas if you're heading east on the Long Island Expressway.

"Are you here to give me free legal advice?" I ask. "Because I'll take whatever you got at this point, McCall."

He smiles. It only makes him better looking.

Down, girl.

"I want to hire you," he says.

"Oh, no." I smile back at him. "Did *you* shoot somebody?"

He sits down on the courthouse steps and motions for me to join him. Just the two of us out here. Tomorrow will be different. That's when the circus comes to town.

"I want to hire you and Jimmy, even though I can't officially say that I'm hiring you," he says. "And even though I'm aware that you're kind of busy right now."

"I'd only be too busy if I had a life," I say.

"You don't have one? You're great at what you do. And if I can make another observation without getting MeToo'ed, you happen to be great looking."

Down, girl.

"I keep trying to have one. A life. But somehow it never seems to take." I don't even pause before asking, "Are you going to now tell me what you want to hire me for even though you can't technically hire me, or should we order Uber Eats?"

"You get right to it, don't you?" McCall asks.

"Unless this is a billable hour. In which case, take as much time as you need."

He crosses amazingly long legs out in front of him. I notice he's wearing scuffed old loafers. Somehow they make me like him even more. I've never gotten the sense that he's trying too hard, even when I've watched him killing it a few times on Court TV.

"Remember the three people who got shot in Garden City?" he asks. "Six months before Jacobson is accused of wiping out the Gates family."

"I do. Brutal."

Three senseless deaths that time, too. The Carson family. Father, mother, daughter, a sophomore cheerleader at Garden City High. I don't know why I remember the cheerleader piece. But it's stayed with me. A robbery gone wrong. Gone bad and gone tragically wrong.

"Well, you probably also know that the father's mother never let it go until she finally passed," he says, "even though there was never an arrest or even a suspect worth a shit."

"I remember Grandma," I say. "There was a time when she was on TV so much I kept waiting for her to start selling steak knives."

McCall grins. "Well, it turns out Grandma was right."

"She kept saying it wasn't random, that her son's family had been targeted, even though she wouldn't come out and say why. She finally told me why but said that if I went public with it, she'd sue me all the way back to the Ivy League."

"But you're going to tell me."

"Her son gambled. Frequently and badly, as it turns out."

"And not with DraftKings, I take it."

"With Bobby Salvatore, who is still running the biggest book in this part of the world."

"Jimmy's mentioned him a few times in the past. Bad man, right?"

"Very."

"And you guys missed this?"

"Why do you think I'm here?"

"But upstanding district attorneys like yourself aren't allowed to hire people like Jimmy and me to run side investigations."

"We're not. But I promised Grandma," he says. "And there's an exception I believe would cover it."

"The case was never closed, I take it."

"But we'd gotten nothing new in all this time until a guy in another investigation dropped Salvatore's name on us."

"And here you are."

"Here I am."

"I don't mean to be coarse, McCall, but I gotta ask: who pays?"

"Don't worry about it," he says.

"I'm a worrier."

"Grandma liked to plan ahead," he says. "She was ready to go when we found out about the Salvatore connection. When I took it to her, she said, 'I told you so,' and wrote a check. She told me that she was willing to pay whatever it took to find out who took her family."

"This sounds like your crusade, not mine."

"Come on, think of the fun," Gregg McCall says. "While you're trying to get your guy off here, you can help me put somebody else away."

I know all about McCall by now. He's more than just a kick-ass prosecutor. He's also tough and honest. Didn't even go to Columbia on an athletic scholarship. Earned himself one for academics. Could have gone to a big basketball school. His parents were set on him being Ivy League. Worked his way to pay for the rest of college. The opposite of the golden boy I'm currently representing, all in all.

"I know we're supposed to be on opposing sides," McCall says. "But if I can make an exception..."

I finish his thought. "So can I."

"I'm asking you to help me do something we should have done at the time. Find the truth."

"You ought to know that my client just now asked me if

I thought he was telling the truth. I told him that I wasn't interested in the truth." I shrug. "But I lied."

"If you agree to do this, we'll kind of be strange bedfellows."

"You wish," I say.

Actually, *I* wish.

"I know asking you to take on something extra right now is crazy," he says.

"Kind of my thing."

THREE

ON MY WAY HOME, I call Jimmy Cunniff at the tavern. He used to get drunk there in summers when he'd get a couple of days off and need to get out of the city, day-trip to the beach and party at night. Now he owns the business, but not the building, though his landlord is not just an old friend but also someone, in Jimmy's words, who's not rent-gouging scum.

A Hamptons rarity, if you must know.

Jimmy's not just an ex-cop, having been booted out of the NYPD for what he will maintain until Jesus comes back was a righteous shooting, and killing, of a drug dealer named Angel Reyes. He's also a former Golden Gloves boxer and, back in the day, someone who had short stories published in long-gone literary magazines. The beer people should have put Jimmy out there as the most interesting man in the world.

He's also my best friend.

I tell him about Gregg McCall's visit, and his offer, and him telling me we can name our own price, within reason, because Grandma is paying.

"You think we can handle two at once?" Jimmy asks.

"We've done it before."

"Not like with these two," he says, and I know he's right about that.

"Two triple homicides," Jimmy Cunniff says. "But not twice the fun."

"Who knows, maybe solving one will show us how to solve the other. Maybe we'll even slog our way to the truth. Look at it that way."

"I don't know why you even had to ask if I was on board," Jimmy says. "You knew I'd be in as soon as you were. And you were in as soon as McCall asked you to be."

"Kind of."

"Stop here and we'll celebrate," he says.

I tell Jimmy I'll take a rain check. I have to go straight home; I need to train.

"Wait, you're still fixed on doing that crazy biathlon, even now?"

"I just informed Mr. McCall that crazy is kind of my thing," I say.

"Mine, too."

"There's that."

"Are you doing this thing for McCall because you want to or because the hunky DA is the one who asked you to?"

"What is this, a grand jury?"

"Gonna take that as a yes on the hunk."

"Hard no, actually," I say. "I couldn't do that to him."

"Do what?"

"Me," I say.

There was a little slowdown at the light in Wainscott, but now Route 27 is wide-open as I make my way east.

"For one thing," I tell Jimmy, "Gregg McCall seems so happy."

"Wait," Jimmy says. "Both your ex-husbands are happy."

"Now they are."

13

FOUR

MY TWO-BEDROOM SALTBOX is at the end of a cul-de-sac past the train tracks for the Long Island Railroad. North side of the highway, as we like to say Out Here. The less glamorous side, especially as close to the trains as I am.

My neighbors are mostly year-rounders. Fine with me. Summer People make me want to run back to my apartment in the West Village and hide out there until fall.

There is still enough light when I've changed into my Mets sweatshirt, the late-spring temperature down in the fifties tonight. I put on my running shoes, grab my air rifle, and get back into the car to head a few miles north and east of my house to the area known as the Springs. My favorite hiking trail runs through a rural area by Gardiners Bay.

Competing in a no-snow biathlon is the goal of my endless training. Trail running. Shooting. More running. More shooting. A perfect event for a loner like me, and one who prides herself on being a good shot. My dad taught me. He's the one who started calling me Calamity Jane when he saw what I could do at the range.

Little did he know that carrying a gun would one day

become a necessary part of my job. Just not in court. Though sometimes I wish.

I park my Prius Prime in a small, secluded lot near Three Mile Harbor and start jogging deep into the woods. I've placed small targets on trees maybe half a mile apart.

Fancy people don't go to this remote corner of the Hamptons, maybe because they can't find a party, or a photographer. The sound of the air rifle being fired won't scare the decent people out here, who don't hike or jog in the early evening. If somebody does make a call, by now just about all the local cops know it's me. Calamity Jane.

I use the stopwatch on my phone to log my times. I'm determined to enter the late-summer biathlon in Pennsylvania, an event Jimmy has sworn only I have ever heard about. Or care about. He asked why I didn't go for the real biathlon.

"If you ever see me on skis, find my real gun and shoot *me* with it."

I know I'm only competing against myself. But I've been a jock my whole life, from age ten when I beat all the boys and won Long Island's NFL Punt, Pass, and Kick contest, telling my dad I was going to be the first girl ever to quarterback the Jets. I remember him grinning and saying, "Honey, we've had plenty of those on the Jets since Joe Namath was our QB."

Later I was Hockey East Rookie of the Year at BC. That was also where I really learned how to fight. And haven't stopped since. Fighting for rich clients, not-so-rich ones, fighting when I'm doing pro bono work back in the city for victims who deserve a chance. And deserve being repped by somebody like me. Fighting with prosecutors, judges, even the cops sometimes, as much as I generally love cops, maybe because of an ex-cop like Jimmy Cunniff.

Occasionally fighting with two husbands.

Makes no difference to me.

You want to have a fight?

Let's drop the gloves and do this.

I'm feeling it even more than usual tonight, pushing myself, hitting my targets like a champion. I stop at the end of the trail, kneel, empty the gun one final time. Twelve hundred BBs fired in all.

But I'm not done. Not yet. Still feeling it. *Let's do this.* I reload. Hit all the targets on the way back, sorry I've run out of light. And BBs. What's the old line? Rage against the dying of the light? I wasn't much of a poet, but my father, Jack, the Marine and career bartender, liked Dylan Thomas. Maybe because of the way the guy could drink. My mother, Mary, who spent so much of her marriage waiting for my father to come home from the bar, having long ago buried her dreams of being a writer, had died of ovarian cancer when I was ten. I'd always thought I had gotten my humanity from her, my sense of fairness, of making things right. It was different with my father the Marine, who always taught me that if you weren't the one on the attack, the other guy was. His own definition of humanity, just with much harder edges. He lasted longer than our mom did, until he dropped dead of a heart attack one night on a barroom floor.

It's dark by the time I get back to the car. I'm thinking about having one cold one with Jimmy. But then I think about making the half-hour drive over to the bar in Sag Harbor and back, and how I really do need a good night's sleep, knowing I'm going to be a little busy in the morning, even before I head to court.

I drink my last bottle of water, get behind the wheel, toss the rifle onto the back seat, knowing my real gun, the Glock, is locked safely in the glove compartment. I have a second one at home. A girl can't have too many.

I feel like I used to feel in college, the night before a big game. I think about what the room will look like tomorrow. What it will feel like. Where Rob Jacobson will be and where I'll be and where the jury will be.

I've got my opening statement committed to memory. Even so, I pull up the copy stored on my phone. I slide the seat back, lean back, begin to read it over again, keep reading until I feel my eyes starting to close.

When I wake up, it's morning.

Also By James Patterson

ALEX CROSS NOVELS

Along Came a Spider • Kiss the Girls • Jack and Jill • Cat and Mouse • Pop Goes the Weasel • Roses are Red • Violets are Blue • Four Blind Mice • The Big Bad Wolf • London Bridges • Mary, Mary • Cross • Double Cross • Cross Country • Alex Cross's Trial (*with Richard DiLallo*) • I, Alex Cross • Cross Fire • Kill Alex Cross • Merry Christmas, Alex Cross • Alex Cross, Run • Cross My Heart • Hope to Die • Cross Justice • Cross the Line • The People vs. Alex Cross • Target: Alex Cross • Criss Cross • Deadly Cross • Fear No Evil • Triple Cross • Alex Cross Must Die

THE WOMEN'S MURDER CLUB SERIES

1st to Die (*with Andrew Gross*) • 2nd Chance (*with Andrew Gross*) • 3rd Degree (*with Andrew Gross*) • 4th of July (*with Maxine Paetro*) • The 5th Horseman (*with Maxine Paetro*) • The 6th Target (*with Maxine Paetro*) • 7th Heaven (*with Maxine Paetro*) • 8th Confession (*with Maxine Paetro*) • 9th Judgement (*with Maxine Paetro*) • 10th Anniversary (*with Maxine Paetro*) • 11th Hour (*with Maxine Paetro*) • 12th of Never (*with Maxine Paetro*) • Unlucky 13 (*with Maxine Paetro*) • 14th Deadly Sin (*with Maxine Paetro*) • 15th Affair (*with Maxine Paetro*) • 16th Seduction (*with Maxine Paetro*) • 17th Suspect (*with Maxine Paetro*) • 18th Abduction (*with Maxine Paetro*) • 19th Christmas (*with Maxine Paetro*) • 20th Victim (*with Maxine Paetro*) • 21st Birthday (*with Maxine Paetro*) • 22 Seconds (*with Maxine Paetro*) • 23rd Midnight (*with Maxine Paetro*)

DETECTIVE MICHAEL BENNETT SERIES

Step on a Crack (*with Michael Ledwidge*) • Run for Your Life (*with Michael Ledwidge*) • Worst Case (*with Michael Ledwidge*) • Tick Tock (*with Michael Ledwidge*) • I, Michael Bennett (*with Michael Ledwidge*) • Gone (*with Michael Ledwidge*) • Burn (*with Michael Ledwidge*) • Alert (*with Michael Ledwidge*) • Bullseye (*with Michael Ledwidge*) • Haunted (*with James O. Born*) • Ambush (*with James O. Born*) • Blindside (*with James O. Born*) • The Russian (*with James O. Born*) • Shattered (*with James O. Born*) • Obsessed (*with James O. Born*)

PRIVATE NOVELS

Private (*with Maxine Paetro*) • Private London (*with Mark Pearson*) • Private Games (*with Mark Sullivan*) • Private: No. 1 Suspect (*with Maxine Paetro*) • Private Berlin (*with Mark Sullivan*) • Private Down Under (*with Michael White*) • Private L.A. (*with Mark Sullivan*) • Private India (*with Ashwin Sanghi*) • Private Vegas (*with Maxine*

Paetro) • Private Sydney (*with Kathryn Fox*) • Private Paris (*with Mark Sullivan*) • The Games (*with Mark Sullivan*) • Private Delhi (*with Ashwin Sanghi*) • Private Princess (*with Rees Jones*) • Private Moscow (*with Adam Hamdy*) • Private Rogue (*with Adam Hamdy*) • Private Beijing (*with Adam Hamdy*) • Private Rome (*with Adam Hamdy*)

NYPD RED SERIES

NYPD Red (*with Marshall Karp*) • NYPD Red 2 (*with Marshall Karp*) • NYPD Red 3 (*with Marshall Karp*) • NYPD Red 4 (*with Marshall Karp*) • NYPD Red 5 (*with Marshall Karp*) • NYPD Red 6 (*with Marshall Karp*)

DETECTIVE HARRIET BLUE SERIES

Never Never (*with Candice Fox*) • Fifty Fifty (*with Candice Fox*) • Liar Liar (*with Candice Fox*) • Hush Hush (*with Candice Fox*)

INSTINCT SERIES

Instinct (*with Howard Roughan, previously published as* Murder Games) • Killer Instinct (*with Howard Roughan*) • Steal (*with Howard Roughan*)

THE BLACK BOOK SERIES

The Black Book (*with David Ellis*) • The Red Book (*with David Ellis*) • Escape (*with David Ellis*)

STAND-ALONE THRILLERS

The Thomas Berryman Number • Hide and Seek • Black Market • The Midnight Club • Sail (*with Howard Roughan*) • Swimsuit (*with Maxine Paetro*) • Don't Blink (*with Howard Roughan*) • Postcard Killers (*with Liza Marklund*) • Toys (*with Neil McMahon*) • Now You See Her (*with Michael Ledwidge*) • Kill Me If You Can (*with Marshall Karp*) • Guilty Wives (*with David Ellis*) • Zoo (*with Michael Ledwidge*) • Second Honeymoon (*with Howard Roughan*) • Mistress (*with David Ellis*) • Invisible (*with David Ellis*) • Truth or Die (*with Howard Roughan*) • Murder House (*with David Ellis*) • The Store (*with Richard DiLallo*) • Texas Ranger (*with Andrew Bourelle*) • The President is Missing (*with Bill Clinton*) • Revenge (*with Andrew Holmes*) • Juror No. 3 (*with Nancy Allen*) • The First Lady (*with Brendan DuBois*) • The Chef (*with Max DiLallo*) • Out of Sight (*with Brendan DuBois*) • Unsolved (*with David Ellis*) • The Inn (*with Candice Fox*) • Lost (*with James O. Born*) • Texas Outlaw (*with Andrew Bourelle*) • The Summer House (*with Brendan DuBois*) • 1st Case (*with Chris Tebbetts*) • Cajun Justice (*with Tucker Axum*)• The Midwife Murders (*with Richard DiLallo*) • The Coast-to-Coast Murders (*with J.D. Barker*) • Three Women Disappear (*with Shan Serafin*) • The President's Daughter (*with Bill Clinton*) • The Shadow (*with Brian Sitts*) • The Noise (*with J.D. Barker*) • 2 Sisters Detective Agency (*with Candice Fox*) • Jailhouse Lawyer (*with Nancy Allen*) • The Horsewoman (*with Mike Lupica*) • Run Rose Run (*with Dolly Parton*) • Death of the Black Widow (*with J.D. Barker*) •

The Ninth Month (*with Richard DiLallo*) • The Girl in the Castle (*with Emily Raymond*) • Blowback (*with Brendan DuBois*) • The Twelve Topsy-Turvy, Very Messy Days of Christmas (*with Tad Safran*) • The Perfect Assassin (*with Brian Sitts*) • House of Wolves (*with Mike Lupica*) • Countdown (*with Brendan DuBois*) • Cross Down (*with Brendan DuBois*) • Circle of Death (*with Brian Sitts*) • Lion & Lamb (*with Duane Swierczynski*) • 12 Months to Live (*with Mike Lupica*)

NON-FICTION

Torn Apart (*with Hal and Cory Friedman*) • The Murder of King Tut (*with Martin Dugard*) • All-American Murder (*with Alex Abramovich and Mike Harvkey*) • The Kennedy Curse (*with Cynthia Fagen*) • The Last Days of John Lennon (*with Casey Sherman and Dave Wedge*) • Walk in My Combat Boots (*with Matt Eversmann and Chris Mooney*) • ER Nurses (*with Matt Eversmann*) • James Patterson by James Patterson: The Stories of My Life • Diana, William and Harry (*with Chris Mooney*) • American Cops (*with Matt Eversmann*)

MURDER IS FOREVER TRUE CRIME

Murder, Interrupted (*with Alex Abramovich and Christopher Charles*) • Home Sweet Murder (*with Andrew Bourelle and Scott Slaven*) • Murder Beyond the Grave (*with Andrew Bourelle and Christopher Charles*) • Murder Thy Neighbour (*with Andrew Bourelle and Max DiLallo*) • Murder of Innocence (*with Max DiLallo and Andrew Bourelle*) • Till Murder Do Us Part (*with Andrew Bourelle and Max DiLallo*)

COLLECTIONS

Triple Threat (*with Max DiLallo and Andrew Bourelle*) • Kill or Be Killed (*with Maxine Paetro, Rees Jones, Shan Serafin and Emily Raymond*) • The Moores are Missing (*with Loren D. Estleman, Sam Hawken and Ed Chatterton*) • The Family Lawyer (*with Robert Rotstein, Christopher Charles and Rachel Howzell Hall*) • Murder in Paradise (*with Doug Allyn, Connor Hyde and Duane Swierczynski*) • The House Next Door (*with Susan DiLallo, Max DiLallo and Brendan DuBois*) • 13-Minute Murder (*with Shan Serafin, Christopher Farnsworth and Scott Slaven*) • The River Murders (*with James O. Born*) • The Palm Beach Murders (*with James O. Born, Duane Swierczynski and Tim Arnold*) • Paris Detective • 3 Days to Live • 23 ½ Lies (*with Maxine Paetro*)

For more information about James Patterson's novels,
visit www.penguin.co.uk.